C000065044

The Interpreter

Isabella Pallavicini

Grosvenor House
Publishing Limited

All rights reserved
Copyright © Isabella Pallavicini, 2022

The right of Isabella Pallavicini to be identified as the author of this
work has been asserted in accordance with Section 78
of the Copyright, Designs and Patents Act 1988

"Der Dolmetscher" by Isabella Pallavicini,
Translated into English by Rachel Farmer

The book cover is copyright to Isabella Pallavicini

This book is published by
Grosvenor House Publishing Ltd
Link House
140 The Broadway, Tolworth, Surrey, KT6 7HT.
www.grosvenorhousepublishing.co.uk

This book is sold subject to the conditions that it shall not, by way of
trade or otherwise, be lent, resold, hired out or otherwise circulated
without the author's or publisher's prior consent in any form of binding or
cover other than that in which it is published and
without a similar condition including this condition being imposed
on the subsequent purchaser.

This book is a work of fiction. Any resemblance to
people or events, past or present, is purely coincidental.

A CIP record for this book
is available from the British Library

ISBN 978-1-83975-874-4

For those who survived.

For those who didn't.

*And for my father, whose recollections
inspired me to write this book.*

For Yvonne,
Enjoy the reading!
Isabella

Content

The Dorigo Family before WW2

Sicily, Italy Vittorio Dorigo (*nonno*)-Piacenza Lombardi (*nonna*) (*1868) (*1870)			
New York, USA Luciano (*1895)- Alice Morris	*Basel, Switzerland* Umberto (*1897)- Maria Bettega	*Sicily, Italy* Maria (*1898)- Toni Poletti	*Como, Italy* Chiara (*1900)- Mauro Conti
Vincenzo/Vince (*1918) Pietro/Pete (*1919)	Enzo (*1921) Rinaldo (*1928)	Luca (*1919) Roberto (*1920) Zia (*1924)	Alfredo (*1918) Bianca (*1920)

Do you know the land
Where the lemon trees bloom,
And among the dark leaves
The golden oranges glow?
A gentle wind blows from the blue sky,
The myrtle is silent and the laurel stands tall,
Do you know it?
There, there
I would go with you, O my beloved!

Johann Wolfgang von Goethe: Mignon (1786)

Prologue

Sicily, 1930

"Cu è surdu, orbu e taci, campa cent'anni 'mpaci."

"He who is deaf, blind and dumb lives a hundred years in peace."

Sicilian proverb

Luca and I ran as fast as we could.

"Don't look round—follow me! We can hide down in the village!"

The stony track led into a narrow lane. In the shade of the first row of houses, we paused a moment to catch our breath. A dark red trail of blood ran down Luca's calf, a film of dry dust over it.

"My leg hurts! Savio, that *fanculo* got me right on the shin with his catapult. Where are those bastards? Let's get our own back!"

Inch by inch, we crept along the wall of the house. A gate to an inner courtyard stood open. "Quick, in here!" The gate closed softly behind us. A narrow crack allowed us to keep watch on the lane.

I was staying with my grandparents in Sicily for the summer holidays. My father had emigrated to Switzerland as a young man to take a job at a textile factory. While he was there, he met my mother, who came from Northern Italy. My *nonno* had actually wanted my father to take over his wine shop where he sold Marsala, the Sicilian fortified wine, but my father wanted to get into the textile industry. I could never figure out why. But that's how Sicily became my second home. I enjoyed playing with my cousins, being spoiled rotten by my *nonna* and driving around in my nonno's new car. I found swimming in the sea and the long, warm summer nights a welcome change from the cool summers in Switzerland. All of us children were given a lot of freedom here, and every day was a new adventure for me. We were always on the go. We played hide and seek among the vineyards, built huts and rode donkeys. I got on especially well with my cousin Luca. He was ten years old, one year older than me. Naturally, he let me join his gang, the *lupi*. Luca's friend Cesare had just given the *orsi* a good beating. I had looked on from a distance as they lured Franco, the leader of the orsi, into a trap. Franco Soglieri was a real thorn in our side. He and his cronies would always pick on Luca's brother Roberto. I felt really sorry for Roberto. He was always quiet and accommodating. He wouldn't hurt a fly. His role in the gang was that of a follower, and he steered well clear of any fights as he was rather small, weedy and weak, tending instead to shrink fearfully into the background. It drove Luca mad as hell when his brother was attacked by the orsi yet again. Now he had got his own back. "Revenge is sweet," was his lesson to me.

Now the orsi were after us. We lay low behind the gate, making no sound.

"They're coming, those idiots!" hissed Luca. "But they'll never find us."

I took over guard duty from Luca, keeping watch over the lane, and leaned tensely against the gate. I could well understand Roberto's aversion to playing at gangs; I wasn't particularly fond of it either, but I didn't want to let Luca down. I felt honoured that he had brought me along with him, but I was scared. I heard the voices of Mario and Salvatore as they ran after Franco and his gang, hurling insults as they went.

"Do you think Franco will get us back?" I wondered apprehensively.

"They probably think we ran to the cave. We've outsmarted them yet again."

We waited a moment longer until the voices had died away.

"They've gone. They're probably down by the piazza. Come on! Let's catch them off guard!" Luca whispered.

We found the perfect hiding place in the alcove just inside the entrance to the church. A sound put us on high alert, and we froze, listening intently. We heard footsteps, the squeak of a bench. Luca padded noiselessly to the thick woollen curtain that separated the church's entrance from the nave and opened it a crack before tiptoeing back to the alcove.

"The priest. He sat down on a bench in one of the confessionals."

Breathing a sigh of relief, we crouched in the cool shade of the church walls. The heavy oak portal was slightly ajar. We squinted into the piazza. Old men sat around little tables at the Domenico bar, in the shade of the canopy of leaves overhead, engrossed in their games of cards. The bead curtain in front of the bar swayed gently in the afternoon breeze. At the corner of the bar stood two Carabinieri, puffing appreciatively on their cigarettes. A sudden burst of laughter rang out from three old women dressed in black, who were sitting on a rickety bench and chatting cheerily away to each other.

"Our honourable friends have surrendered," Luca gloated in a whisper, the corners of his mouth curling into a satisfied grin. We giggled with pride, clapping our hands quietly with glee at our victory.

Luca turned his gaze back to the piazza. Then, abruptly, he grew serious. "Enzo, there's something in the air. Look. The piazza is almost empty all of a sudden."

He was right. The card players were nowhere to be seen. And the women had retreated back into their houses. Only the Carabinieri were still visible at the far end of the square. They ambled down the Via della Madonna, before disappearing from view.

"The heat probably got too much for them," Luca said, leaning back. He pulled his cap down over his face, indicating that he wanted to be left alone. I shuffled over to the corner too, feeling a pleasant tiredness wash over me. But no sooner had my limbs started to relax than I heard a deafening bang.

"What was that?" I cried, aghast.

It felt as if we had been struck by lightning. The echo from the bang resounded through the narrow streets that surrounded the piazza, reverberating back off the walls of the houses. We peered cautiously through the crack of the open oak door, our gazes combing the skies. Fear gripped me, causing my breath to catch in my chest.

"Luca, what was that?" I yelled again.

"*Sta' zitto!* That was a gunshot!"

I looked at him, confused.

"The bar," he murmured.

As soon as he said it, the bar's bead curtain swung open, and a stocky, well-dressed man stepped out into the piazza. His three-piece suit was custom tailored, and his pointed black-and-white shoes were made of the finest leather.

Deep in thought, I noted that his outfit seemed somewhat excessive for a normal weekday. The brim of his hat was drawn down low over his face. We couldn't make out his eyes. He strode leisurely towards the church. With his right index finger, he casually lifted the brim of his hat. For a split second, we caught sight of his black, almond-shaped eyes lurking beneath bushy, close-set eyebrows. Quick as a flash, we slipped through the woollen curtain and hid behind a marble block sporting a statue of Saint Albert of Trapani. Then we heard the creak of the church portal and, at almost the same moment, the squeaking of the wooden bench again. We crouched behind the marble block, frozen to the spot. My heart was pounding in my throat. The man strode purposefully through the woollen curtain, just as the priest was stepping out of the confessional.

"*Signore!* You startled me," he called out in surprise.

"Calm yourself, Padre. I was just coming to see you. It's about time I made another donation to the church," said the man softly.

Only the outlines of the two men were visible in the dim light. As a faint beam of sunlight fell on the priest, I could make out his anxious face. Tiny beads of sweat gleamed on his forehead. His hands shook as the man held out a stack of banknotes.

"Here, Padre!" said the man forcefully.

"That's very generous of you, signore!" stammered the priest.

"Good afternoon," said the man, taking his leave. He swept hurriedly out of the church and across the piazza. One after another, the old men re-emerged from the bar. They sat down under the leafy canopy and started playing their card games again, as if nothing had happened. The three women came back out of their houses, and the Carabinieri materialised once again at the far end of the square. They crossed paths with the man, and they nodded silently to one another. A moment later, a black car drew up. We could just make out the man climbing into it and driving away.

Sicily, 1936

"Enzo, where are you?"

The steps drew nearer, and the rustling of the vine leaves grew louder. A shadow scurried past. Then all was still. Now I could make her out through the foliage. She was looking around, but she couldn't see me. I stayed where I was, rooted to the spot, not moving a muscle. But soon I couldn't keep it up any longer and started stretching my upper body. She heard the noise but couldn't tell where it came from. Quick as a flash, I ducked down and cast about for a stone. I raised my arm in slow motion, then sent the stone spinning, lightning fast, into the vineyard. She started. Then she crept quietly away in the direction of the sound. Soon, she had disappeared completely into the greenery.

Finally, she was gone!

I searched for the way out of the vineyard. It was like a labyrinth, but I knew every nook and cranny. Luca and I used to play hide and seek here—we used to race up the hill to the olive grove.

I strolled along the rows of olive trees, the loud chirruping of the cicadas ringing in my ears. This was where we had concocted our plans to make mischief. I leant against a gnarled trunk and let my mind wander. The sun burnt hot on my face, and I squinted into the azure sky. A flock of birds soared towards the sea.

My cousin Zia always wanted to play with me, as if I were still a little boy. She never gave me a moment's peace. She clung onto me as if she would never let go. But I had to leave in four weeks. That's just the way it was. *Would I stay in Sicily if I had the choice?* I wondered. But there was no point dwelling on pointless thoughts. I didn't belong here—at least, not really. I could be happy here. My many relatives would welcome me with open arms, feed me and put a roof over my head. But I'd miss my school and my friends. I wanted to make something of myself, like my father. I wanted to follow in his footsteps: study in Germany, become a textile engineer, then run my own factory one day. Then I would drive a car and build my dream villa in Sicily, high above the cliffs of Taormina or Agrigento. I would come on holiday here in the summer. Nonna would cry happy tears, and Nonno would clap me proudly on the shoulder.

I sat up. My gaze fell on Aunt Maria's yellow stone house. The green shutters were all closed to keep the midday heat at bay. A veranda, shaded by vines growing overhead, was the main hub of activity in the summer months. People would gather there around long tables, eating, drinking and making merry until the small hours. Now, in the afternoon, everything was silent and still, as if no one was in the house. Everyone was taking *una pennichella*. My stomach rumbled with hunger.

I suddenly realised I had missed lunch, which was invariably a lavish affair. How annoying. Perhaps I could sneak into the kitchen. There were always various dishes left over. I could do with a plate of pasta, I decided.

I made my way through the garden, past the overhanging tomato plants, dark green courgettes, long beanstalks and a bed of herbs. The fragrant scent of basil was my favourite.

The door was open, but all was silent. Softly, I slipped down the corridor and into the kitchen. I spotted a plateful of pasta and a loaf of bread on the table. My aunt must have saved them for me. How kind of her! I quickly grabbed a fork from the drawer, fetched a glass and filled it with wine. I relished being able to eat alone and undisturbed, but it rarely ever happened, if at all. It was almost always very noisy over meals, with everyone shouting over one another, and they would usually just talk politics or gripe about other people anyway.

My moment of peace was short lived. I heard footsteps approaching down the corridor and muffled laughter. Before I could figure out who it was, she was standing right in front of me.

"Enzo, where have you been hiding? We've been looking all over for you!" Zia exclaimed.

A girl appeared behind her, smiling shyly at me. She eyed me astutely with her dark eyes, her thick black hair tumbling loosely over her slim shoulders and framing her pretty face.

"Ciao," I said, my mouth still full.

She giggled surreptitiously.

"Who are you?" I asked, trying to act as if I weren't paying her much attention.

"Oh, my dearest cousin seems to be taking an interest in you!" cried Zia excitedly.

"I'm Francesca, from next door."

Zia laughed out loud. "From next door! Francesca's very modest, isn't she, Enzo?"

"Yes, I'm the modest neighbour!"

"Enzo's no good with names, Francesca, especially not the most important ones."

"Stop it, Zia. Don't make fun of me," I retorted coolly. "Tell me, Francesca, which neighbourhood family do you belong to?"

"The most important, richest, most respected family in all of Sicily!" gushed Zia before Francesca could answer.

"It's a pleasure to meet you! Are you coming to the family gathering tonight? It would be lovely to have you."

Francesca said she would be there, and Zia beamed at me.

She was always assuring me I was her favourite cousin.

After I had eaten, I set off back to Nonna's house. The stony path meandered its way up the hillside to the summit, where my grandparents' proud, grand villa stood. This sprawling estate, bursting with olive groves, vineyards and citrus orchards, had been in the family for generations. I picked an orange. It was wonderfully juicy and thirst-quenching! No wonder they were known as the fruit of the gods.

I heard the thrum of an engine and saw a shiny new Lancia Astra as it rounded the corner. The light grey car wheezed its way up the hill and drew up in front of me.

"Hey, Enzo! Ciao! I hardly recognised you! Are you spending the holidays with your nonna again? How's it going in Switzerland?"

I didn't recognise the face of this impeccably dressed old gentleman, but I assumed he was one of my grandparents' neighbours.

"Switzerland? Oh, it's fine. My dad found a good job at a factory, and my mum is working too."

"Your mum is working too? Life certainly is different up there in the North!"

I must have looked at the car with interest because he exclaimed proudly, "Great car, eh? It's the latest Lancia, a Tipo Bocca Cabriolet."

"Yes, it's a really great car."

"Say hello to your dad for me!"

"From who, if you don't mind me asking?"

"Oh dear, my boy, you really are almost like a foreigner here. Tell him Salvatore says hello!"

I looked at him quizzically.

"*Ciao, ragazzo!*"

The engine revved, the wheels spun in the sand for a moment, then the car drove off and vanished in a cloud of dust. Salvatore. I had no idea who that could be. He was probably one of the big names in the neighbourhood, just like Zia had said. I ran the rest of the way up the hill to the house. Nonna was sitting on the bench outside.

"Enzo, darling! Where on earth were you?"

"Ciao, Nonna! I was down at *zia* Maria's and stopped for something to eat. Then I bumped into Salvatore. He drove past me in his car."

"Salvatore Soglieri." Nonna repeated the name flatly.

"He told me to say hello to Dad for him. I don't know the man at all, but he knows everything about us."

"Everyone knows everything about everyone around here, my love. Some people like it, some begrudge it. It's always been this way. Salvatore went to school with your dad in the *Convitto* in Palermo. Salvatore's family owns a lot of land in our area. He's an important neighbour, sweetheart." My grandmother hauled herself wearily to her feet and shuffled into the living room. "Come here, Enzo, let me show you something." She took a framed photo from the bookcase and held it out to me. In the picture were around fifty boys, dressed in uniform and standing to attention in front of the Convitto Nationale di Palermo. I had to squint at the photo to make out my dad.

Nonna pointed out where Salvatore was standing. "You know, Enzo, my love, there aren't any good schools here like there are in Switzerland. Children that want to make something of themselves and whose parents can afford it get sent to boarding school. It's important for them to get an education. Yes, and Salvatore is a very important man. He and his family own the salt mines. He makes a fortune from them. He's constantly going off to Palermo in his new car to make business deals and meet with other influential people."

"Were Dad and Salvatore good friends at school?"

Nonna looked at the photo thoughtfully. "No, quite the opposite. They couldn't stand each other and were envious of one another."

"Dad, envious? I can't picture that at all! He always seems so poised, calm and level-headed, unlike my mum."

Nonna burst out laughing. "Oh yes, your dear mum! Umberto can count himself lucky to have such a wonderful wife. Even though she comes from Northern Italy, more's the pity. Your dad didn't like how Salvatore was always showing off. I almost think Salvatore was part of the reason your dad went to Milan to learn the textile trade. He wanted to show him he could make something of himself too."

Nonna pointed to a photo on the wall.

"Your cousins in New York, Vincenzo and Pietro, when they were barely out of nappies. Cute, aren't they? And look at them now! Luciano sent me this photo last month."

"You mean Vince and Pete? That's what people call them in America."

"I know, Enzo, but their real names are still Italian."

The first thing that struck me was the restaurant sign; *La Siciliana* was written in curved letters above the entrance. Vince was leaning against the doorframe, dressed in pristine white. He had always set great store in his appearance. And he was certainly well aware of his own attractiveness. He was looking haughtily down at his younger brother. Pete's shrewd eyes were looking directly at the camera. He looked rather weedy and small beside his older brother, but I knew he was very intelligent. Three years ago, they had come to Sicily for a visit while I was there for my summer holidays. Luca and Vince were constantly getting on each other's nerves. They turned every little thing into a competition. Pete, on the other hand, was very agreeable and friendly.

In the other photo, the whole family was posing in front of a red Cadillac. Aunt Alice looked like a film star with her dark sunglasses, red lipstick and silk headscarf. Uncle Luciano was wearing dark sunglasses too. His delighted laugh showed just how proud he was of his new ride.

There was a knock at the door. Anna looked in. "*Signora*, when should we serve dinner? We've made the pasta, the tomato sauce is ready, the vegetables have been washed, and the roast roll is in the oven, a *farsu magru*. Manolo also bought fresh sardines and sea bass at the market. We're going to fry them in butter and serve them with fresh bread. And for dessert we've got cassata and fresh cannoli from Pasticceria Lungomare!"

"Wonderful," said my grandmother appreciatively. "Let me see!" She stood up and disappeared with Anna into the kitchen.

"Nonna, where's Luca?" I called after her.

"I don't know, Enzo! Luca is always off somewhere. God knows what he's up to this time."

Anna cut in. "He went to the beach."

I snatched up my swimming things, jumped on my bike and cycled down the hill. I loved feeling the wind in my hair as I rode. The highway was lined with vineyards as far as the eye could see. My grandfather owned one of the largest Marsala distilleries in Sicily. *Shame the grapes won't be harvested until later in the summer,*

I thought. Luca had told me how everyone pitched in during harvest time, and when the work was done, the whole village would be in a festive mood, indulging in wine, food, music and dancing.

My uncle's bike rattled along the windswept road. I panted my way up the final hill. Not far now, and it was all downhill from here. I freewheeled down towards the small bay at top speed. Before me lay the sea, deep blue and stretching out to the horizon, little waves gently rippling its surface in the blazing heat. The salty scent of the ocean filled my nostrils. I lay the bike down by the side of the road. A steep footpath snaked over the cliffs and down to the bay. I spotted Luca over by the rocks and headed towards him. He was hunting for crabs, and he already had about ten of them in his basket.

"I need to cool off before we go fishing," he said. His fit, muscular body was tanned. Luca could take on anyone—he was a real athlete.

"If you want to go places in the army, you don't just need to be smart. You need endurance and physical fitness too. It helps you to be assertive and keep a clear head. There are so many officers with a one-track mind—all they think about is drinking and stuffing their faces. They walk around with their big potbellies, their heads foggy with wine, making all the wrong decisions."

"And what do you think of Mussolini?" I asked.

"Oh, I don't bother too much about politics. In the army, I can get the best pilot training there is. That's all I care about. My father isn't too keen on it. He wants me to take over his company one day. But I want to fly fighter jets. The speed and the buzzing in your limbs as you soar through the air—there's no feeling like it. I'm totally addicted already!" His eyes sparkled with passion. It suited Luca. Even as a young boy, he had always had the drive to prove himself. He was the ringleader of our gang and had often put his foot down to get his own way. I remembered the first time we had raced each other on our bikes. He was always faster and bolder—he just had more of a knack for it. I loved my cousin more than anything. He was like a big brother to me. And I admired him.

"What does your father think of Mussolini?" I persisted.

"He doesn't say this publicly, but in private he hates the Fascists. He never says it outright, but he alludes to it, and I understand him. He's worried about the future. He is always reserved and tries to please everyone. He doesn't want to rock the boat. It annoys me. He's constantly fawning over his important friends. I don't think they're real friends at all. They're just using him. That's one of the reasons I don't want to waste my time with the company. If I did, I'd only get sucked into the endless vortex of favours and get smothered."

I knew what he meant.

"Of course, Mussolini has the big landowners, like my father, in his sights. Mussolini wants farming reform. He wants the big landowners to lease out plots of their land to farmers. And he has this crazy idea, as my father calls it, of creating a monument to himself by building the *borghi*. It's a construction project involving various buildings for the farming community. My father says that's all well and good, but it will only lead to chaos. And I think my dad's right. Come on, let's go for a swim!"

We jumped into the water and raced to the rocks. The sunlight glanced off the turquoise water and shone right down to the sandy ocean floor. I dived down and spotted a starfish on a stone. A shoal of tiny fish drifted past my face. Just as I was about to come up for air, I noticed something under a fragment of rock. I hurried back to the surface.

"Luca! Something's moving behind the rocks!"

Luca dived down and swam around the rocks. A moray eel slithered out of a hollow and disappeared behind the boulder. We dived down again and again to watch it. We spotted some crayfish too. Luca bravely reached his hand into a crevice that had a long, worm-like arm protruding from it. An octopus had crawled inside. No sooner had Luca reached out to grab it than the water was stained black. Soon, we could barely see anything at all. Luca had had his fun goading the octopus.

We bobbed back up to the surface and swam over to a rowing boat in the bay. Luca hauled it into the water. "Let's row out to a cave!"

We clambered into the boat, and Luca worked the oars with gusto.

"Look at all the shoals of fish! Is there a fishing rod on this boat?"

"No, but we could come back at night and use a net to fish for *calamari*. When you shine a fishing light at them, great shoals of them swim towards the light. There's a full moon in a week's time—that'll be the best time. The sea will be calm then too."

We steered the boat round a rocky bluff, and Luca rowed slowly through the entrance of a large cave. The water lapped against the rock face, tiny crabs clinging to its sharp edges. The splash of the oars made a hollow sound and echoed back at us. All at once, the cave narrowed. Luca drew in the oars and allowed the boat to glide noiselessly onward. Dappled light danced across the white rock formations. The sun was still able to light up the cave, even this far in.

"Close your eyes, Enzo. In two minutes, you'll get a surprise!"

I covered my face with my hands.

"Now, check it out! Open your eyes!"

My jaw dropped in astonishment. A grotto the size of a cathedral opened up before us, with a small stretch of sandy beach at the far end. Luca steered the boat towards it. We climbed out and marvelled at the beauty of the rock formations, as if we were in a place of worship.

"Did you discover this cave yourself?"

"Yes. One night, when I was fishing with Roberto. The sea was choppy, and we were struggling to make it to the bay. We rowed into a random cave and discovered this little beach. During the storm, the sea level rose a little, but it didn't matter. The entrance to the cave is so tall, you can row out again at any time."

After a while, we sat back down in the boat, pushed off from the beach and glided back through the entrance into the evening sun.

The tables were decked out in white, lanterns illuminating the splendid summer garden, and the aperitif was being handed round. Nonno Vittorio was sitting on the veranda. He had grown older since my last visit. His hips were giving him grief, and he had been using a walking stick to get around for some time now. In spite of this, he was still running his Marsala business as enthusiastically as ever. He would visit press houses, taste the wares, or have himself driven through the vineyards in a cart. He enjoyed spending his autumn years admiring his Marsala empire and observing with satisfaction how his long years of hard work building up the business had paid off. The sweet wine was exported as far as England. Now he could bask in his success and relish in the prestige he had acquired as a result. Wealth brought him influential friends and ties to the worlds of politics and business. Dressed in stately attire of white linen trousers and pointed shoes, he was smoking a cigar and conversing with his friend Michele Fiori and the latter's son Antonio. The older gentleman owned the largest tuna factory in Sicily. He had recently handed over the reins to his sons Antonio and Giuseppe.

Michele and Vittorio had been friends since childhood and had both worked hard in their youth to build up their fathers' businesses. While my grandfather was busy expanding the Marsala wine business by cultivating, processing and exporting the product far beyond our country's borders, Michele managed to create the first tuna factory out of a small fishing business. His unique method of preserving tuna in cans was a ground-breaking innovation, which had given Sicily's economy a major boost. His sons Antonio and Giuseppe had continued to invest in the business and had recently purchased a shipping fleet on the Adriatic. Antonio evidently enjoyed life in the upper echelons of society. He loved good food and expensive champagne, and he nursed an insatiable passion for the sea. All his free time was spent sailing round Sicily on a luxury yacht. He knew every port and every bay and would go cave diving in search of crayfish and lobster. Once a year, he would set off for a couple of weeks on a sailing trip along the Amalfi Coast on the mainland and would drop anchor near the international jet set in Positano or Sorrento, where he would meet clients from around the world and invite them onto his yacht. Then he would proudly take them to Elba or Sardinia to play golf and close deals with British, French and German businessmen. The fact that he was a bachelor didn't bother him one jot. On the contrary, he loved how women were always throwing themselves at his feet.

Tanned, of sturdy build, and dressed in sporty sailing attire, Antonio was deep in conversation with Luigi Gentile, a bank manager from Palermo. Luigi Gentile was an interesting conversation partner, not only because he was up to speed with the latest news on politics and business. He also dedicated his free time to literature and writing novels. He had a genteel, intellectual air about him. His clothes were cut from fine fabrics and his suits made at Brioni couture house in Rome. The Gentile family was very well regarded among the uppermost circles of Palermo society. My nonna was on the best of terms with his wife Gabriela. They would go to Palermo together and shop for shoes and clothes, drink coffee and swap the latest town gossip. "Despite their wealth and reputation, the Gentiles are a good family, real friends you can rely on," Nonna insisted. "They've remained honest and respectful."

Antonio's brother Giuseppe and his wife Laura entered the throng, exchanging delighted greetings with the other guests. Giuseppe was the spitting image of his brother Antonio, but they were different as night and day. While Antonio cultivated relationships between the Fiori firm and its customers, both at home and abroad, Giuseppe busied himself with the nuts and bolts of running the factory. He still enjoyed fishing with a rod and line from a rowing boat. And until recently, he had gone out on every big tuna catch and pitched in to help. He loved working closely with the fishermen.

"So, Luigi, how's business at the bank?" Giuseppe asked the bank manager.

"Could be better. The share markets are recovering more slowly than anticipated. Too many restrictions from the government. And they're talking about increasing taxes. Damn those Fascists! They'll ruin us yet! The land reforms are causing nothing but trouble, and who are the ones ultimately giving the government their loose change?"

"You said it, Luigi!" replied Vittorio. "If it weren't for us, the country would have been bankrupt long ago. Ultimately, we're the ones who have contributed the most to rebuilding this country after the war, getting the economy back on its feet and boosting trade. Where would we be without our exports! Almost all of us took a nasty blow from the crisis six years ago, but we got our businesses up and running again. And look at the North—nothing but problems. The Fiat plants are reporting a forty-percent drop in business. At least we can export our Marsala to rich English people." He raised his glass.

"*Salute*, to the best Marsala in the world! Ah, here comes my grandson from Switzerland!" I heard my grandfather say as I stepped onto the terrace.

"Say, Vittorio, does your son Umberto happen to have any connections at the Swiss banks? We could get him some good business, don't you think? Lucrative business deals at that! I'm sure they would welcome our custom," Antonio quipped.

"But seriously, if the Fascists make our lives any harder, we'll need to start worrying about our money," Luigi retorted.

"Secure investments are in high demand these days."

I glanced into the kitchen. The maids were hurrying about, under Aunt Maria's instructions, busily compiling their delicious dishes. The fresh aroma of roast meat and rosemary filled the room. Pasta dough was being rolled out, cut, boiled in water and topped with tomato sauce. There was chicken roasting in lemon and herbs, fish on the grill, and a beef roast simmering in red wine. I loved this bustle of activity. I grabbed a glass of wine and sat down at the table.

Anna, the cook, brought in the appetisers: *arancini*, small stuffed rice balls, olives, tomatoes, anchovies and *sfincione*, fresh bread with olive oil. My cousins Roberto and Luca were sitting down at the end of the table. The two brothers couldn't have been more different. Luca was tall and powerfully built, with a confident, impudent air about him. He revelled in his family's status. At seventeen, he already gave the impression of a young lord of the manor. In between puffs of his cigarette, he led the conversation, not allowing any other opinion to prevail; he was grand, impressive and eloquent. As ambitious and adventurous as he was, he was bound to achieve his aims without much difficulty. He wanted to aim high—that's what he always said. His wild, curly hair testified to his unbridled thirst for adventure, and his dark, almond-shaped eyes were beguilingly beautiful. Even as a young child, he had always been the centre of attention, and his open, affectionate manner made him universally popular. If he defied them or tried to get his own way, they would always relent. People found it funny when he stamped angrily on the floor; they would lift him up, kiss his cute curls and forgive him his mischievous fancies.

Beside him sat his brother Roberto—slight, silent, introverted. As a child, he had buried himself in books and loved nothing more than to be left alone in his room to read. He was often sickly—a weak immune system, according to the doctors. At ten years old, he'd had a close brush with death when he spent four weeks in bed with pneumonia. As if by a miracle, his high fever gradually fell, his coughing subsided, and after more than four weeks, he finally felt himself again. After that, he often read the Bible and grew increasingly fascinated by spiritual literature. He later went on to devote himself entirely to studying the Bible and ecclesiastical history. For years now, he had been helping out at Mass to support the frail old village priest. He attended boarding school at the Convitto di Palermo—the best in his year—and was determined to make it to the seminary in Rome when he had completed his schooling. Despite his modest demeanour, he had set his career sights high: the Vatican. His dreams—wholly unimposing, yet utterly determined—all focused on advancing in the clergy. He was currently talking to Silvana, Giuseppe Fiori's daughter, in a quiet, somewhat aloof manner. He hardly ever looked at the girl, as if looking at her posed a threat to him. Luca often acted out and showed him up when it came to women. I felt sorry for Roberto, in a way. He always seemed so completely in Luca's shadow, even though his parents were bursting with pride at the thought of having a future priest in the family. He would be following in the footsteps of his great uncle, who had been the province's priest. And, like his great uncle, he would place his family under the protection of the Church. Don Pascuale, head priest of the Basilica in Palermo, had contacts in Rome and had already ensured that Roberto could enter the seminary there.

"So, Enzo, how was crab catching yesterday?" My uncle Toni sat down next to me.

"It was great, *zio*!" I replied.

Uncle Toni was an amiable character. He was the right-hand man in my grandfather's business, as none of his sons wanted to go into the Marsala trade. My father went north to learn the textile trade, and Uncle Luciano emigrated to America. Toni had started working in my grandfather's vineyards and press houses as a boy. After he married my aunt, Nonno gave him a management position. Now, he practically ran the whole company, but he still considered my nonno to be the boss. Toni didn't make any of his own decisions; he always consulted Nonno on them first. Nonno counted himself lucky—Toni had become like a son to him. Working together in the Marsala business had given the two men an unbreakable bond. But there was one thing they disagreed on, and they often had heated discussions about it. Toni wanted to defy the mafia and stop paying them money. However, my nonno just wanted to be left in peace, so he always paid what was demanded of him. There was no way he was going to mess with the mafia. It was only with difficulty that he managed to persuade Toni that he had no choice; on the contrary, if he didn't play along, he would put himself, his family and his business in jeopardy.

"You should come with me to the wine press house while you're still here." Toni looked at me with interest.

"I'd be happy to, *zio*. I've always wanted to find out more about your Marsala business. Luca usually wants to go down to the sea, but I'll try and convince him."

"Oh, Luca has no interest in these things, sadly. He may have grown up with it, but now he has other ideas. And he's a dreamer. I would prefer him to think about his future. No good will come of going into the military. In fact, if the political problems come to a head, who knows…"

A friendly middle-aged woman appeared in the doorway, arm in arm with Aunt Maria. They were in high spirits, chatting away affectionately.

Luca waved at me. I sat down next to him.

"That's Francesca's mother, Carlotta Rizzotto," he whispered surreptitiously.

"Where's her husband?"

"Leonardo Rizzotto was killed in a car accident a couple of years ago. A tragic affair." As Luca quietly continued telling the story, I watched my cousin Zia. She was chattering away merrily with her friend Francesca. They strolled among the sumptuous bougainvillea bushes, accompanied by a petite young girl. The girl picked a flower and arranged it dreamily in her hair.

"Who's the pretty girl next to Zia and Francesca?" I asked Luca.

"That's Francesca's younger sister, Carina. I think she's the most beautiful girl in all of Sicily!" he gushed.

"Luca, you're in love! I'm right, aren't I?"

"Come and sit down, children!" My nonna reached for her cane. Maria helped her out of her lawn chair. Then she stood there a moment, gazing with satisfaction upon her family as they proceeded to the big table. Nonno Vittorio took his seat, as usual, at the head of the table, and his guests seated themselves to his left and right. People were feasting, drinking, laughing. Luca handed out cigarettes, and I smoked along with everyone else, although the tobacco scratched my throat. The faint evening breeze felt pleasantly cool.

Sometime after midnight, a car drew up and a short, youngish man climbed out. Toni hurried over to him.

"What do you want? We're eating dinner!" he snapped brusquely.

"Oh, come on now, Toni. I just want to speak to Vittorio for a moment."

"Leave him alone. It's late. You can come back tomorrow!"

"Eh, *non capisci*—it's important!"

Toni came back and whispered something into Nonno's ear. At that, my grandfather stood up and headed over to the car. In the semi-darkness, I could only see the silhouettes of the two figures, talking softly. After a while, Nonno returned and sat back down at the head of the table. The car drove slowly away down the drive.

29

Michele Fiori looked at Vittorio quizzically.

"Carlo Gambino wants to meet me tomorrow. It's about the export costs. Has he spoken to you too?" Nonno asked tensely.

"No, but he probably will soon. What can we do about it? He's going to want to increase the costs and everything else that goes along with it," said Michele gloomily.

"Yes, probably. I'll let you know what he wants."

"Thanks, Vittorio. I've always been able to count on you."

The church bells roused me from sleep.

"Time to get up, Enzo!"

Aunt Maria was standing at the bedroom door. She was elegantly dressed and ready for Sunday Mass. I stumbled out of bed, gave myself a quick scrub in the washbasin and pulled on a white shirt. Anna had kindly set out a cup of coffee for me on the kitchen table. Luca honked his horn. I stepped out into the dazzling sunlight.

"Did you sleep well and rest up?" he asked, grinning. "Everyone else is at the church already. We need to hurry."

The car screeched along the winding road. Soon after, we arrived in the forecourt. We leapt out of the car and managed to squeeze into the rearmost pew just in time. The elderly priest stepped through the church door with Roberto following behind, solemnly carrying a cross. Two altar boys trailed in their wake. The congregation rose to their feet and joined their voices in song.

Luca nudged me. "Look, Francesca is here! And there's her beautiful sister Carina sitting next to her."

My eyes strayed to the fifth row of pews. I could make out Francesca's profile among the women dressed in black. Her hair was pinned back, accentuating her high cheekbones. Her dark, sad eyes rested devoutly on the priest's face. Her melancholy expression gave me pause for thought. I remembered my discussion with Luca the previous evening. Her father, Leonardo Rizzotto, was killed in a car accident the previous year. Was she thinking of him right now? Francesca's father had been politically active in the fight against the mafia. His death had caused quite a stir, as his friends had insisted he'd been murdered, and that the mafia had rigged his car with explosives. Investigations were launched, but in the end, his wife gave up hope and just wanted to be left in peace—the criminal investigators couldn't bring her husband back, after all. She resigned herself to living the rest of her days as a widow. Her daughters took care of her, and that enabled her to bear the pain. At the time, she had failed to convince her husband that politics was like playing with fire, and that he could quickly get burnt. And what she had always feared ended up coming to pass. She felt paralysed, marooned amid circumstances that she could have prevented. What woman didn't see right through all the feuds and power plays among the men in this society? But there was next to nothing she could say about it—on the contrary, she was urged to keep her mouth shut and do her duty. Her personal opinion was not wanted. Not only would she have made herself unpopular, but she would also have shown her husband up—the worst offence of all. And that, in turn, would have caused her husband to fly into a rage, and he would have taken it out on her, aggressively, thoughtlessly, unscrupulously, just like the men who destroyed him, only behind closed doors, in his own house. An action that society deemed perfectly legitimate would have spelled the end for Francesca's mother. She was better off keeping quiet and looking on helplessly as her husband made political gains in parliament, leaving him increasingly at the mercy of a hostile opposition. Public threats were made against him, but he took it all in his stride, believing his opponents were no match for him. Soon, he was receiving death threats in writing, which Carlotta Rizzotto found extremely alarming. Yet, her husband could not be dissuaded from carrying on as if nothing had happened. The tension had grown between her and her husband, and he had become noticeably more aggressive when anyone mentioned the subject to him. He didn't want to admit that he had more enemies than friends.

The Mass bell rang. After the prayer, the priest administered Communion, with Roberto holding the wine out for him. The priest's movements were calm and controlled. The women in their black garb kneeled softly to pray in their pews. Their portly husbands were on the other side, their faces a mask of boredom and longing for the moment they could stand up and head to the bar.

"The tuna fishing ritual is happening tomorrow. I'm meeting Matteo in front of the *tonnara* in Favignana at seven. Are you coming?" whispered Luca.

Luca had often told me about this, especially the bloody slaughter of the tuna. Sometimes just hearing about it made me feel sick, but there was no way I could pass up this offer. It was considered a rite of passage for men to take part, after all, and I didn't want to look like a wimp.

"I want to go and visit a wine press house with your father while I'm here on holiday. Do you want to come with me?"

Luca stared at me in disbelief. "You're better off going alone, Enzo. Press houses are way too boring for me."

"*Nel nome del Padre, del Figlio e dello Spirito Santo. Amen.*"

Mass was over. The chiming of the church bells was exactly what the men had been waiting for. They made their way impatiently towards the exit. Their wives trooped along behind, whispering quietly.

Luca tugged at my sleeve. "Wait!" His eyes sought out Carina in the throng of women. He winked at her, and she smiled shyly.

"Flirting again, little brother?" came a voice from behind him. Zia gave him a look of mock reproach. "Give it a rest, Luca! It's not proper to wink at ladies in church."

The Mattanza

The forecourt of *Tonnara Fiori*, the huge tuna factory, was bustling with activity.

"Luca! Good to see you! And you brought your cousin? Ciao, I'm Matteo." Matteo gave me a friendly hug with his muscular arms, then hugged Luca with just as much enthusiasm. Matteo was the factory founder's grandson and a good friend of Luca's. It pleased him no end that I was going to take part in the *mattanza*, the traditional tuna fishing ritual that took place off the coast of Sicily and Sardinia, and he was visibly proud to be able to show me round the factory. Luca greeted Gioacchino, one of the oldest fishermen. He was wearing blue overalls and sat hunched over on a wooden crate by the entrance. His weather-beaten face told of many years at sea. He was watching us keenly, his deep blue eyes as sharp as ever in spite of his 78 years. He smiled at us good-naturedly when he heard it would be my first mattanza.

Huge great chimneys towered above the imposing factory building. Behind the iron gates lay an inner courtyard surrounded by towering pine trees. The building was an impressive sight inside as well. Gothic arches traversed the high ceiling, and I could make out an F in the centre of the wrought iron windows. We entered the vestibule, which had an exit leading out to the sea. Thick ropes hung from the ceiling.

"The tuna are hauled in through the door here, then the fish are beheaded and hung up on the ropes so the blood can drain out."

In the next room, the *batteria*, copper kettles were suspended in a row over coal fires.

"This is where we cook the tuna. We use everything: the eyes, the blood, the oil and the bones. Nothing is thrown away," explained Matteo. He led us on into the *galleria*, which had a statue of the Virgin Mary by the entrance.

"This is where the workers fill cans with the tuna mixed with olive oil. There are two types of cans. The yellow ones, the *ventresca*, contain the tuna belly. The green cans, the *tarantello*, contain the meat from the fish's abdomen."

Matteo also showed us the carpentry workshop where wooden shipping crates were put together.

The office of the *rais*, which we were now approaching, was a small, dark room.

I had learnt from Luca that the rais was not just the boss of the entire team of fishermen, overseeing the fish traps and deciding when the tuna would be killed. Rais was an old, reverential Arabic term meaning sultan.

A single light bulb hung over the rickety table, and we could make out an imposing figure in the low light. A middle-aged man with hands as big as tiger paws was propped on his elbow over the morning paper. The air was thick with cigarette smoke. Clemente had been the rais of Favignana for twelve years. He was highly esteemed and treated with reverence, not only by the fishermen and *tonnarotti*, but among the population at large. These tuna catches always had a high yield, which gave the Fiori tuna factory's finances a boost. The many lucrative *mattanze* helped the company double in size, raise its export quotas and increase the tonnarotti's salaries. The people of Favignana could count themselves lucky to have access to such prosperity. The rais traditionally enjoyed considerable social standing, but Clemente was in a league of his own, as many of Favignana's residents, particularly the older ones, attributed the successful tuna catches to his prodigious skills. But he had remained humble in spite of this. When Michele Fiori, the owner of the tuna factory, wanted to provide him with somewhere to live on his grand estate, Clemente refused. He preferred to reside in a small cottage by the harbour, right next to the tonnara. He helped repair the nets, tie them back together with flax twine and grease them up, before they were laid out on the hill by the harbour, attached to the floats, then loaded onto the big longboat and sunk in just the right spot off the coast. It brought Clemente great joy to see that the fishermen didn't shy away from this hard work. In fact, they were proud to be part of this annual spectacle. They were deeply attached to the mythological significance and ancient tradition of tuna fishing. During the mattanza, they were at one with the tuna, with its life, its loving and dying, its coming into being and passing away. It was a never-ending cycle, converging miraculously at its climax: the mattanza.

"Luca!" came Clemente's deep voice. His powerful frame straightened up behind the rickety table, and he gave Luca a hug.

"I brought my cousin Enzo along with me."

Clemente held out a bear-like hand for me to shake. I felt very small and nondescript next to him.

"The mattanza is happening tomorrow. You can go on board the *Vascello*," he said proudly.

Luca winked at me. "It would be an honour, Clemente!" He set two bottles of Marsala down on the table. "As a little thank you."

Later, we were sitting in the *locanda*, where the tonnarotti met after work. Photographs hung on the chalk-white walls. Matteo pointed to the most prominent picture. "That's my father after he caught the biggest tuna of all time." I could hardly believe my eyes. There stood a tall young man, holding the head of a colossal monster in his hand. One of his feet was resting on the fish's body, which lay on the ground. The tuna was bigger than the man himself, who was looking intently at the camera.

"That's incredible!" I exclaimed.

"The tuna weighed over two hundred kilos," Matteo explained proudly. "It was backbreaking work heaving it into the boat. The animals tend to lash out wildly, even with rigor mortis already setting in."

I secretly hoped I would be able to watch the spectacle from afar so the tuna's flailing fins wouldn't knock me overboard.

"Two weeks ago, we barely caught four hundred fish. That was disappointing," complained Matteo.

"There should be plenty tomorrow. Clemente went out with Maurizio earlier to count the fish. They said over two thousand swam into the *bastardella*."

I shot Luca a questioning look.

"The tuna are guided into a net cage underwater. The net cage has different chambers where the fish are held until the mattanza. The bastardella is the last chamber before the *camera morta*, the chamber of death. This chamber has a net floor, which is then lifted during the mattanza. You're in for a surprise!" Luca grinned.

It all kicked off the next morning.

"Guess what! We're sailing up to the camera morta in the *Vascello*, the biggest longboat in the fleet. We'll be able to watch the action close up," Luca explained.

Everyone gathered in the tonnara just after sunrise. As the rais came in through the curved entrance, a sudden hush fell. Behind him, six men strode pensively to the end of the floating pier, where longboats of various sizes were moored. The rais joined the men in the smallest boat. Their calloused hands dipped the oars into the water. A smell of salt and fish wafted through the sea air. The rais's boat ploughed on, the others forming a line, prow to stern, that trailed along behind it. A small tugboat, the only one with a motor, dragged us out into the water. With every movement, I could feel us drawing nearer to that special spot in the middle of the ocean. It was as if our boats were pulled towards the tuna by an irresistible magnetic force. The tension was building, and I had the impression the tuna were dragging the boats along behind them. The sun was already beating mercilessly down upon us.

"Hopefully I won't get seasick."

The rais began to recite his litany: "*Na sarvirriggina a matri ri dii ri Tràpani!*" It was a Hail Mary for the Madonna of Trapani. This was followed by the Lord's Prayer and prayers to the saints requesting a good catch.

The tonnarotti responded: "Holy Creator, we ask you for eternal peace after our deaths!"

I was completely awestruck by the song. The cries of the men were heartrending.

Luca turned to me. "We're getting close to the nets. These are knotted together over several weeks and are arranged in a specific formation along the tuna's migration route before being sunk down into the sea.

When the net cage is opened under the water, the tuna are lured into the trap. The net cage consists of several chambers where the tuna are divided into groups and kept captive until the day they are killed. The underwater chambers are separated by a collapsible door made of netting. When it is opened, it drops down and rolls up on the seabed. The men can then use ropes to pull it up and close it again."

Our boat drew into position by the camera morta, the chamber of death. The fishermen pulled up the net and attached it to their boats. The middle section of the net could reach up to thirty metres beneath the surface. Three or four boats arranged themselves along each of its edges, leaving only the eastern side open. The men watched the tuna and waited until they swam in. When the fish were inside the chamber of death, a boat was positioned on the eastern edge of the square to close it off. Only the rais still remained in the middle of this square formation. He raised his arms and gave the command for the men to pull up the net, whereupon the forty men started lifting the net evenly out of the water from the sides of their longboats. At the same time, the tonnarotti sang an unfamiliar song with loud, booming voices, pulling more and more of the net out of the water as they bellowed.

Suddenly, flitting shadows started to appear. Ripples sliced the surface of the water and jagged dorsal fins glided this way and that. The shouts of the men morphed into throaty calls as more and more fish came into view. The tuna writhed faster and faster as the voices of the tonnarotti grew more and more ecstatic. The bigger the fish, the more loudly and passionately the men's voices roared. The rais gave the order to kill, whereupon the men drew their gaffs in unison and struck the animals with all their might. The gaffs hooked into the firm flesh of the tuna, and the foaming surf turned pink as the fish were hoisted onto the gunwale, rhythmic cries filling the air. The creatures flailed their fins wildly, shaking uncontrollably from the pain of the gaffs striking their bodies. Several of the men fell over each other as they scrambled to avoid the flapping fins. The stench of blood and fish oil rolled over me like a cloud. I felt nauseous at the sight of so much blood, and the barbaric cries and the slaughter filled me with revulsion. I clung to the railing and let myself be swept away into a timeless limbo, where life and death came face to face.

Luca's dark eyes were locked on the carnage. His torso was leaning over the edge of the boat to look the tuna in the eye. I could feel the fish juddering and thrashing around in mortal terror. Blood poured from their jaws, where the tonnarotti had stuck their gaffs. More and more blood flowed into the water, dying it first pink, then red, then finally a deep crimson. The men's muscular forearms grasped at the bleeding bodies and hauled them into the longboat. The smell of sweat and salt mingled with the stench of blood from the wounded fish. I felt as if my stomach were turning somersaults. The staring eyes of the giant fish horrified me. I turned and vomited over the back of the longboat. As I hung over the railing, the men continued to pull the net up further and further in rhythmic jerks. The bottom of the net was already visible. The last of the tuna were flailing around in the hollow of the net as it grew smaller and smaller.

The rais was the first to climb out of the boat and wade through the blood-red slush. Two more stout men followed him, and together they seized the last of the tuna with their gaffs. The fish fought for their lives. One of the men was struck with the thrashing tail of a dying fish. He gasped for air and dragged himself painfully back to the longboat. The fish struggled tirelessly for their freedom as the men tore and dragged at the nets until the jerking spasms finally died away. Hooting and crying out with joy, the tonnarotti leapt into the bloody water and rolled around in it. They celebrated their victory—their triumph—and wallowed around in high spirits.

"How can they swim in all that blood?" I asked Luca in dismay.

"Come on, Enzo. Don't give me that look! It's the greatest feeling, diving into that holy water. Just remember, the fish mated here before they were caught. That's the feeling the tonnarotti are trying to capture when they jump into the water. They say swimming in the bloody water of the mattanza gives you extraordinary powers."

"So why aren't you jumping in then? Knowing you, I bet you'd like to get some of that love water for yourself," I teased him.

"Only tonnarotti are allowed. More's the pity!"

Beginning My Studies in Cottbus, 1941

It was a bright, cloudless autumn day, and the woods were draped in gold. I watched the landscape curiously as it rolled by outside the train window, gradually transforming into open farmland. Sunflowers blazed in between yellow stubble fields, and rows upon rows of cabbages stretched as far as the eye could see. The even rhythm of the rolling wheels lulled me into a comfortable doze.

My memories of the past few weeks wouldn't leave me in peace. Over and over again, my thoughts kept returning to the letter confirming my place at the textile engineering school, my joy—then the packing. Mum had mixed feelings about saying goodbye. She was worried about me going to study in a country that was at war. Not to mention the grief over the loss of my beloved father.

He had always been very sickly, often catching colds, and he had had a cough for as long as I could remember. The doctors put it down to his weak immune system. He drank a glass of red wine every day, as it was supposed to be good for the blood. In actual fact, he just loved sitting down with a glass of wine at the end of a long, tiring day at the factory. It was part of our Sicilian tradition. One night, he suddenly developed a high fever. Mum called the doctor straight away, and he had my father transferred to hospital immediately. He lay in the hospital bed, weak, pale and feeble. I still remember, clear as day, how happy he was to see me.

"My dear Enzo, I'm so proud of you! You're smart, and you learn fast. You're bound to make something of yourself."

The sterile atmosphere of the hospital and the nurses and doctors dressed in white made me uncomfortable whenever I visited. But the worst thing was the sight of my father. There was no sparkle, no light in his eyes, just an immense tiredness and exhaustion looking back at me. After a few days, he seemed to be getting better. He was able to stand up, and he was starting to gradually recover his strength. But, quite suddenly, his fever worsened, and within an hour it was so high that a nurse called us in. Mum went to the hospital and stayed there with him. He died in the early hours of the morning.

I wept bitterly because I hadn't had the chance to say goodbye. Mum had called me just before and told me hurriedly, "Come as quick as you can." I let my little brother sleep. I couldn't help fearing the worst but didn't want to believe it. I threw my coat on in a rush and ran to the hospital as fast as I could. I was too late by mere minutes. The sight of my dead father sent me into a state of shock. My throat felt constricted—I couldn't make a sound as tears streamed down my face. I felt utterly wretched. My father was dead. Never again would I be able to go for our favourite walk by the stream, nor would I be able to hear his reassuring voice calling me to get up in the morning. Never again would I be able to talk to him about the latest power looms, nor listen to his treasure trove of expert knowledge on how I could best learn and master the craft, perhaps even develop new innovations and learn all about the machines. When my father talked to me about the textile trade, his fascination was palpable. I could practically feel the different fabrics beneath my fingers. But that was over now. No more exciting conversations, no more encouraging words.

"Tickets, please!"

The voice roused me from my thoughts. The conductor was accompanied by two SS soldiers. I hastily rummaged in my waistcoat pocket. "Here you go!"

The conductor peered closely at the ticket. "You come from Switzerland. Do you have an entry permit?"

I reached into my pocket again and handed him my passport with the entry document. The SS soldiers also seemed interested in my passport.

"You're an Italian citizen travelling from Switzerland? Ah, here's your visa. A student visa. Are you going to Cottbus to study?" asked the smaller of the two SS soldiers.

"Yes, at the textile engineer training college."

"How long will you be staying?" The larger of the two soldiers gave me a piercing look.

"Two semesters."

The soldiers dismissed me with a wave of the hand and continued on their way.

"Thirty more minutes to Cottbus Central Station!" announced the conductor.

I tucked my documents away again. Relieved, I looked out at the landscape, which was starting to look much less rural. Terraced houses and small factories streaked by, separated by roads and alleyways. I could make out two cars and a military truck on the country road, then another cart. Everyone else was travelling by bicycle or on foot.

With a screech of brakes, the train pulled into Cottbus Central Station. I looked out of the window. Soldiers were saying farewell to their loved ones—women and children—as new soldiers arrived. It was raining. I hauled my trunk from the luggage rack and pushed my way through the crowd.

I took the tram to Potsdamer Platz, then it was a five-minute walk to Bonnaskenplatz. I marvelled at the grand houses and huge buildings. It was a shame that all the shops seemed to be closed or standing empty. A queue of about fifty women snaked along Kaufhausstrasse, leading up to a bakery. They were clutching food coupons in their hands.

I could hardly wait to take my seat in the lecture theatre of the textile engineer training college and learn about the latest technological advances, to study how all the different fabrics were made and become intimately acquainted with the pattern design process. This training would open up a whole range of career possibilities for me.

Frau Pöllnitz, my landlady, greeted me warmly and led me to my room. It was spacious and contained a wardrobe, desk and washstand.

"Blackout is at 5 p.m. Please bear that in mind. If you hear an air-raid siren, run to the cellar as quick as you can. All the residents of the house gather in the air-raid shelter down there. Dinner is about to be served. Please can you come to the table in ten minutes?"

"Yes, gladly."

Frau Pöllnitz left the room. I washed myself in the washbasin, which felt good after my long journey. As I combed my hair, I contemplated my reflection in the mirror. I had never liked my long, thin nose. But my long eyelashes and my dark, almond-shaped eyes made me at least somewhat presentable. In fact, my facial features were refined, almost aristocratic—but that nose still bothered me. I applied a little pomade to my close-cropped hair, put on a clean shirt and made my way to the living room. It was thick with the smell of cabbage soup. I was shown to my seat. A young man was already sitting at the table. We exchanged greetings. Lars was from Norway.

"How was the train journey?" he asked.

"Uneventful. I had to change in Leipzig. The stations and trains were jam-packed."

Lars told me how he had been questioned by the SS men. They had scrutinised his passport and visa very closely.

"I had a bad feeling about it. I'm sure they thought I was a spy!"

We laughed. Right off the bat, Lars and I got on like a house on fire. We chatted away at length. He was also planning to study at the training college. He told me about his family in Norway. His father worked at the cloth mill, while his mother worked as a nurse. They were also completely self-sufficient. "We have a pig farm in our garden, and we converted the lawn into a vegetable plot," he said with a touch of irony. "And what brings you to Cottbus?" he asked me, intrigued.

"My father worked in the textile industry. He worked in a large weaving mill, the same one where I completed my apprenticeship. I think I want to go into business for myself at some point, so I want to gain more knowledge. Sadly, my father died of pneumonia six months ago."

"Oh, how awful! I'm so sorry."

"Yes, it was a shock for me, and for my little brother and my mother. At first, I thought I should defer my studies for a year, but my mother thought she would be okay. She sews clothes for children and earns a little money that way."

"Living conditions in Switzerland must not be that bad yet."

"It's fine, but they have introduced food coupons, and we only have very limited consumer goods available. Have you seen the long queues for the butchers and bakeries here? I can't help wondering what's going to happen. Frau Pöllnitz thinks she has enough coupons for us to have meat once a week. The problem will be getting hold of sugar and coffee. I brought chocolate with me from Switzerland."

We talked well into the night, and I felt as though I had already made a new friend.

The next day, we walked along Kaufhausstrasse towards Potsdamer Platz. There was another huge queue of people waiting outside the general store. Around the corner, we passed a market garden. There were not many flowers here, but all the more fruit trees, tomato plants, bean poles and lettuce seedlings. The remaining window displays on the once-bustling shopping street were half empty and were a sorry sight. We headed across the Marktplatz. Potatoes, carrots, cabbage and turnips stretched as far as the eye could see.

I was reminded of the markets in Sicily. The smells of the different varieties of fruits and vegetables, the colours of the tomatoes, peppers and courgettes—a paradise beyond compare. There were delights to be sampled everywhere you turned. My favourite was the salami and olive seller. Just thinking about it made my mouth water. Then the fresh chicken, the fish and seafood... I was brought back to the present with a bump, as an SS official suddenly appeared in front of us, asking what we were doing here. We showed him our identity cards, and he went on his way.

"What would have happened to us if we'd been Germans? Would he have dragged us off to war there and then?" asked Lars in a whisper.

"Lucky we had our identity cards and visas on us, otherwise he might not have believed us. Come on, we'd better hurry up. The training college is round the corner over there."

The large lecture theatre was a hive of activity. It was filled with heated discussions, punctuated by bursts of laughter. The students seemed to be in high spirits. When the gong sounded, we all crowded into the huge room. The lecturer came briskly through the door and slammed it behind him to get everybody's attention. Immediately, there was absolute silence. He greeted us briefly and then had us all introduce ourselves with our name and country of origin. Many people were from northern countries like Iceland, Sweden and Norway, along with a man from Afghanistan and two students from Sudeten Germany. I was particularly glad to see four of my compatriots, who, like me, had made their way here from Switzerland to complete their studies. The student sitting next to me, whose name was Wolfgang, came from Cottbus. He told me about his father, who ran the tailor's in town. "If you get bored in the evenings, come down to the Kolping Society. We play cards and make music together."

I gave my enthusiastic assent, keen not to spend my evenings alone in my room. Wolfgang clapped his hands when he heard I had even brought a violin with me.

I liked the school a lot, especially the pattern design and dressing classes.

The following week, I started a work placement in one of the nearby weaving mills. I soon discovered that I was one of the most highly trained of all the students. Because I had been working in the factory since I was fifteen, first as a labourer, then as an apprentice, my experience put me ahead of many others in the group. I knew my way around a power loom and a twisting machine, and I was familiar with pattern design. One professor took me aside and told me quietly that my knowledge was excellent, and that I would probably find the work placement boring. He was wondering whether, instead of the work placement, he might be able to find somewhere else to put me.

"Oh, how thoughtful of you, Enzo, to bring me such beautiful flowers! Please, come in and sit down! Wolfgang has been waiting impatiently for you to arrive."

Wolfgang's mother clasped my hand warmly in greeting. She was handsomely dressed, and she led me through the tiled entryway with a spring in her step. The walls gleamed bright white, and the ceilings were adorned with stucco. The house, with its tasteful furnishings, gave the impression of elegance and wealth. The entrance hall was decorated with antique French furniture. A Venetian mirror hung on the wall in a copperplate frame featuring images related to weaving and spinning. A magnificent glass door led into the next room. In the centre of the room stood an antique bust on a small Louis XV table. I heard Wolfgang's voice, along with the clacking of his crutches. "Enzo! Great to have you with us. Come and sit down! Let's have a drink to give you a proper welcome!"

He opened a cabinet and withdrew two crystal glasses with gold trim. The glass door swung open, and an older, plump woman appeared. She beamed at us amiably. "You must be our Swiss guest! Welcome! What would you like to drink?"

"Bring us some champagne, please, Frieda! Thank you."

We made ourselves comfortable at the long table. Wolfgang told me about his job at his father's workshop. Before the war broke out, he had mainly sewn suits and evening gowns for wealthy customers from all over Germany, but for two years now he had been forced to make officers' apparel and uniforms for senior military personnel. Good thing too, he said, because that meant his father wasn't drafted. And Wolfgang's disability meant there was no question of him having to go to the Front either. But several of his friends had been deployed, and I could hear the concern in his voice.

"We can count ourselves lucky that we can dedicate ourselves to our studies. I'm excited for our work placements next week," I said.

"You might find it rather boring. The other German students are coming straight from school. They have no idea about weaving machines, let alone what working in a factory is like. You'll certainly be able to show them a thing or two! And nobody knows more about looms than you," said Wolfgang enthusiastically.

"Lars, the Norwegian who's renting one of the other rooms where I live in Bonnaskenstrasse, also has experience working in his father's factory. He makes particularly fine fabrics out of wool. Oh yeah, and Ismail from Afghanistan was telling me that he worked at Christy in England."

"Christy is a world-renowned company, apparently. What do they make?"

"Mainly terry towels, as far as I can tell."

The glass doors swung open again, and Frieda the housekeeper brought in plates and silverware. She deftly set the table, then laid out platters of cold cuts and cheese and brought us fresh bread, pork dripping and tea. I was ravenous. Frieda rang the bell to summon everyone to the table.

The other family members greeted me warmly. Wolfgang's father took his seat at the head of the table. He was a middle-aged man with a diminutive stature. His grey-flecked hair was combed severely back, and the thin strands shone with pomade. His fine facial features were soft and even. He spoke quietly, and his clean, manicured hands lay sedately on the table. To his right sat Wolfgang's mother, steering the conversation round the table with her easy manner and creating a relaxed atmosphere with her humorous interjections. Her friendly demeanour made me feel instantly at home in this distinguished house. She told me about Wolfgang's siblings, including his brother Wilhelm, who was completing his officer training and was currently stationed with a military unit in Brandenburg.

"We hope he won't have to go to the Front. The situation in Russia is dreadful, and I can only pray he won't be deployed there," she said, concerned.

"Please, let's not talk about it," Wolfgang's father objected. "Luise is coming this weekend. She needs to prepare for her final school examinations. I can't wait to have our girl here with us."

Wolfgang's sister Luise attended a boarding school and only came home to visit one weekend a month.

"My sister plays the piano well. We often play together in the orchestral society. And we could do with a violin in our little orchestra too," said Wolfgang.

"Oh, you play the violin?" his mother asked with interest.

"Yes, I play in an orchestra back home. Wolfgang is very excited that I brought my violin with me. Of course, I would love to play in the Kolping orchestra."

"Join us at St Stephen's Church on Sunday evening. We're meeting at 7 p.m. for orchestra rehearsals. I will find some sheet music for you!"

St Stephen's church was a neogothic building with multicoloured windows and a heavy oak door at the main entrance. Wolfgang was already chatting away happily with his friends when I entered the sacristy.

"Enzo! There you are! Friends, we have some reinforcements! What do you think, Enzo? First or second violin?"

"Hello! I'll try second violin to start with," I replied.

"Then allow me to introduce you to our first violin, Franz Schulze," Wolfgang exclaimed delightedly.

"Oh, I've risen through the ranks rather quickly there. Enzo, I'm happy to give you responsibility for first violin." Franz looked at me inquiringly.

"You don't need to intimidate our new member right off the bat, Franz. Don't worry, Enzo. We all play as equals here."

"Quite. There's enough hierarchy out there. In here, anarchy reigns supreme!"

"You don't need to go overboard, Julius! Enzo, allow me to introduce you to Julius Binder, oboe."

"Hello, Enzo! Nice to meet you."

"I'm Monika Lange on the clarinet, and that's Elsbeth Fischer."

"Hello, Enzo. Pleasure to meet you! I play clarinet too," Elsbeth said in greeting.

"Cellist Heinz Köhler here! Hello, Enzo."

"And last but not least, let me introduce you to my beloved sister, Luise!"

"Hello, Enzo! I've already heard so much about you," she said.

"All good things, I hope," I said, grinning.

"Of course." Luise gave me a friendly smile.

"We could do with more female reinforcements, Luise. What happened to your friends Klara and Barbara? Aren't they coming anymore?"

"Oh, Klara decided to get more involved in the *Bundesjugend*."

"Pff, she should ditch that! Has she gone mad?" Julius exclaimed.

"Not so loud, Julius. Careful what you say. Keep your thoughts to yourself," Wolfgang rebuked him.

"Jeez, can't we even have our own opinions anymore? I just mean, it's a real shame she won't be playing music with us anymore."

"You took a shine to that Klara, didn't you, Julius?"

Laughter filled the room, and Julius tried to hide his blushes.

"Of course, guys! But now I know she's in the Hitler Youth, I must admit I'm glad I didn't kiss her after all. I wouldn't want to kiss a traitor!"

We chatted some more, then sat down and played a couple of pieces of Mozart and Schubert. It wasn't until late in the evening that we left the church and proceeded to Wolfgang's house. We stayed there a while longer, and did so at our subsequent meetings too, sometimes sitting together until midnight discussing anything and everything.

Frau Pöllnitz was busy in the kitchen with the radio on quietly. A German military march was playing. I sat down at the breakfast table, and Lars took a seat beside me shortly afterwards. In the background, we could hear the rest of the radio programme: *Newsreel, 8 October 1941: Mass rally in the Berlin Sports Palace for the opening of the third Winter War Relief Fund. The Führer himself came to Berlin during new large-scale operations on the Eastern Front to speak to the German people in honour of this event.*

Then came a chorus of loud cheers and applause.

First, Reich Minister Dr Goebbels gave a full statement of accounts for the 1940–41 Winter War Relief Fund. While around 358 million Reichsmarks were collected in 1933, total donations have continued to increase, with the 1940–41 Winter War Relief Fund amounting to 916,240,000 Reichsmarks. Then the Führer arrived in front of the Sports Palace, the old battleground of the Berlin National Socialists.

The people cheered; music and shouting could be heard.

In his great speech, the Führer delivered a crushing reckoning to the Bolshevik war criminals. The Führer stressed that every action in the Eastern Campaign had gone according to plan, just like in Poland, Norway, in the West, and in the Balkans. They had only been wrong about one thing: the scale of the Soviet Union's extensive preparations against Germany and Europe. That could be stated loud and clear now, since that opponent had already been broken and would never recover.

Applause rang out.

He lauded the great victories our soldiers had won against this ferocious, bestial, brutal enemy with its formidable armaments. No words could do their achievements justice. Those who sacrificed themselves at the Front, said the Führer, could never be repaid for their service. What our homeland has achieved must one day also stand the test of history. Everyone knows what is rightly demanded of them at this time and what it is their duty to give.

Then the national anthem began to play...

Lars and I ate our breakfast in silence. Frau Pöllnitz always listened to the weekly newsreel very attentively. I watched her as she did the washing up and saw how tense she was when the latest war report was read out. She was always complaining about the food coupons, which grew more and more paltry by the day, and she didn't like only being able to cook simple meals for us. I liked her. She was very caring and worried about us students a lot. I was sorry she had to spend hours and hours standing in line every day to get food for us. Lars had recently received a package with a large tub of lard. Since he was from Norway, we teased him, asking if he was sure it was lard and not cod liver oil. He shared the large tub with me and Frau Pöllnitz. At supper, we spread a thick layer of it on our bread.

The weeks I had already spent in Cottbus had absolutely flown by. I felt at home with Frau Pöllnitz, the lectures at the training college were interesting, and the work placement was a doddle. Every time Frau Pöllnitz listened to the weekly newsreel, I secretly thanked my lucky stars I was studying and not caught up in the war.

It had snowed overnight, and the windows were laced with frost. The snow on the rooves of Cottbus sparkled in the pale sunlight. It was Sunday. I could make out a smattering of footprints on the pavement. The tram glided silently by. It was the beginning of December, and the students were talking about going home over Christmas. I had planned to do so too, but I hadn't counted on several people asking me to bring back 'gifts' from Switzerland. Of course, I definitely wanted to bring back several cartons of cigarettes, as well as chocolate and coffee. But the 'gifts' my friends wanted were in another league altogether. First of all, Wolfgang asked me if I could bring him back a gold watch.

I couldn't remember how it happened, but it was as if I were jinxed; one person after another asked me for a watch, including Frau Pöllnitz, the librarian at the training college, the materials administrator—even Wolfgang's mother praised the quality of Swiss watches. In total, I was tasked with bringing back ten watches! Then the girls wanted stockings and silk. Luise asked me to bring back ten metres of pink silk! How was I supposed to get all that into the country? But I wanted to do it for the people who had become my friends and who had made me feel at home.

The weekly music rehearsals were an enjoyable distraction from my intensive day-to-day life as a student. I made new friends, and before long, a new girlfriend too. Luise and I met now and then to go for walks. I was sorry to say goodbye to her on 22 December.

"It's only two weeks, Enzo," she said, trying to cheer me up. We promised to write to one another.

I was supposed to return on 3 January for the start of the new term at the college. But things took a rather different turn...

Dear Luise, Basel, 25 December 1941

When I arrived home, I discovered a letter that has left me angered and frustrated. The Ministry of Foreign Affairs sent me a letter from the Italian army drafting me with immediate effect. Because I am an Italian citizen, even though I live in Switzerland, I must do my duty and travel to Italy. I went to speak to the authorities directly, as I do not want to give up my studies, nor do I want to leave my mother and younger brother on their own. But every argument I brought forth was dismissed. They told me I could recommence my studies after the war, and they would ensure my mother received a widow's pension while I was without an income. I'm still angry and am struggling to accept that I am to travel to Italy next week. I think it is cruel that I'm being patronised and told what to do. Above all, I'm upset that now, out of the blue, I'm expected to just give up my studies when it seems to me that I have only just begun. And I will miss you in particular. Is it not a tragic fate to be so suddenly separated from everything I love? I felt so at ease with you all. It was as if I'd found a new home, a new family, and speaking to Wolfgang and my other classmates made me discover a true passion for textiles and my studies, which are now to be so abruptly cut short. I can hardly believe it! What's more, I simply can't imagine how I will manage in the Italian army. I've never been to a military training school, and I've certainly never handled a weapon. It goes completely against the grain for me to get involved in this now. I want nothing to do with this whole war business. This uncertain situation makes me really nervous; it frightens me. I have to go to Novara in Piedmont on Monday to see the army doctor. I'm going to get the doctor to declare me unfit to go to war! That's my plan.

Keep your fingers crossed that I'll soon be back in Cottbus, and give my very best wishes to your brother Wolfgang!

With love,

Your Enzo

Start of Military Service in Rome, 1942

The army doctor pressed a cold stethoscope to my chest.

"Tip top. You are healthy and strong and can start your military training as of tomorrow."

"Is there any chance you could deem me unfit?" I asked.

The doctor looked at me, surprised. He was middle-aged, short and haggard. Thin strands of hair stood out on the collar of his coat. His cadaverous face was laced with deep wrinkles. "I was born and raised in Switzerland. Apart from holidays I spent with my relatives in Italy, I don't have any connection to this country. Plus, I'm having to interrupt my studies and leave my recently widowed mother and younger brother alone. If I'm here doing military service, I'm unable to look after them, let alone support them financially. And in Italy, there's a law that says the eldest son of a widow doesn't have to do military service. It's my right, *dottore*!" I said, trying to convince him.

"My dear boy, we are at war. Different laws apply now." He fiddled nervously with his stethoscope, then turned away and sat down at his desk.

The doctor's lack of understanding enraged me.

"I'm begging you, write me a doctor's note proving I'm unfit! I often suffer from colds."

He stood up impatiently and raised his voice. "I'm sorry for you and your widowed mother, but my hands are tied. I have to do my duty. Young sir, we are at war! You can count yourself lucky you will be remaining in Italy, not being sent to the Eastern Front."

I was on a train to Rieti, feeling exasperated and powerless. I had been assigned to the air force and would be spending the next two months completing my recruit training there. This damned war! It had absolutely nothing to do with me. That army doctor was a chicken, scared to risk his reputation. It was his fault I was having to break off my studies! I should have bribed him. This was Italy after all. I was even more annoyed that I hadn't thought of buttering him up with a generous sum of money. I'm sure he would have taken it and let me go. What an idiot I was! I had money on me, and plenty of it. The longer I thought about the situation, the more furious I became. I could have torn my hair out at the fact I was throwing away my future so rashly, sacrificing it to the military and the war. I bitterly acknowledged that there was nothing I could do about it now. I'd missed my chance!

I tried to console myself with the thought that the army doctor might have denounced me for attempted bribery. They could have sent me to jail, or worse, a labour camp.

During the first role call at the military training school in Rieti, northeast of Rome, we all had our passports and identity cards taken away. I was then given an Italian army badge.

The time there dragged by slowly and painstakingly. The only enjoyable moments were when I received letters from Luise. She wrote to me often, and I to her. I very much looked forward to receiving post from her, and I could hardly wait until I had a moment of calm to read her detailed and entertaining letters. Wolfgang always wrote a few lines of his own, which usually caused me more pain than joy. He described his interesting lectures in great detail, which only heightened my desire to get back there as soon as possible.

I found the letters from my mother both comforting and encouraging. She wrote that I shouldn't worry myself, and that she was managing perfectly fine on her own. *"Just focus on what you have to do, then the time will pass quickly, and hopefully, the war will soon be over."*

The recruits were assigned their positions. I was ordered by the Ministry of Aviation to work as an interpreter at Centocelle Airport in Rome.

"Welcome to Rome, Enzo Dorigo! I'm Tenente Rossi. I'm glad to have you with us. Please, sit. Would you like a cup of coffee?"

"I'd love one!"

The lieutenant called for his assistant, then offered me a cigarette. He leaned back in his office chair in a relaxed manner. What a pleasant welcome from my superior! He looked at me with interest through his black horn-rimmed glasses and smiled.

"You come from Switzerland and have relatives in Sicily, correct?" He seemed to be well informed. "I'm glad to have someone at my side who speaks German. We have some problems here between our unit and the Germans. I'm convinced you will be able to help us build a rapport with them. Please let me know how the conversations are going. If you notice anything untoward, make sure you tell me."

"Yes, of course, lieutenant!" I wondered what this was all about, and whether I was being asked to turn spy.

As if he could read my mind, he said: "Don't worry. It's really just about making sure there's a good atmosphere. Maurizio will show you what you'll be doing." He handed me an envelope. "Your interpreter ID is in here. Carry it on you at all times and use it to prove your identity."

The building where the food was stored was right next to Centocelle military airfield. Maurizio was standing at the entrance. He was shorter than me, but he looked powerful and strong.

"You speak perfect Italian—that's great. Until now, I've been having to deal with a German who only pretended to speak Italian. I could hardly understand a word he was saying. Would you believe it, he complained to Tenente Rossi that I couldn't understand him?"

Maurizio made a dismissive gesture with his hand. "The German shouted at me, and his colleague laughed at me. I knew they were insulting me. Then he would say things like *aslok*."

I couldn't help laughing. The way Maurizio pronounced the swearword was hilarious.

"Don't laugh at me!" Maurizio's cheeks reddened. His small, dark eyes flashed angrily beneath his bushy eyebrows that met in the middle above his nose. "Tell me what he said?"

I could sense he was about to throw a fit of rage, but what could I do about it?

"*Fanculo*."

Maurizio's neck tensed. "The next time I see that German, I'll smash his face in!"

Indignant, he strode ahead of me through the warehouse. Now I understood why I needed to listen to what people were saying. Relations between the Germans and Italians were certainly strained. Neither side showed any respect for the other, simply because of the language barrier. It was ridiculous! I saw the enraged Maurizio before me, facing a brusque German, and realised: it wasn't just the language that was the problem, but rather a clash between two very different cultures. Southerners were encountering northerners. The Italian temperament was colliding with German arrogance. I glanced at the incomplete, illegible inventory list and could envision how the Germans would react to it—not to mention the German Wehrmacht, where propriety and perfection were the order of the day.

I knew instantly that I would befriend the Germans. Not only did I speak their language, but I also understood their nature and their sense of order and reliability. Likewise, I also saw myself in the Italians. I understood their way of life. Amiability and zest for life were second nature to me. At that moment, I knew that I didn't just master two languages—I carried two homelands within myself. I felt at home in one while longing for the other.

"No need to get upset, Maurizio! I'll deal with the Germans from now on."

Maurizio stopped walking. "I'm so glad. You'll certainly be wanting something in return for your services." He winked at me.

"Sure. How about some cigarettes?"

A smile flitted over his face.

"Come on, I'll show you the warehouses!"

He explained to me in detail where each food item was stored. Once a week, fresh vegetables, potatoes and eggs were delivered. I had to check the delivery notes and hand over the desired items to the Germans.

We reached a large storeroom in which stacks of crates were piled high along the left-hand wall.

"Maurizio, ciao! *Come va?*"

Maurizio waved at the driver. "*Ti piace la macchina?*" he quipped. "My friend Tomaso. He spends half his working hours driving the transport trolley around. This is where food is moved around, sorted and loaded into the trolley by the tonne. Behind the building are the lorries that distribute the food to the troops. You'll sometimes need to take inventory or check where each consignment is going. Then the Germans collect the food."

"Where is the office?" I asked.

"On the second floor. I assume you'll be spending most of your time there, as there's a lot of paperwork to be getting on with. But at least we don't have to rampage about in the mud like the infantrymen."

"Yes, I agree with you. I think I have it easy, being able to work here. Do I need to translate the paperwork?"

"No idea! Tenente Rossi can explain in more detail. I can already tell you're going to be a good intermediary, Enzo!"

Maurizio suddenly seemed to be in a good mood. He told me his family lived in Rome and his parents ran a hotel in the city centre.

"That's handy. You can go on holiday right round the corner. I have a cousin here in Rome. He's a priest at the Vatican."

Maurizio stopped abruptly where he stood and looked at me sharply. "Your cousin is a priest at the Vatican? You can count yourself lucky! Families with a connection to the Vatican are very highly regarded in Rome," he said reverently.

I seemed to have got into his good books.

Working in the office was an easy job, and I had enough free time to explore the city. I took a rickety bus towards the centre. The summer heat made me feel like I was on holiday.

I spotted the Colosseum through the grimy window. On a whim, I got off at the next stop and bought an admission ticket. The balmy sunlight filtered in through the arches that gave onto the stands. I imagined the throngs of people surging through these aisles, pushing their way outwards into the stands, mingling ecstatically with thousands of other people, and shrieking when the powerful, muscular figures of the gladiators appeared. In that moment, before one of them stepped into the arena, he was a hero, adored by all, an object of lust. How would he have felt beneath the curious stares of the onlookers? The loud cheers spurred him on; he knew it was a matter of life and death.

"Excuse me, signore. We are closing in ten minutes!"

What a shame, I thought. But I decided to come back and look at everything in this enormous building. I headed to the exit and boarded the next bus to St Peter's Basilica.

St Peter's Square was swarming with people. There were soldiers standing around the obelisk that dominated the centre of the square. A group of nuns were gathered by a fountain. Opposite stood another perfectly symmetrical fountain. Children were running around, chasing the pigeons.

I was overwhelmed. Giant colonnades flanked the square like protective arms, curving in a symmetrical arc up to the basilica. The deep clanging of the bells rang majestically out over the vast area. A sweep of Corinthian columns formed the façade of the church. Above them stood thirteen statues, the apostles with Christ and John the Baptist. Awestruck, I strolled through the colonnade towards the steps leading up to the cathedral. The great nave was surrounded by wide aisles. I stopped in front of the Pietà. Until then, I had only seen Michelangelo's marble sculptures in pictures. My mother kept a small picture of the Pietà in her prayer book. Even just that image had fascinated me. But seeing the sculpture up close, in the flesh, was incredible. What a masterpiece! Every vein, every muscle had been chiselled out of the stone with perfect precision. Maria's grief at the death of her son was etched into her face, and the dead body of Jesus looked unbelievably realistic.

I walked on past the statue of Saint Peter and arrived at the dome. I felt miniscule beneath this monumental vault. Great mosaics of the four evangelists were set against a golden background. I could scarcely imagine how the dome had been built and decorated at that dizzying height. I headed to the baldachin, which traversed the grave of Saint Peter. Seventy-seven oil lamps were lined up around it. The sea of light exuded a reverent atmosphere. I sat down on a bench and thought of Roberto, who worked here. I felt almost envious of him. He spent his working hours in this oasis of harmony and quiet, while war raged outside. Then the envy disappeared almost as soon as it had come—in spite of everything, I didn't want to be a priest. It was a calling, one that Roberto was made for.

I headed back across the square and turned down a narrow alley near the Via Romana. A Swiss guardsman in a blue uniform was standing before a nondescript door.

"Good afternoon. I have an appointment with Monsignor Roberto Dorigo."

I was led down a long passageway. Thick red carpets swallowed the sound of our footsteps. The atmosphere was calm, quiet, almost holy.

Roberto greeted me with exuberant warmth. "Let's drink a toast to the fact that my Swiss cousin is stationed in Rome!" He fetched two glasses and a bottle of grappa from the cupboard.

"I'm still not truly Swiss, otherwise I wouldn't be here, Roberto. But, of course, I'm delighted to see you and hear all the news of our family. I would rather have stayed in Germany to complete my studies, though."

"I can well understand that. We all hate this war. Luca is a fighter pilot now. He is stationed at the fighter pilot training camp in Castiglione and has a leadership role in his regiment," he explained.

"He made it, then. His dream came true. Even as a boy, he used to talk about becoming a pilot."

"The whole family is proud of him, apart from my father. You know he doesn't like how Luca has made a name for himself in the military. For Luca, it's purely a career move—he doesn't give a toss about the military. He just enjoys flying. And, well, you know him—he's a dreamer. He doesn't like the Germans, and he hates the Fascists even more. But he loves the fighter jets and doesn't think there's any danger. In fact, he doesn't think much about it at all. He's just fascinated by the speed and the freedom up in the air. It's like a drug for him. He recently spent a weekend here. He spent the whole time raving about his work. I'm a little worried about him, but there's no point. He's become a real daredevil." Roberto poured us both some more grappa. We drank it down in one gulp. He told me about his work, about the Vatican, the neutral speck at the heart of the war. "If you have any problems or if anything happens to you... you're safe here!"

"Thank you, Roberto. There won't be much happening at the food depot. I'm actually glad that I'm able to sit in an office and haven't been drafted into active service. But the Italian military postal service doesn't seem to be working. The letters from my German girlfriend take almost a month to arrive, and my letters don't seem to be getting to her at all. It's annoying. You write something that takes two months to arrive, and by then it's so out of date that it's hardly worth sharing it at all. I need to find another way."

"What other way is there? Perhaps via the air force airmail service. But how would that work?" Roberto laughed out loud. "Sorry, Enzo, I don't want to make fun of you. But I can't help you there either. You would need to chase down a German post convoy and make it take your letters to Germany. Maybe the German unit at the food depot would be able to help you? Or you could give your letters to a soldier who could post them for you."

"You've just given me a great idea, Roberto! I don't need to give them to a German soldier, I can send them myself via the German army postal service. Terrific, thank you! I have to go. Listen, let me take you to the Trattoria dell'Orso on Saturday evening!"

I was so delighted at the thought of sending the letters that I set off straight away. When Roberto had mentioned the German postal service, I remembered that there was a German army letter box at the main railway station, right next to the side entrance. I wanted to hurry so I could write a letter straight away and head to the post box!

Dear Luise, Rome, 14 July 1942

I hope this letter will reach you a little more quickly. I'm planning to post it in a German military letter box at the main railway station in Rome. My cousin Roberto gave me the idea. Please let me know when you receive it. I hope you are doing better. How long do you have to remain on bed rest? I think of you often and hope you get well soon from your bout of influenza.

My work in the office is not taxing. There's a lot of paperwork to complete—I have to take inventory of the food items and do translations. Today, I met my cousin Roberto, the priest at the Vatican. That was a pleasant change of scene. I wish you a swift recovery from the bottom of my heart. It must be boring spending every day in bed. Give my best wishes to your brother Wolfgang.

With love, your Enzo

I hastily stuffed the letter into an envelope together with the other letters. Then I fetched a bicycle from the storeroom and rode to the train station. A train had just arrived from Milan. People were surging towards the exit, suitcases in tow, while others shoved their way through the carriage doors, the faster among them snapping up the remaining seats before the train set off on its onward journey to Calabria. A young Italian soldier was hanging out of the window to kiss his wife goodbye. I pushed my bicycle in front of me. I could hardly make out the letter box in all the hustle and bustle. Then I remembered it had been put behind a pillar. Perfect. I leant the bicycle against a pole. I briefly looked around me, then extracted the envelope from my jacket pocket and slipped it through the slot. I looked around again, on high alert. No one seemed to have noticed. Feeling elated and in good spirits, I cycled back to barracks.

Maurizio was relaxing on his bed.

"Come on, Enzo. Have a seat here with me. Do you have a cigarette for me? Ah, *amico*, you're a gem."

"Gustav slipped me two packs yesterday. Do you know Gustav?"

"Yes, *Gustavo*. He gave me a bar of chocolate, just like that. He said the army chocolate was inedible. I thought it was fine—even my mum ate some."

"That's saying something, if your mum ate it," I chuckled.

I listened to Maurizio's chitchat with satisfaction. Since I had been talking to the Germans and interpreting for them, he had been showing his affable, friendly side.

A brusque knock made us jump.

"*Entre!*" called Maurizio, jumping to his feet.

Corporale Nunzio was standing at the door. "Enzo Dorigo, go to the command post immediately!"

Maurizio gave me a quizzical look. I gave a tense salute and followed the corporal. His quick march made me uneasy. He didn't say a word to me. At headquarters, I came face to face with Tenente Mazarone and four other military officers.

"Enzo Dorigo, you are under suspicion of espionage. Corporale Zizzi caught you sending correspondence via the German military postal service. Explain yourself! You belong to the Italian army and have nothing to do with the German post!"

A thought flashed through my mind: *my God, someone actually ratted me out!*

"I... I was only sending a letter to my girlfriend in Germany," I nervously tried to explain. The four soldiers laughed.

"Quiet!" The lieutenant gave me a piercing look. "A German girlfriend? You will need to explain that to me in more detail!"

It was embarrassing giving a detailed explanation, and I felt like a schoolboy who has pulled a naughty prank. But it was serious. They were accusing me of espionage. I was placed under arrest for 24 hours in an army barracks, under the supervision of two soldiers. That evening, I was subjected to a two-hour interrogation about my family's history and my childhood, and I had to provide the names and places of residence of all my relatives in Switzerland and Italy.

What if there were more consequences and I ended up in jail? I started to grow afraid. The worst thing I could imagine was that my family would be dragged into this mess. When I mentioned the names of my Sicilian relatives, the corporal's ears pricked up.

"Vittorio Dorigo is your grandfather?" The corporal chuckled. "Dorigo Marsala is the best in the country." He cleared his throat, and his snarling tone of voice transformed instantly into a friendly one. "Now, Enzo, your unlawful actions will have consequences. We are going to transfer you. Your linguistic abilities will be useful elsewhere. The Ministry of Aviation is summoning you to Lampedusa. A German radar station is being built there. You will be deployed there as an interpreter and will need to instruct the Italian unit on how to use this equipment. The German radar specialist will brief you when you get there. And next time you go to Sicily, bring me back a bottle of your grandfather's Marsala. That's an order!"

Finally, I was allowed to leave. I felt wretched. They were treating me like a criminal. Years ago, under Mussolini's military regime, criminals had been exiled to Lampedusa, an island off the coast of Africa, far from any civilisation. I couldn't believe I was being deported there.

I packed my things and said goodbye to Maurizio.

"The colonel wants to see you before you go. Boy, am I going to miss you, Enzo! Now I'll have to handle the Germans again. I hope you'll be ordered back here soon. Come to my house for a holiday. You can stay with my family anytime."

"I'd love to, Maurizio. Take care!"

Despondently, I trudged over to the office of my superior.

"I'm sorry you're being transferred. It's a bit of a blow, especially as you've created such a friendly relationship between the military units here at headquarters. I'm very sorry to have to hand you over to Lampedusa."

He looked tired and overworked. I was embarrassed, and once again I had the irksome feeling that I had risked too much. Friendly superiors like Lieutenant Rossi were few and far between. Even Maurizio with his fiery temper had grown increasingly mellow. He had even tried to learn a few scraps of German, mainly because it helped him get things from the soldiers. But he soon realised that the Germans were people too, young men just like him. He had even invited me and Gustav round to his house once. We had been given a warm welcome and had been fed as if we were part of the family.

I shifted from one foot to the other. I knew Colonel Rossi was extremely disappointed in me. But I had a few aces up my sleeve too. He needed me as an interpreter just as much as the military unit in Lampedusa. They were all dependent on us to translate.

"I would be grateful if you could order me back here soon. I'm sure I will only be needed on the island for a short while. I'm guessing you can arrange that."

The colonel shook his head. "Whatever may have happened, I know that you are an intelligent young man. And you've got talent! Interpreters like you aren't exactly ten a penny. Unfortunately, when you come back is out of my hands, but I'll talk to my superior about it in a few weeks."

Lampedusa, Autumn 1942

I had gradually grown used to the idea that I would be departing for a remote island. After spending a long time weighing up the pros and cons, I came to the conclusion that there was, in fact, a bright side to all this. I would be far from the worst of the war and would be right by the sea. I could spend my free time swimming and fishing, and it was only a small leap to go and spend a holiday in Sicily with my relatives.

The boat glided slowly through the waves. The sky was cloudless, and the bright sunlight glittered on the surface of the water. Somehow, I felt free and light-hearted, almost in a holiday mood. The boat was bustling with activity. Before we headed to Lampedusa, we were dropping off some German soldiers on the island of Pantelleria first. There was a large aircraft hangar there. We approached the harbour.

The squad was saluted by an officer, who gave them a briefing. Who would be picking me up? Probably no one, I realised sullenly. I wasn't part of the German or the Italian unit. My superiors were in Rome. Italian soldiers were now boarding the boat. We had to move together to allow enough space for everyone.

"Hey, I don't know you. Who are you?" asked one of my fellow passengers.

"I'm Enzo. Who are you?"

"Marcello. You look so fresh and unjaded. Have you just been drafted?"

"No," I said, laughing. "I've just come back from holiday in Sicily. I was in Rome, and now my services are required in Lampedusa—I'm an interpreter."

"Great, comrade. We're headed the same way. We're also stationed on Lampedusa. We're keeping an eye on what's happening on the African coast. Do you have any cigarettes?"

I opened my jacket pocket and took out a pack.

"Thanks, *amico*. Cigarettes are getting scarce. We have to ration them carefully. You can't get anything on the island at all. We have a couple of cases of wine, tins and cigarettes, so we can get by for the time being. The Germans seemed to be better stocked than us, right, Michele?"

"Yeah, definitely. They're always smoking, and one evening I saw them holding bottles of beer. So annoying that I can't speak German, or I would have asked one of them if I could at least have a swig."

Everyone laughed. "Oh, Michele, beer is just for the Germans. *Vino, vino, amore mio!* What could be better?

Apart from grappa, of course, which gets me blotto that much faster. Tell me, Enzo, how long are you going to stay?" The laughter grew louder still.

"You appear to be drunk already, Sergio," Marcello retorted.

"What a stupid question! Everyone knows how long we have to stay, or do we need to jog your memory on political matters? The great enemy is moving closer, and we're the bait," Michele said.

"What do you mean, bait? We'll fight them off. You'll see!"

"You're bonkers, Sergio. Fight them off? It's nonsense, stupid babble, lousy propaganda from the higher-ups in government. Us, fight them off? Do you know how strong their army is? Do you know how many soldiers are in the American army alone? We might as well pack our bags now!" Michele's voice grew louder and louder.

"Calm yourself, amico." Marcello put his arm around him in a friendly gesture. The atmosphere grew more subdued until, suddenly, the boat stopped short.

"This damned war," muttered Michele softly.

Sergio was unperturbed. "Whatever. We've got a cushy number on this island. Who's there already?"

"That's just it, amico, we're completely isolated there, marooned, exiled! But tell me, Enzo, which military unit do you belong to exactly?"

Michele was now looking at me with a friendly expression. His anger had subsided somewhat.

"Good question," I said.

Again, my remark was met with roars of laughter. "He's a spy hiding behind an Italian uniform! I can't quite place your accent, Enzo. Where are you from?" Marcello asked, amused.

"I'm from Switzerland!"

"*Uno svizzero in Sicilia!* I can't stand it any longer! You're pulling our legs, right? But I have to say one thing—your Italian isn't so bad for a mountain-dweller. Can you swim?"

They all clutched their stomachs with laughter. The boys were puzzled by me—it was great fun.

"So, it's like this, guys: I was born and raised in Switzerland, but my family comes from Sicily," I explained.

"*Ahhh, bravo, bravo, siciliano!*" Some of the soldiers applauded.

"But because on paper and in my heart"—as I spoke, I lay my hand on my heart in a gesture of feigned reverence—"I am an Italian…"

"*Siciliano, amico!*" Sergio corrected me.

"Siciliano, of course. I was lucky enough to be drafted into the war."

"We have such a kind military regime, don't we? They're going north and crossing the Swiss border to fetch boys for the war. *Fanculo!*" Sergio made pejorative finger gestures.

"Yeah, that's what I thought too," I said. "I love coming to Italy, but not in this uniform. At first, I was stationed in Rome, at Centocelle Airport. Now they're sending me here to interpret during the installation of the radar system."

"So you'll be instructing us on how to use the radar system?" asked Sergio.

"Exactly!"

"Welcome to the gang, amico. We're happy to have a svizzero among us! Do you have any chocolate?"

We approached the island of Lampedusa. The craggy, white rocks along the coast levelled out towards the east, where the harbour was situated in a sheltered bay. The street leading up to the harbour was lined with palm trees.

At the dock, I was greeted by two German soldiers.

"Hello, I'm Werner. Mechanic. And this is Klaus, our radar specialist."

We drove west in an open-topped jeep towards the *Albero Sole*, the highest point on the island. The route took us along a dusty gravel road and snaked its way up the hill in a series of hairpin bends. Apart from a couple of flowering maquis bushes, the landscape was barren and threaded with rocky ravines. Giant cacti were growing along the sides of the road.

"We're quite isolated up here. The commanders live down by the harbour. If you ever want to drive down to the village, I can take you on my motorbike."

"Werner loves his motorbike," Klaus interrupted.

Werner laughed, and his white teeth flashed against his tanned face. He was wearing a pair of modern sunglasses. I spotted a long scar on his right forearm.

"What happened?" I asked.

"Oh, it was a while ago now. There was an altercation, and someone tried to slash my arm." He grinned as if he had told a joke. "It seems to run in our family. My father was a commander in Africa. He suffered lacerations to his face in a crash landing. Now he has a scar too."

"And where is your father now?"

"He's at home. He was severely injured and is in a wheelchair." Werner's face darkened. He deftly steered the jeep around the potholes in the road. We were approaching the highest point, where you had a clear view of the ocean. I thought about Werner's father. It must be terrible. My father was dead. If he were still alive, he would certainly have been drafted too. Unthinkable.

"I would love to join you on a motorbike tour of the island," I said, breaking the silence.

Werner smiled. "There isn't much to see here. This is the only road that goes to the harbour, but we have to run errands every now and then, so we fill up the sidecar. It's very handy."

"How far is it?"

"It's around twelve kilometres from the harbour to the Albero Sole. We're almost at the top now. The radar is being built behind the two military barracks."

"We'll give you a tour of the island from our rubber dinghy," Klaus cut in. "Going round the coast is a bit of an adventure, isn't it, Werner?"

They both nodded cryptically.

Werner parked the jeep in front of the barracks. Only as I climbed out did I notice the torrid heat.

"We're just off the coast of Africa, hence the climate. But you'll soon get used to it."

Werner took my suitcase out of my hand and led me into the barracks. There was a small kitchen with a dining table and chairs, and the sleeping areas were next to them.

"We get deliveries of drinking water and wood for cooking once a week. We need to fetch the water with the tanker truck and then pump it into the tank behind the barracks," Werner explained.

"It really is a desert island. It doesn't even have water on it."

"You said it. And you can count yourself lucky you didn't arrive in the height of summer. It was practically unbearable. Would you like a little tour of the island?"

We trekked over the barren hillside. Lizards were basking on the rocks, which were surrounded by maquis bushes. We were above the cliffs, and the turquoise water was so clear that you could see all the way to the bottom. Werner pointed to a rocky outcrop.

"Check out the view! The thin black line on the horizon is the African coast."

Werner had already been on the island for two weeks, and already seemed to know every nook and cranny. He told me how not much equipment had arrived on the island thus far, so we couldn't start building the radar system yet. "The rest of the deliveries should arrive in the next two weeks, then we can get started. But we won't get bored. There is a beautiful beach down there where we can go swimming. Our unit has a small rubber dinghy. We've already explored the coast several times and discovered hidden caves and bays. There are rabbits on that small island over there, the Isola dei Conigli. Klaus and I went hunting over there and shot one," he said enthusiastically.

"Did you roast it?"

"Of course!"

"Now I understand why it's called the Isola dei Conigli. Unbelievable that such a small island has rabbits on it."

"And further up on the long beach is where the turtles hatch. I saw a huge one when out swimming once. That was quite something. It was ginormous!" He took a bag of small explosive bombs out of his pocket. "Homemade!" he quipped. "Let's go down to the bay, and then I'll show you how we fish out here."

We steered the dinghy out of the bay. As we reached the open sea, Werner pulled the oars in.

"Ready?" He placed a small explosive in my hand and lit the fuse. With all the strength I could muster, I flung it out to sea as far as I could. As soon as it hit the water, it detonated with a dull bang. We stood there, mesmerised, our eyes scanning the surface. The waves created by the detonation slowly ebbed away. Beneath the thin plume of smoke, more and more white fish started appearing, rising to the ocean's surface amid the gentle rocking of the waves. We counted them. Twenty fish! There was one large tuna among them. We heaved the fish into the boat using a hand net.

"That's more than enough, Enzo! What are we going to do with all these fish? I'm hungry, sure, but twenty fish?" He grinned. We gleefully celebrated our catch like mischievous schoolchildren.

"I know!" I piped up. "We'll grill the fish up here on Albero Sole and invite the Italian squad to come and eat with us. That's around twenty men. They can bring bread and wine for us in return."

"Brilliant, Enzo! Great idea!"

I appraised our improvised cooking station in the barracks.

"We'll need to cook in two or three shifts. Do we have enough wood?" Werner went to look. There were only a couple of logs left. "That won't be enough. What shall we do now?"

No sooner had the question been asked than Klaus appeared in the doorway. "Great catch!"

"Yes, but we just realised we don't have enough wood to build a fire. There's no wood on the island."

"No problem, friends. There are plenty of olive trees!" Klaus fetched an axe and set about chopping the olive tree behind the barracks into kindling. Klaus was the strongest one of us. He grew up as a farmer's son in Bavaria, and as such he was practically minded and able to tackle most problems. Once, when the jeep wouldn't start, he was the one who instantly knew what needed fixing.

After we had got into the nitty gritty of how the fish should be cooked, Werner fetched the motorcycle. It was a BMW R 75 with sidecar.

"This is my first time on a motorbike."

"Well then, enjoy!" Werner swung himself onto the seat, and I positioned myself behind him.

The Italian team gladly accepted our invitation. We bought lemons, onions and tomatoes at the greengrocer and fetched our ration of tins and cigarettes.

What a feast! We grilled the tuna, gilt-head sea bream and sardines. We boiled the tiny squid in water, then fried them in a pan with onions and olive oil.

A middle-aged Italian officer came to stand beside me.

"*Buona sera!* What would you like? Sardines, tuna, bream?" Klaus and I were in charge of the fish, while Werner sliced up bread and poured the wine.

"I like sardines the best. There's nothing better than sardines with a hunk of bread. Thank you for the delicious meal and good company. I'm Island Commander Bernini."

"*Piacere*. I'm Enzo Dorigo. Please, help yourself!"

"Pleased to meet you. You're from Switzerland, I hear."

"Yes, but my grandparents, uncle, aunts and cousins live in Sicily. I often spent my holidays there as a child."

"We're happy to have a translator with us on the island. Even though the German team is only staying as long as it takes to install the equipment—at least, that's the plan anyway—it's very helpful. You're on good terms with both sides. It's nice to see," he said appreciatively.

"Thank you! I've become good friends with both teams. Where are you from?"

"I'm from Rome. My whole family lives in Rome, which is sadly rather far away. It's not easy to send and receive letters from here. The post ship only comes once or twice a month. I miss my family, but then we all do. That's why I'm enjoying this sociable evening so much. It'll help me keep going a while longer!"

Dear Luise, Lampedusa, 24 September 1942

I'm actually really happy the Ministry of Aviation ordered me out here to the island. What could be more pleasant than lying in the sun and letting my gaze wander over the crystal-clear blue sea, occasionally diving into the cool water? That's what I do here in my time off. The German soldiers have a small inflatable dinghy. I have already made two German friends: Werner, who I'm sharing a room with at the barracks, and Klaus, a radar specialist. The construction of the radar station is going swimmingly. We're each on duty for six hours a day. We should be finished within a week. Then we need to keep an eye on the airspace from Malta and North Africa to detect any enemy aircraft and report them via radio. The telephone exchange is located on the highest point of the island. It's a really important communication channel. Unfortunately, I can't tell you any more than that. How are you? Have you recovered from your cold? I've been thinking of you.

With love, your Enzo

Dear Enzo, Cottbus, 20 October 1942

I am writing to you from the bunker. I have already spent the whole afternoon down here in the fire brigade's basement. Sirens are wailing because the bombers are approaching. Everyone is huddling tensely on blankets and straw mattresses in this dark cellar. A faint lamp is giving us some light. It smells musty, like damp and cold. I wish I were sitting in the cellar of our family home, but I couldn't make it back in time. I was brought here directly by two soldiers. They aren't letting anyone else out into the street. Mum and Dad have already packed their bags and are planning to travel west in the next few days, to stay with our relatives in Dusseldorf. Mum says we don't know how long the trains will keep running for. Dad will close his tailor's shop, and he and Wolfgang will go and help out in my uncle's shop in Dusseldorf. I can work at the hospital there. I've already been given permission. Sadly, I'm going to have to cut my studies short, but I'm glad to be of use at the hospital, and the practical work will be a good learning experience. Oh, how I wish this war would end soon. So many of our friends have been called up. I think of you every day, and it makes me sad not to know how long we will have to wait for each other. My mum is concerned about my health. You know I have been plagued by a cough and cold for weeks now, and I sometimes get asthma attacks still, especially in the damp cellar. My parents are considering sending me to Switzerland for a health cure. I am protesting against this, as I want to do at least something useful in this time of crisis. If I'm just sitting in a sanatorium, I'm sure to be bored, and I won't be of any use to anyone. By the way, we can no longer practise the violin either. Our chamber orchestra no longer exists, because everyone is gone apart from Wolfgang and me; they have all left or been drafted. Do you remember Daniel? He came to our orchestra rehearsal once. His parents ran the jewellers' shop in Bonnaskenplatz. It was a well-known shop selling jewellery and watches. One day, it was suddenly closed, and we never saw Daniel again after that. We don't know where he went. His whole family seems to have disappeared. There are various rumours flying around that they were abducted along with the other Jews. What a terrible thought! I simply can't fathom how such a well-respected family can suddenly be gone like that. Mum said they no longer felt at ease in this town since so many shops had closed. The food coupons are growing increasingly scant, and buying food takes a huge amount of time. We often have to queue up for hours just to buy the bare essentials. At least the postal service is still running, even though it takes a long time. Your letters make me so happy. They are my greatest treasures. I read them over and over again and try to imagine you going fishing in the sea under the warmth of the sun. And I dream of being by your side. Write to me again soon!

With love, your Luise

The radar was completed in the next few weeks. The 28 German soldiers worked with 22 men from the Italian unit, the Felino Group, together. First, we constructed a round stone building to house the surveillance posts. Then we had to assemble the radar, which was delivered as separate components. We positioned them on the stone building and connected them to the screen. The German lieutenant was with us all day to check the process was running smoothly, before returning to the village in the evenings, to his accommodation near the harbour. Then he was relieved by an Italian superior. When we were done, Werner and I gave the Italian commander and two of his group instructions on how to operate the equipment. Werner explained in German, and I would translate his explanations into Italian. It worked very well. Soon, the plant was put into operation. We worked around the clock in three shifts.

The radar allowed us to monitor air traffic from the Mediterranean area over Malta. If enemy aircraft were sighted, we had to raise the alarm via the German telephone exchange immediately.

Klaus and I were sitting in front of the screen.

"You've really got this thing down!" I praised him.

"I had to do six weeks' training. Even as a young boy, I used to love taking radios apart and putting them back together," he laughed. "The new Freya radar is an interesting development. If we weren't using it to wage war, I would say it was fun. I had to break off my studies at the Technical University in Munich. That was a real pain."

"Same for me. We're not the only ones."

"Yeah, I know. It's still a pain, though."

The radar was a newer design. With a wavelength of only one or two metres, it was capable of detecting even smaller objects.

I glanced at the screen. "Klaus, look at that. There are some dark dots there." The dots were moving slowly away from the African coast in the direction of Malta and the Italian mainland. Quick as a flash, Klaus grabbed the telephone receiver.

"Enemy aircraft over Malta on course for Italy!" he barked into it.

I heard Werner's voice: "I'll pass it on right away." Then he hung up. The German telephone exchange was 400 metres above the radar surveillance station. The communication channel spanned from the German war headquarters, the 'Wolf's Lair', to Munich, Rome and Taormina, where Commander-in-Chief Kesselring was stationed. From Sicily, it headed via Lampedusa to North Africa, to the command post of General Field Marshal Rommel.

"Enzo, you're up!" Klaus gave me the receiver.

I had to pass the news on to the Italian telephone exchange at the harbour. In no time at all, every airport and civilian institution in Italy had been alerted.

It was early morning, just as I was heading from the barracks towards the radar station, when I noticed a small boy behind the building. He was hunting for cigarette butts and picking them up.

"Hey, you there, what are you doing with the cigarette butts?"

The boy gave a start when he saw me. "I'm bringing them to the village. I can exchange them for eggs and flour there," he answered shyly. Then he ran away, as if he were embarrassed that I caught him in his search.

I told my colleagues about the encounter with the boy. Now we knew how to get hold of eggs. We immediately collected up the cigarette butts and put them into a tin until we had enough to exchange them for eggs. But I did feel sorry for the little boy. Now he had no source of income anymore. I suggested to my colleagues that we should give him half the cigarette butts, as he certainly needed the eggs more than we did.

One morning, the boy knocked on the door of my barrack. "*Buon giorno*," he called. "Commandante Vascello Bernini sent me. I'm supposed to take you to him. He wants to talk to you."

I headed with him down to the village, to the island commander's quarters in a small villa right by the beach. He was sitting on the veranda behind the house.

"Thank you, Enzo!" he said. He told the boy he could collect some flour and eggs from the cook.

He poured me a strong coffee and told me that, as a navy colonel, he had command of the harbour and the shipping traffic between the islands. He inquired whether both teams on the Albero Sole were also working well together. I informed him about the friendly relationship between the two units, and about setting up the radar and telephone exchange. He continued the discussion by asking whether the German military telephone line could access the Italian city network.

"Would it be possible for me to call my family in Rome?" he asked softly. He was acutely aware that it would be no easy undertaking.

"I would be very glad to organise that for you, Commandante, but first I need to check with the team at the German exchange whether that would be possible or not. If so, I'll probably need permission from the German commander too." I promised to make an inquiry without delay.

It turned out that it was possible to access the civilian network in Rome from the city's German Wehrmacht line, and the German lieutenant gave us permission to try, as long as we maintained utmost secrecy. Bernini's driver brought the Commandante up to Albero Sole.

"Enzo, I'm very grateful to you for having made this possible."

I led him to the cubbyhole where he would be able to access the communication channel. Werner was in there, sitting at the desk on which the radio and three telephone receivers were located.

"Please, commander, take a seat." Werner and Bernini dialled the numbers. Just as the Commandante heard ringing on the other end of the line, Werner shouted, "Stop! Hang up! *Führungsblitzgespräch!*" We hung up the receivers immediately. We watched the flashing red light, spellbound.

"When the red light is on, that means there is a connection between the Führer and Kesselring or Rommel, and we all need to stay off the line. The *Führungsblitzgespräche*, or command-flash-calls, are strictly confidential. Listening in could cost you your life," explained Werner.

We waited over two hours until we could access the network again. Commandante Bernini was over the moon to talk to his family. He visited six times, and three of those times we were able to connect him with his family.

It was 24 December 1942. Christmas Eve. I was heading down to see the postman in the village. We had been waiting in vain for the packet ship for over a week now. My mum had written to me two months ago to say she would be sending me a package for Christmas. There was a new clerk working in the post office.

"Show me your ID!" he said roughly.

"I only have my service book; they took my passport away."

"Your service book doesn't have a photo of you. How do I know you're actually Enzo Dorigo? Unfortunately, I can't take your letters. That's the rule.

We can only send letters abroad if we can see a verified identification document."

"My service book has always been accepted before. And your predecessor always took my letters," I retorted.

He ignored me and resumed his stamping.

"Listen, signore, my mother is a widow, and she's worried about me. She's expecting my letters. Please, can't you have a bit of sympathy?" I held out a cigarette.

Reluctantly, he stopped stamping and took the cigarette. "Bring me a whole pack next time! Come back this afternoon. The packet ship won't arrive till 5 p.m., and perhaps your package will be on it." He took the letters and shuffled over to the postbag with them. That was my first encounter with him. I always had to bribe him with cigarettes after that.

We had been wondering what to do on Christmas Eve for days now. Sergio, the little boy, had promised to get minced meat and potatoes for us. We were planning on frying some meatballs and serving them with potato salad. I was really looking forward to the day off.

I fetched my swimming trunks and ran to the bay. Werner had already climbed into the boat, and Klaus was rowing steadily through the breakers.

"Hey, wait for me! I'm coming too!"

I jumped through the surf and swam the last stretch. It was only when I was already in the boat that I noticed

I'd forgotten to take off my wristwatch. How annoying! I quickly took it off and dried it, but after two hours, it had stopped. Salt water had penetrated the case and damaged the mechanism. My beloved watch, which my parents had given me for my confirmation, was broken. I regretted my carelessness for a long time; it was a piece of home, an article of great value, and a personal companion. From now on, I would have to rely on others to know what time it was.

"Don't be cross, Enzo. We're going on a very special trip today."

"Where?" Werner and Klaus had probably just found another cave.

"Wait and see! It's going to be really exciting! Are you a good diver, Enzo? You're in for a surprise!" Klaus steered the dinghy in the direction of the small island called Isola dei Conigli, which was overgrown with maquis bushes.

"Are you planning on shooting a rabbit?" I asked but noticed at once that there was no rifle in the boat.

"We're heading to the east coast of the island," Klaus hinted.

And then I saw it! Before us lay a stranded freighter.

"Quite something, don't you think?" cried Werner in excitement.

"How long has it been here?"

"No idea, but we'll find out soon enough."

I felt a bit uneasy as we approached the half-sunken ship. We leaned over the edge of the dinghy to look at the seabed. The water was clear and calm.

"See there, where the galley is open? We're going to dive in!" Werner exclaimed enthusiastically.

"You want to dive into the ship?"

"Of course. And we've come prepared!" Klaus rummaged in a linen bag and brought out three sets of diving goggles. "I borrowed them from Marcello. I think there are a few people in the Italian unit who have diving equipment." He even had flippers with him. "You see, Enzo, we have it all planned out. The midday sun is shining directly on the opening, so we'll have plenty of light."

It was really exciting. First, Werner and I dived down to scope it out. We jumped down on the port side and pulled ourselves along the ship's rail to the entrance, which was open. Shoals of fish shot out of the belly of the freighter. We swam through a narrow passage that led to a stairway, behind which was an open cupboard. To our amazement, we saw it was full of rifles. We took two each and swam back.

"That was close!" We both gasped for air and breathed deeply. "I didn't think I'd have enough air, but we made it! Your turn, Klaus. There are more rifles in there. Go and get two for yourself," Werner urged.

I sat down in the boat and inspected the weapon. It was a German Wehrmacht rifle. A while later, Klaus and Werner dived back down to the wreck and brought back four more guns.

"Guys, this wreck can be our new hobby!" Werner was ecstatic.

We rowed back to the beach where we lay on the warm sand, smoking and chatting awhile. Suddenly, Werner spotted something. "Wait, be quiet a second. Look at that!" He stood up to get a closer look at something floating in the surf. "It looks pretty bloated, but it's probably not a bomb," he said.

Klaus took his binoculars out of his trouser pocket. "Now we'll be able to see exactly what it is." No sooner had he made out the floating object than he fell silent.

"What is it, Klaus? What can you see?" I asked.

"Look for yourself!" was his gruff reply. He wretched, then vomited.

"I can imagine what it is," said Werner.

I only had to look through the binoculars for a moment before I knew: it was a drowned corpse. Werner set off immediately to inform navy command, while Klaus and I waited on the beach. We hid the rifles in a cave so the Italian marines wouldn't see what we had found in the wreck. That evening, we learnt that the drowned man was an English pilot who had been shot down.

The next day, I only had to work in the morning, so I decided to go for a walk on the cliffs in the afternoon. The sun was high in the sky, and it was still warm and summery. I was looking forward to relaxing in the sun and writing a letter to Luise. I sat down on a rocky ledge and looked out at the deep blue sea. The gentle breeze ruffled the surface of the water, forming little white waves. Further out, I spotted a school of dolphins—there must have been around twenty of them. I couldn't help smiling to myself as I watched them caper about. It looked as though they were racing each other as they leapt. The tranquil scene was soon interrupted by the hum of two transport planes heading for the airfield. *Good*, I thought, *some more supplies*. Barely two seconds passed before I spotted three British fighter planes chasing the transport planes. I heard one bullet after another, and in an instant, both transport planes had crashed into the sea.

"Oh no, how awful!" I felt completely helpless. I stared at the sea in disbelief, watching all those people drowning. Tears were streaming down my face.

As well as civilians, the transport planes were also carrying soldiers returning from leave. I could have been among them, flying back from visiting my grandparents in Sicily. This damned war! I realised it hadn't really felt tangible for us island soldiers until now. We may have been watching enemy planes in our surveillance of the airspace, but it somehow felt as though they were far away and would leave us in peace—at least, that's what we thought. I felt uncomfortable. I stood up, my legs trembling. My heart was pounding in my throat. I ran as fast as I could to report what had just happened.

It was another week until the packet ship arrived. My great joy at the package and letters that arrived was short lived. Wolfgang's letter contained the terrible news that Luise had died in hospital from pneumonia.

Vince and Pete Dorigo
in New York, 1942

Vincenzo Dorigo considered his reflection in the mirror as he buttoned up his white shirt over his protective vest. He noted with satisfaction that his handsome physique was already superior to that of Peppe Gambino.

"I can take him on," he told himself, his dark eyes flashing. He grabbed his revolver and slipped it carefully into the waistband of his trousers, then he slowly put on his jacket and left the house.

Before he climbed into his Pontiac Streamliner, he took a quick look around him. The street was practically deserted. It was Sunday, and most people would be sitting at home around noon to eat a big meal with their families. He lit a cigarette and sat down in the car. As he drove, the events of the previous day ran through his head. His father had asked to see him alone in his office. He knew right away that this would be about a meeting. The Gambino family wanted to speak with him and Giancarlo Costello.

"You know, Vincenzo, we're on good terms with the Gambinos. They're dangerous and ruthless. But we need to find a way to deal with them. It's about our liquor imports. Our restaurants count on us to get the drinks in at a reasonable price. The situation with the cargo ships on the East Coast has escalated. The Gambinos now control New York's harbour and all imports along with it, especially alcohol. I was thinking, *figlio*, maybe we should have someone tailing you," Luciano said worriedly.

"Just leave it, Papà, I'll go alone. If I have someone with me, it'll look like I don't trust them. You know how sly the Gambinos are. I can take Peppe, that *bastardo*!"

"Control yourself, Vincenzo! Keep things calm and civilised, understood?" His father gave him a sharp look. "The last thing we need is an altercation. I'm warning you!"

"Yeah, yeah, Papà. I'll keep things calm and casual. If I feel that the offer is unreasonable, I can say I need to discuss it with you. And Gianni will be there too," he told his father soothingly.

They both knew, without it needing to be said, that the restaurants in Manhattan, Brooklyn and Queens couldn't exist if they didn't pay dues to the Gambino family. Thinking about it annoyed Vincenzo, but he had to control himself, even if Peppe Gambino decided to show his condescending, arrogant nature once again.

He approached the harbour. Gigantic passenger ships were lined up along the jetty. Further north were the docks with all the tankers and merchant vessels. He stopped in front of a small, nondescript dockside pub. It was a dirty area, and the stench of oil and tar hung in the air. Giancarlo Costello was waiting impatiently for him at the bar. Vince was glad to have his friend with him when he met Peppe Gambino. Giancarlo Costello's family ran a large liquor import business, as well as several restaurants in Manhattan.

"There you are at last, Vince!" He clapped him on the back, then headed to a table by the entrance, where they could see the bustling activity in the port.

"Thanks for coming. This is a serious matter."

Vincenzo gave him a questioning look.

"There are going to be fewer liquor imports. For all of us to benefit, we have to work together, *capisci*? The Gambino family has taken care of the unions." Giancarlo's face darkened.

"I heard 26 men were murdered. Was that really necessary?" asked Vincenzo defiantly.

"Leave it. It's not our problem, Vince. It's nothing to do with us. You know…" He paused, looked out of the window to make sure no one was approaching the pub, then whispered, "The Gambinos are making short work of it. They alone are responsible for this. The union is simply getting too big. The Gambinos don't want their control over the harbour to be taken from under their noses. And after all, if we can get a fast, reliable liquor supply, that benefits us too."

A black Buick pulled up outside the entrance. Vincenzo and Giancarlo scrutinised the car to try and see how many people were in it.

"He's brought Joe with him," Giancarlo observed.

"Joe's harmless."

Peppe Gambino stepped through the doorway, his chest thrust out. He always walked like that, as if it could make him seem more impressive and powerful. His brother Joe was somewhat taller, but with the same bulky build. It was impossible not to see the resemblance between the brothers.

They had wine brought to the table.

"My father's the one who wanted this meeting, not me," Peppe began the conversation, sounding bored. "Either way, I'm sure you can guess that it's about the port."

Vincenzo and Giancarlo said nothing.

He doesn't just look stupid, he is *stupid too*, thought Vincenzo. "You'll need to explain in more detail," he said calmly.

Peppe looked at Joe.

"We've got problems," Joe explained. "German U-boats have sunk several cargo ships off the East Coast and in the Atlantic. Of course, the navy should be sending warships to escort the cargo ships. Then there are the spies and saboteurs, but we have a horse in the race too. We need your help to secure the liquor imports, though."

"What kind of help? What will it cost?" asked Giancarlo directly.

"You won't pay any more than you do now. We still have other sources. In fact, the government wants our help. An FBI agent will be in touch with you soon, Vince."

Vince was going to ask what all this was about, when suddenly a deafening explosion rang out from the port, and seconds later, great billows of smoke had filled the sky. The whole pub felt like it was vibrating. Glasses shattered behind the bar, and the waiter sought refuge under the counter.

"*Dio mio!*" cried Joe, and he ran to the exit.

The others followed him.

"Down there, by the passenger ships!" Giancarlo exclaimed. The largest ship of them all was engulfed in smoke. Because of the strong wind, the flames were already licking the upper decks.

"That's the SS *Normandie*!" Vince shouted.

Dockworkers, passers-by, marines and whole families were thronging to Pier 88 where the luxury steamer had been moored. The fire brigade fought through the crowds and tried to put out the flames from all sides, while shrieking sailors escaped in a panic from inside the ship.

Peppe pushed his way towards Vince. He smelled of garlic and sweat. "I have something urgent I need to follow up on. So, like I said, you're going to get a call."

Before Vincenzo could respond, Peppe and Joe had vanished into the crowd. Vince called Giancarlo over.

"Listen, I don't trust this. What do they want from us?"

Giancarlo shook his head. "No idea, Vince. But what do you think of this fire on the biggest luxury liner in the world?"

"I wouldn't be surprised if the Gambinos had something to do with that too," Vincenzo said disdainfully. They watched the ship start to tilt sideways under the weight of all the water from the firefighters' hoses.

"Maybe it was saboteurs," Giancarlo wondered.

They left the crowd of onlookers and headed home.

No sooner had they entered than they were greeted by Pietro, Vincenzo's brother. "I need to tell you my plan, Vince!" he exclaimed, excited.

"Go on, then!"

They went into the living room.

"I need a whisky, Gianni." Vincenzo fetched two glasses and filled them to the brim. They clinked glasses. "Now tell us, what have you got in mind, Pete?"

"I want to be where the action is!"

Vincenzo looked at his brother in bewilderment.

"You've lost your mind, Pietro. Why do you want to enlist?" Vincenzo looked over to Giancarlo, who agreed with him.

"We can't let that happen, Vince! Your brother is far too naïve to appreciate how dangerous an invasion will be."

"Listen, surely you don't mean to tell me that you don't care what happens to our homeland?" scoffed Pietro indignantly.

"Of course we care, but there are other ways to make a difference. You don't need to sign up to serve on the front lines," his older brother cautioned him.

"You're not going to change my mind. I haven't spent the past six months at Chesapeake Military Training Camp for nothing. I want to use my training and do my part. So, now leave me alone!" Annoyed, he left the living room and slammed the door behind him.

Vincenzo refilled his glass and drank it down in one gulp. "I don't want to lose my brother to those big-headed Germans."

"Or the Italians. They have to fight on the Germans' side," Giancarlo objected.

"No, no, according to the latest information, many Italians are planning to switch sides," Vincenzo explained. "But that does give me an idea how we can keep Pietro happy. We'll let him tag along, but then earmark him for another job after he lands."

Giancarlo smiled at him, then grinned. "Oh, I understand. You want to arrange something for him, Vince."

"Exactly. And Gianni, you can make sure that everything to do with the military is sorted before the ship sails."

Satisfied, Vincenzo clapped Giancarlo on the shoulder.

Luciano Dorigo was sitting at the head of the table. A thick Cabañas cigar hung lopsidedly from the corner of his mouth. The outline of his face was just visible through the smoke.

"Come in, everyone. Have a seat! Laura! Where's the food? *Subito*, the guests are here. We're hungry!"

Out of the kitchen came a shrill voice. "*Due minuti, signori!*" A short, plump woman hurried to the table with a bread basket and plates. There was a tomato sauce stain on her apron. She scurried back into the kitchen, and a moment later she re-emerged with a pot of fresh pasta. She placed it on the table, and her gold teeth glinted in the glare from the lamp as she smiled and wished them, "*Buon apetito!*"

"Pour the wine, Vincenzo!" Luciano ordered.

Vincenzo, Luciano's eldest son, jumped to his feet and filled the glasses with a flourish.

"Salvatore, your Nero d'Avola is delicious! And how's business?" Luciano asked.

Salvatore Costello cleared his throat. "It could be better. There are a couple of minor problems at the port, but we're working on getting them under control." Salvatore, a friend of Luciano's, ran one of the largest liquor importing businesses in New York.

Vincenzo pointed to a newspaper article that lay open on the table. The cover page of the *New York Times* showed an image of the SS *Normandie* engulfed in flames and smoke.

"The SS *Normandie* in flames. The biggest, most luxurious luxury liner of all time," Luciano mused. "To think we sailed to Le Havre in her only four years ago. They said she was more beautiful than the RMS *Queen Mary*. Alice was very excited at any rate. And the crossing only took around four days. I can't believe that perfect passenger ship has burnt to a crisp. She was a floating work of art, designed in the Art Deco style. There were gigantic mirrors framed in gold and silver hanging on the wall panels in the dining room. After dinner, we went to the theatre, which had room for 380 people in the audience. During the day, we had a great time in the swimming pools—there was even one outdoors. Alice loved the 80-metre-long shopping street with its rows of select boutiques." Luciano looked thoughtfully at the picture in the newspaper.

"Why did it drop anchor in New York and never return to Le Havre?" Vince asked.

"The American government seized the ship after war broke out. Then the *Normandie* lay at port for a while not being used for anything, until the navy decided to convert it to be used for transporting troops," Luciano explained. "But now to the two of you. What do you have to tell us, Vince, Giancarlo?" He looked at them inquiringly.

Vince gestured to Giancarlo that he should speak.

"The war is wearing on and on, and the government wants to gain a foothold in Italy. Because of our connections to the military, we were able to get hold of some leaked information. The Allies are planning an invasion in Europe, and Churchill is putting more and more pressure on Roosevelt to secure a dominant position in the Mediterranean first, via an invasion of Sicily."

"In Sicily? How's that going to work?" Luciano asked, surprised. Luciano Dorigo had emigrated to New York in his youth. His father Vittorio had planned for him to take over his Marsala empire, but, like so many others of his generation, he dreamt of a new life in America. He worked his way up as a kitchen boy and waiter, until he was able to open his first restaurant in Manhattan. Now, twenty years later, he owned seven restaurants and sold liqueurs and champagne on the side.

"The Allied forces are talking about an amphibious landing," Giancarlo reported.

"No aerial attack on Rome?"

"They'll probably do that at the same time." Giancarlo paused.

Vince picked up where he left off. "Picture this: I get a call from a Mr Walker. At first, I thought it was a trap, one of our own pretending to be a *funzionario*. I didn't quite know what to make of it, especially after meeting with Peppe and Joe Gambino. But I soon realised something was wrong."

"We were careful," Giancarlo interrupted.

"Yes, very. We always took every possible security precaution for our meetings."

"Where did you meet him?" asked Salvatore.

"We were smart enough not to pick the usual place down by the Hudson River. Our meetings needed to remain a secret, by hook or by crook. We met in a factory off the beaten track in New Jersey. Twenty of our men were standing guard."

"Did he come without protection? Are you absolutely sure you weren't being watched?" Luciano couldn't suppress his anger. Tiny beads of sweat hung on his temples, throbbing up and down in rhythmic time with his pulse, which, along with his gritted teeth, gave away that he was trying to keep his composure.

"Papà, we were extremely careful. We had people watching the entire length of road that led up to the factory. I hope you trust us to have a meeting like that under control." Vincenzo gave an appreciative drag on his cigarette, leaned back in his chair, his demeanour oozing confidence, and seemed pleased to have told his story to his father and the other men.

"Now, what did Mr Walker want?"

"He's an FBI agent."

"Dio mio! You'll ruin us! I don't want any more dealings with the FBI!" cried Salvatore angrily.

"Calm down, *pazienza*! You'll see, this connection will be extremely useful to us. In times like these, we need to be looking for friends everywhere—we're smart enough to realise that. The question is, how do we do it? That's the crux of the matter. We won't just be careful—no, we're the *più intelligenti* in this whole scheme, don't you see? We're the ones who will benefit in the end. And we should always keep that in mind, no matter what it costs. We're smart enough that we can take what we need and lose nothing in the process. Nothing at all. *Nulla, basta*. We make the rules. *Siam i padroni!*" The corner of Vincenzo's mouth twisted into a contemptuous smile.

"Get your head out of the clouds, Vincenzo! What's it all about?" Luciano asked roughly.

"Mr Watson wants to work with us on a secret mission."

"A secret mission?" Luciano couldn't hide his curiosity.

Vincenzo gestured with his hand and said quietly, "The Allies want us to help plan the landing in Sicily. They need our information and connections. And you know what that means, Papà? *We* hold all the cards! They'll bring the necessary vehicles and weapons and so on, and we'll supply the right people."

Luciano's face lit up with satisfaction, and he said, "We're going to destroy them, the damned Fascists and everyone involved in the Fascist machine!" Suddenly, they were all doubled over with laughter, patting each other on the back and toasting this pie in the sky with their whisky glasses.

Then, all at once, Luciano grew very grave and raised his hand. "Folks, let's not forget that this is a very dangerous undertaking. This alliance could cost us our necks one day. As long as it's still wartime, they can use us, but what about when the war is over? Then they'll point the finger at us and accuse us of everything." He cleared his throat. The smoke from his Cabañas cigar helped him think more clearly. "We need collateral. But how? What do you think, Salvatore?"

Salvatore didn't think for long. "We should ask Giorgio Bonnano."

"Giorgio Bonnano?" Luciano let out a bark of laughter and sprang up from his chair. "He's in the clink!" He lost his temper and flew into a rage: "That's going too far! It's not like we're friends with him! Quite the opposite!"

"I think Mr Watson seeks out every possible contact and then commissions those who suit him best, and that's the ones who can get him the best information," Vincenzo objected.

"Mr Watson is a shrewd man, I can tell you that much," said Giancarlo. "And by the way, he also raised the issue of security at the ports along the East Coast, but the Gambinos are taking care of that. They're going to deploy spies too."

"As long as the Gambinos keep their distance, I can live with that, but we need to keep a close eye on this Mr Watson. We need to make sure we can trust him." Luciano's temper gradually subsided, then he stood up and paced the room, thinking hard. "For a start, I want you to make some inquiries, Gianni, and get me all possible information on Mr Watson, who he works with, how much he knows about our *famiglia*, and what course his life has taken so far. Then we'll see."

That put an end to the conversation. Exhausted, Luciano flopped down into an armchair. When everyone had left, Vincenzo approached him and said, "Papà, in two weeks I'm going to be going away for a while." He bent down close to his father and whispered something in his ear.

Giorgio Bonnano was relaxing on his Louis XV sofa. He was wearing a silk dressing gown and had just shaved when Fred Walker and Vincenzo arrived. His guard bowed reverently and left the room. He gestured serenely with his hand, indicating that they should sit down.

"Ah, Fred! Who would have thought you'd seek me out again? You want something from me, correct?" The angular features of his face twisted into a scornful grin. "Who sent you?"

"Not the government this time, Giorgio. They don't know anything about this. I'm on a secret mission from a top military official—I can't tell you his name. We need your help." Giorgio reached for a cigarette.

"And what do you have to do with this, boy? You're a Dorigo, aren't you?" He eyed Vincenzo.

"I'm Vincenzo, and I have an assignment to carry out. In Sicily." Vince tried to appear casual, but he couldn't hide the fact he was slightly nervous in the presence of this mafia boss, who had already spent ten years locked up in one of America's most infamous high-security prisons. Vince felt both admiration and aversion for Giorgio Bonnano. For a long time now, he had been feared across the whole of New York. Vince remembered how his father had always warned him to avoid any kind of confrontation with the Bonnano family. Although Vince's father dabbled in illegal liquor imports, he always insisted that he was an honourable man and would remain so, whereas Bonnano was embroiled in drug trafficking and prostitution. And that had cost him dear in the end. Living behind bars was no life, even in a five-star lockup like this one.

Fred Walker took out a map and spread it out before them. "In July, the Allies want to land in Sicily and on the Italian coast. They want to free Italy from the Fascists and Germans. There are plans for a secret mission with the codeword 'Husky'. The US Naval Intelligence Service needs contacts—your contacts—to make sure we have the right support in place. We need clear land routes, food, shelter and people we can rely on. Vincenzo will go ahead and take charge of everything."

Giorgio gazed at the map dreamily. "*Bella Sicilia!* I was born up here, in Castellammare. My dear nonna raised me for the first few years until it got too dangerous, then my father took me to New York. My grandfather was the local *padrino*. Everyone respected him, and they sometimes even kissed my hand. He let me ride the donkey and often took me to Palermo to eat ice cream. By the way, my late mother's sister still lives in the village. Her son, Giuliano, was banished back to Castellammare because of an incident on the Lower East Side." He lit a cigarette absentmindedly.

"Are you on board?" Fred interrupted him.

Bonnano suddenly became very serious and businesslike. "Nothing would make me happier. Those damned Fascists need to be stamped out!" He grew thoughtful, then the left-hand corner of his mouth twitched into a faint smirk. "I assume I can expect something in return. When the war is over, I mean." He leant back haughtily in his chair.

"We can discuss that later. It's certainly possible," Walker replied, feigning friendliness.

"Good, Fred. I'll give you a list of people that will be well suited for your plans. My nephew Giuliano especially. He's well respected, intelligent and hates the Fascists. Not only can he put you in touch with his contacts, but he also has a lot of people on hand who can come at short notice and help out in an emergency."

Fred leaned back in his chair and smiled. "I knew we could count on you!"

Wedding in Rome, 1942

"I need to express my deepest sympathies." Luca looked at me with compassion. "I'm really glad you're here with us. The holiday will do you good." He started the jeep, and we drove towards the Vatican. I told him about my deployment on Lampedusa, then the subject turned to Carina. Luca grinned. "We're getting married!" I must have looked at him in astonishment. "Honestly, why is everyone so surprised? Who knows how long the war is going to last? We want to tie the knot here in Rome. Roberto is going to marry us." He gazed out of the window dreamily. I gave him a sideways glance. He was still the same daredevil. Of course, that's how he had gone against his family. I was a little jealous of him.

"Do you want to be my best man? Now that you're here on holiday? After all, you're my best friend, Enzo." I didn't answer right away. I had just lost my girlfriend and wasn't in the mood to talk about a wedding. "I understand if you don't want to, Enzo. The timing is…"

"Forget about that, Luca," I cut him off. "Of course I'll be the best man at your wedding."

At the Vatican, Roberto and Luca were making the final preparations for the wedding, when a guardsman knocked roughly at the door. "*Monsignore*, a British refugee, a prisoner of war, is at the main entrance. He is asking to be admitted. The guard is awaiting further instructions!"

Roberto dialled the number of the British ambassador to the Holy See, Sir D'Arcy Osborne. "Sir, please come to my office immediately."

The refugee was brought into the reception room. When Roberto entered with the other men, he stood up, gave a small bow and spoke. "Gentlemen, monsignore, I am Sam Derry, a major of the Royal Artillery. I escaped from a prisoner-of-war camp in Chieti."

Sir D'Arcy Osborne looked him up and down. "You aren't wearing a uniform. Can you prove who you are?"

"I'm sorry, sir, my identity documents were taken by the Germans at the prison camp. I acquired civilian clothing so as not to draw attention to myself."

"And how did you get here, Major Derry?"

"On foot and by bicycle!"

A short laugh spread through the group.

"I was able to hide on a train and jump out near Frascati. Then I walked from there. On the outskirts of Rome, I stole a bicycle. I beg you, grant me a place to stay here in the Vatican! Us refugees aren't safe anywhere. You can't imagine how many have escaped and are on the run. The Germans shoot all refugees on sight. I remember you visiting us in prison, monsignore. It was so good to know someone would inform our families where we were."

"Thanks to Radio Vatican, we are able to send word to England—unofficially, you understand."

It was Roberto who came up with the idea of establishing a link via Vatican Radio to the war cabinet in London so that relatives of British soldiers could find out where their sons were imprisoned. Roberto created a list of the prisoners' names and personal information. This meant travelling for two days once a week to the detention camps and visiting the prisoners. He kept a record of the new prisoners so that he could immediately forward their information to the British war ministry via Radio Vatican. This gave countless families peace of mind that their sons hadn't been killed but were imprisoned instead. Roberto was also known for bringing food with him to give to the imprisoned soldiers.

"I think we need to consider this situation carefully, monsignore," said the ambassador. "Major Derry has told us what is happening outside the Vatican, and he has brought home the fact that we really are on neutral ground. We have free rein here. I am only now really realising the options open to us."

"You are absolutely right, sir. Major Derry has given me an idea. But it needs time to ripen, and I will need your support in this matter more than anything, gentlemen!" Roberto cleared his throat. "You can stay here for the time being, Sam Derry." Roberto called a clerk and instructed him to fill a bathtub and provide a monk's robe for Sam Derry.

"We must ensure the Vatican's neutrality," said D'Arcy Osborne. "The Allies will attack sooner or later, and we cannot allow the Vatican City State to be drawn into all that. So far, I haven't been able to achieve much. The British government has other problems to contend with. Perhaps there's a way to come to a diplomatic agreement with the Germans."

"What are the Allies planning? When are they going to attack Rome?" Roberto asked.

"There are plans for a conference between Churchill and Roosevelt in Casablanca. They will make a decision on the matter there. There are points of contention between the two powers. Britain wants to secure the Mediterranean; the Americans would rather intervene in Normandy right away. Sooner or later, they will move onto Rome. But we would like to reach a prior agreement with the Allies that the centre of Rome and the Vatican City State will not come to any harm. Fortunately, Hitler is an art fanatic and will certainly be interested in saving the old buildings from destruction."

The German occupation was gaining more and more control, and Roberto was keen to embark on a secret mission to do something about it. The British ambassador to the Holy See, Sir D'Arcy Osborne, and the young major Sam Derry were to become his closest allies in this plan.

Luca and I sat in an adjoining room, waiting for Roberto.

"So, how do you feel on your last day as a bachelor?" I asked mischievously.

"Oh, I can't wait for Carina and me to be together. She works at the hospital here in Rome, so we see each other regularly. We rent a room at weekends from a friend of Roberto's. I'm happy—really happy!"

"You really found yourself the most beautiful girl in all of Sicily, *cugino*!"

"In all of Italy, Enzo!"

Carina was wearing a modest white lace dress and holding a small bouquet of roses in her hand.

I gave Francesca an inquiring look. "What do we actually need to do? I've never been the best man at a wedding before."

"And I've never been maid of honour," she grinned. "Roberto will tell us what to do."

"What do Nonna and Nonno think of them getting married in secret here in Rome?" I asked.

"Zia wrote to me and said that on the one hand, the parents and grandparents are happy about the match, but on the other hand, they are accusing Luca of being foolhardy and selfish. He could have waited until his leave and then got married in Sicily. But Luca doesn't want just any old priest marrying them. It's important to him that Roberto does it. And Roberto can't travel to Sicily at the moment; he has too many responsibilities in the Vatican."

"When the war is over, they can have a huge wedding party in Sicily," I pondered.

"I can get behind that, as long as you come too!"

"Of course. It's tradition for the best man to dance with the maid of honour."

"Oh really?" Francesca smiled, amused.

Roberto read aloud from the Bible. Before he questioned the bride and groom, Luca stood up and recited a poem:

"Quando vedrò nel verno il crine sparso
Aver di neve e di pruina algente,
E 'l seren del mio giorno, or sì lucente,
Col fior de gli anni miei fuggito e sparso;

Al tuo bel nome io non sarò più scarso
De le mie lodi o de l'affetto ardente,
Né fian dal gelo intepidite o spente
Quelle fiamme amorose ond'io son arso.

Ma se rassembro augel palustre e roco,
Cigno parrò lungo il tuo nobel fiume
Ch'abbia l'ore di morte o mai vicine;

E quasi fiamma, che vigore e lume
Ne l'estremo riprenda, inanzi al fine
Risplenderà più chiaro il vivo foco."

"When someday in winter my hair
Shall be covered with snow and icy hoarfrost
And my days, which now are still so bright,
Will have dwindled and passed with the blossom of
    the years,

To thy fair name I shall no longer be meagre
With my praise or ardent affection,
No frost shall ever cool or quench
These loving flames that scorch me.

Like the hoarse bird from the marshes,
I will sing by thy noble river
Like the swan when its hour of death approaches.

And like the flame that recovers
Strength and light once more before the end,
My fire will shine more brightly than ever before."

"Torquato Tasso," he concluded.

We were very moved by his words and the passion
with which he had recited the poem. I didn't know Luca
had such a love of poetry. I felt a profound connection
with him then and was filled with his happiness and
love. Francesca saw how moved I was and gazed at me
lovingly.

At first, I had thought that this wedding was happening
at precisely the wrong moment for me. I was still in a

state of shock over the death of Luise. But now I felt nothing but happiness and peace, and I prayed that Luise would experience this feeling too. And it was as if she were speaking to me, wishing the same peace upon me.

We celebrated long into the night in a tiny *trattoria*. Roberto wore a grey suit and black-and-white leather shoes.

"Is it fun to take off your priest's cassock and wear normal clothes again?" Luca asked, already rather tipsy.

"You know I'm doing this for security reasons, not for fun, Luca," Roberto lectured him.

"I thought the clergy were always well protected. What do the Germans think of the Vatican?"

"I don't want to talk about it here, Luca. It's a delicate matter. We have to be careful."

We changed the subject and started talking about the family. Toni, Luca's father, had become more and more involved in politics and had joined the Fascist party, which had sparked tensions in the household. Nonno wanted him to follow the family's tradition of remaining neutral, but Toni disagreed. My nonno didn't like his friendship with Giulio Gentile one bit. Even Aunt Maria thought it was dangerous. "What's wrong with Giulio Gentile? His parents are good friends with Nonno."

"Giulio is an active party member. He works for the government, and he uses his rank as a lawyer there. And his son Frederico has joined the state police," Francesca explained worriedly.

"Why is he getting involved with the Fascists?" I asked quietly.

"He wants to give up contacts with the important families and fight for independence for the big landowners."

"But you are independent though, right?"

Luca looked at me indulgently. "Wow, you can really tell you didn't grow up in Sicily!" Then he whispered, "My grandfather always paid handsomely so that he would be left alone. Since my father became part of the family, there have been disputes. He doesn't want to continue this tradition any longer. But he doesn't realise that he can't do anything about it—in fact, he's just creating more enemies. Nonno is in despair that one of his sons won't take over the business. Uncle Luciano emigrated to America and your father Umberto to Switzerland, so he only has my father to carry on."

"The connections our nonno made with a certain family always looked very friendly on the surface, but ultimately they were bought so we could live in peace. As for our father, I'm also rather concerned about his political views, and I can't say I agree with them. He doesn't have a clue what he's getting himself into. I pray every day that there won't be a big falling out in our family," said Roberto.

In that moment, I knew there were already political divisions in our family, and that things would probably get even worse. Luca tried to lighten the mood. "Come on, folks, let's celebrate! It's our wedding day, and I don't want anyone moping around, war or no war! How would you like to see my favourite toy?"

Carina rolled her eyes.

"Oh, come on, *amore*! Now that Enzo is here, and you too Roberto, you haven't seen my fighter plane yet!"

In a military truck that Luca had obtained exclusively for his wedding day, we drove to Ciampino military airport outside the city.

Operation 'Husky'—
from Algiers to Sicily

The sun was beating mercilessly down on the city's whitewashed houses. The unbearable heat settled like lead on the soldiers who gathered in the few shady spots. Jeeps sped down the streets between clattering horse-drawn carts, rickety bicycles and squeaking wheelbarrows. Americans, Brits, New Zealanders, Gurkhas, Sinhalese—a hodgepodge of conscripts strolled through the narrow streets, looking for souvenirs at the souk or lying bored in the cafés down by the harbour pier, watching the hustle and bustle of the port, where tankers, transporters, mine destroyers, landing craft, freighters and frigates lay at anchor. One stood out in particular: the USS *Monrovia*, the largest battleship and flagship, commanded by Vice Admiral Hewitt.

Pete was sweating in his army uniform, although he was fortunate enough to be allowed to wear the lighter version consisting of pale khaki trousers and a summer shirt. The artillerymen had it worst, as they had to wear the full combat uniform—that was the rule, an order from General Patton. Anyone who didn't follow this to the letter was punished with a twenty-five-dollar fine. Nonetheless, many people still dared to strip off, the uniform shirt tucked into their belts so that they could quickly pull it on in an emergency.

Wearily, Pete watched the activity in the port, where a steady stream of equipment was being unloaded from the ships. Preparations for the landing in Sicily were in full swing. But the events of the past week still played on his mind.

He couldn't banish the memories of saying his farewells at home, the instructions he had received from Vince, which he had to keep strictly confidential, and the worried face of his mother. The crossing to Algiers went off without a hitch—they only saw enemy aircraft on one occasion but were not attacked. Pete's initial euphoria was abruptly quashed when he learnt that his team would be replaced at the last minute. The soldiers he had trained with for weeks in Chesapeake would now be sent to the Pacific at short notice. Pete realised at once that the people replacing them were not trained to use the army landing craft. These 'civilians', as he saw them, didn't really know what role they would be playing in this war. Many of them claimed they were willing to fight, but after a few days, comments like "Going to war sucks" and "Let's win this war so we can go home quickly" started to trickle through. The naval personnel and soldiers had no idea what exactly the landing plan would entail. Any information on the subject was strictly confidential.

"The landing will only succeed if we have the element of surprise! You are forbidden from sharing any information about where you are or what you are doing. Your letters home should contain irrelevant stories. These rules are set in stone, and you must adhere to them stringently!" Those were their orders.

Officers gave lectures about Sicily and explained that the island had been successfully conquered time and again throughout the centuries. Among other things, they mentioned that the murder rate was seven times higher than in the rest of Italy. Everyone received the 'Soldiers' Guide to Sicily', which explained about the heat, dirt and diseases.

"What a hellhole! How can anyone live there?" one man called out in disgust.

"Oh, don't let a little dirt scare you off. Look at the last page. It has some Italian you can learn. Maybe it'll come in handy."

"Hey, Pete, you can help us out here. Tell me, how should I address a young lady—in the evening, you know."

Pete chuckled. "That's easy! *Buona sera, signorina.*"

Everyone chimed in loudly. "*Due cento lira!*"

Pete couldn't help overhearing a soldier from Kentucky confidently assert, "Folks, you just need three things to make any Italian happy: coffee, cigarettes and women!"

"I'd be happy with that too, what more do you need?"

"Where's your fighting spirit, Jack?"

"In my underpants!"

There was an exuberant atmosphere on board. They were on their way to Algiers, but the closer they got to the North African coast, the quieter the soldiers became. Everyone was well aware that Algiers would only be a stopover before the main battle. Pete wondered what was going through the soldiers' minds. What did they think was in store for them?

Shortly before they arrived, someone quoted General Patton: "When we land, we'll encounter German and Italian soldiers. It is an honour and a privilege to attack and destroy them! The glory of our American weapons, the honour of our homeland and the future of the whole world lies in the hands of every last one of you. Rest assured that you are worthy of this great measure of trust! God is on our side. We will win!"

They spent the rest of the time lazing around in the lifeboats on deck and drinking the brandy they had been given to combat seasickness.

A shot roused Pete abruptly from his daydream. One of the cargo ships had fired off salutes.

It's probably a test run, he thought. He looked at his watch. Where had Joe got to? Pete still couldn't believe his brother Vince had instructed him to join up with Joe Gambino. Joe would be running the show. He had the necessary contacts in Sicily and, although he wasn't a friend of the family, the mission was of paramount importance for their relationship with the Gambinos— and quite apart from this, it would allow Pete to play an active part in combating Fascism, something he wanted of his own accord. His commitment and cooperation would earn the Dorigos respect and high standing in New York society. Since leaving New York, Pete had been seriously wondering whether his brother Vince had got himself caught up in mafia business or whether this mission with Joe Gambino was really just a strategic military operation. Then he suddenly recognised his accomplice in the crowd.

"Joe!" he called to him. He waved and pushed through the throng to a small coffee shop. "There you are at last, Joe!" Pete gave him a friendly handshake.

"Sorry, I had to call on the corporal."

His accomplice, as he called him, beamed at him cheerily. "Come on, let's go. They're expecting us at the Hotel St Georges at half past four. The Allied Forces Headquarters takes up half the city—400 buildings now—including hotels, schools and villas where the Allies are stationed. Just imagine, up to 12,000 people work for AFHQ."

"Unbelievable! No wonder the city's full to bursting."

"Their communication channels probably use at least seven submarine cables," Joe explained.

The Hotel St Georges stood high above the bay. Palm gardens lined the whitewashed colonial-style palace, and balconies and balustrades adorned the imposing façade, which was decorated with mimosas. General Dwight D. Eisenhower was staying in a suite there.

"A bit more comfortable than where we're staying," Pete observed with sarcasm.

An officer asked who they were.

"Pete Dorigo and Joe Gambino."

"Colonel Smith is expecting you." He led them into a room where several military personnel had already gathered. At the front of the hall stood a podium. A hush gradually fell over the hall as an officer stepped up to the lectern. A map of the Mediterranean was projected on the wall with the heading: 'Husky—the landings in Sicily'.

Pete looked around the room. "I thought we'd be meeting Colonel Smith in person," he whispered.

"We need to listen to this introduction first, then we'll be summoned to him." Joe looked at him confidently. He had already been here for a month and knew his way around. All Pete had to do was tag along, but it annoyed him. He didn't want to be henpecked by Joe. But Vince had made it abundantly clear that Pete was never to contradict Joe. An agreement had been made, and he had to comply. It wasn't what Pete had imagined. But, as had happened many times before, his older brother had talked him round in the end. As always, his brother Vince got his own way. That's the way it had been in New York. Despite his father's objections, Vince had recently taken over a nightclub. He claimed it was a good business and that there was lots of money to be made. Pete had listened to the dispute between Vince and his father, who had asked Vince directly what was going on in the nightclub.

"Oh, Dad, just the things that normally go on in a nightclub. Selling drinks, playing music and people enjoying themselves on the dancefloor." Vince's voice had been tinged with its usual dismissive tone.

"Okay, now I want you to tell me who specifically comes to your nightclub. What kind of ladies can be found there?" Before Vince could answer, his father shouted, "If you take prostitutes into your nightclub, then it's over with us—with you and me! You can leave right now and never show your face in our family again! Is that clear?"

Pete kept his nose out of it. He had no interest in the family business; he wanted to study physics at Princeton. But, apart from his mother Alice, no one understood him. "You want to be a physicist? Tinkering around in a lab?" People were always making disparaging comments. No one took him seriously. He hated being under his elder brother's influence, forced to submit to him.

When we're in Sicily, I'll go my own way, he swore to himself as he continued to listen to the instructions for the planned landing in Sicily.

"The naval operation will be carried out on the night of 10 July and will involve two armies, which will land on the southeastern coast of Sicily. There will be over three thousand ships converging in the Mediterranean, making this the most enormous fleet in the history of the world. Half of them will sail from six ports in Algeria and Tunisia under the command of American Lieutenant General George S. Patton. The other half, the British, will arrive from Libya and Egypt under the command of General Sir Bernard Montgomery. A Canadian division will arrive directly from Britain. The Seventh Army under Lieutenant General Patton will invade the Gulf of Gela. We have nine new designs of landing craft and five new types of landing ship on board. This includes the LST, a boat that doubles as a tank on land. This huge expedition will converge in the middle of the ocean, near Malta, on 9 July. First of all, we will take the small island of Pantelleria, the Italian Gibraltar, which is 60 miles southwest of Sicily. Pantelleria is a great strategic location and is equipped with a hangar, so it'll provide an excellent airfield. The British airbases in Malta, 60 miles south of Sicily, will be the site of more aerial combat. Husky will involve landing from both the air and the sea. We will also be launching Operation Ladbroke, which will involve dropping paratroopers from gliders near Syracuse. We will use military gliders for this: the Waco Hadrian, an American glider that will be used to carry equipment, and the Airspeed Horsa, a British one that will be used to transport troops. The deceptive manoeuvres we carried out as part of Operation Mincemeat went like clockwork. Nevertheless, we must be extremely cautious, even though the Axis powers are expecting an attack from Sardinia at the moment. Secrecy is our top priority. Operation Husky's success depends on the element of surprise!"

After the talk was over, Pete and Joe waited for Colonel Smith.

"What was Operation Mincemeat?" whispered Pete.

"Oh, that was a deceptive manoeuvre executed by the British," Joe explained. "It was Churchill's idea. A British submarine floated a corpse dressed in a British major's naval uniform onto the southern coast of Spain. He was carrying a wallet containing forged documents. The Spaniards immediately handed the discovery over to German intelligence, who then took the bait and identified the man as a major who had drowned in a plane crash. They took the documents as proof that the Allies' main attack would go via Sardinia and Greece."

Pete grinned. "That's smart!"

Colonel Smith greeted them with a powerful handshake. His steely blue eyes sized the pair up in an instant. He seemed tense. "Come on!" He led them into a small office and indicated that they should take a seat.

"As you know, this meeting is strictly confidential." There was something noble about his tall, slim figure. Smith turned abruptly and locked the door. Despite this gesture, Pete didn't feel threatened in the slightest; on the contrary, the colonel's military correctness fostered a friendly atmosphere. Joe sat impatiently in his chair and gave Smith an expectant look.

"Now, you've just heard the information about Operation Husky. As I'm sure you know, we will be sending you out ahead of the pack. For six months after the landing, I have been assigned to work in Sicily for the Allied Military Government for Occupied Territories—AMGOT for short—alongside Major General Baron Rennell of Rod. The AMGOT will govern Sicily after the landing. To make sure everything goes off without a hitch, we need you to help us establish contacts in advance. I'm told you speak the local dialect." He gave them a questioning look.

Joe cleared his throat impassively. "Yes, of course. Pete's brother Vince is already in Sicily. He was instructed to get in touch with the right people, as well conducting surveillance in secret."

"We need advice on beaches, bays and mountain passes. It would be very helpful if you could provide sketches and road maps. We will also need information on the movement of troops and where the units are stationed," Smith explained.

"Yes, I already know about that," Joe interrupted him.

"This also includes information on how the ports are operating, as well as the chains of command. The US navy will be in charge of supplying food for the Italians, and the Sicilian Lieutenant Titolo will be able to help you with this. Do you have any questions?"

Joe moved closer and casually folded his arms on the table. "We've been stuck here for a fortnight now. When can we leave?" His impatience was plain for all to see.

"You will fly to Licata the day after tomorrow. Once there, you'll be given further instructions. Your first mission will take place in Licata, and you will need to wire me immediately to let me know how it goes. You are bound by the highest degree of secrecy—towards both military personnel and civilians." He fetched a map from a drawer and spread it out on the table. Joe declared that the Gambino family was one of the most powerful families in Sicily, so they would be best placed to ensure people cooperated with the AMGOT.

"We should only talk in Sicilian from now on, don't you think, Pete?" Joe whispered into his ear.

"*Chiaru!*" Pete retorted drily.

On their flight from Algiers to Licata, Joe's behaviour had abruptly changed. He was now haughty and condescending. Pete had already seen this type of behaviour from him in New York, in the nightclub. Back then, he had also treated his employees with contempt, especially the women. He told Pete he would pull out all the stops when they were in Sicily. Whatever Joe meant by that, he was ruthless. Pete felt more and more powerless, sucked into this spider's web of revenge and sabotage.

They drove from the military airfield in Licata to the port in an open-topped jeep. There, they waited for Tino Titolo. He was a small, stolid man, his round face adorned with a perfectly curved black moustache. He stood impatiently behind a lamp-post, bolt upright as if to lend himself an illusion of power. In his right hand, he held a white handkerchief with which he dabbed beads of sweat from his forehead. His left hand clutched the ivory knob of a walking stick.

"Look, Pete. Titolo is signalling to us."

Pete scoured the harbour promenade but couldn't make him out among the crowd of men.

"The white handkerchief is the signal."

When Titolo caught sight of them, he doffed his ochre-coloured hat. "You must be the two boys I'm waiting for. Come with me!"

Across the street, a black Bugatti limousine was waiting for them. They got into the back seat, and the driver drove them silently along the waterfront, then down a country road. A short while later, they drew up in front of a stately villa.

"You need decent clothes. You'll set off after you've eaten. My driver will take you to some farms, because we need the peasants' help for the mission."

Two hours later, Joe and Pete found themselves back in the limousine wearing black suits complete with hats and pointed leather shoes. The driver seemed to know exactly what he was doing. He drove to several farm estates where, each time, the same scene would play out: as soon as the Bugatti pulled into the driveway, they would ask for the head of the family. Joe had to greet him briefly, show a little silk scarf with the letter B on it, and the men would immediately smile knowingly. Joe would then hand over a piece of paper with the address of the Italian navy headquarters written on it. That was all. Usually other men were summoned too: "*Venite! Saluti di Giorgio Bonnano!*"

They all admired the silk scarf—some even kissed it, then they would hug one another joyfully, laughing and expressing their thanks. It was like a magical object. This all seemed very strange to Pete.

"That's how things work here, Pete," Joe joked.

Shortly after nightfall, they strolled in small groups along the beach. They hid behind the hibiscus bushes in front of the holiday villa that housed the headquarters of the Italian naval command. The raid was short and efficient. First, the riflemen killed the German guards stationed outside the building, then Joe sneaked in and blew up the safe that contained valuable papers. Back at Titolo's mansion, they went through the documents they had obtained. They found sketches of the German and Italian lines of defence on the island, as well as the code books for radio communications.

"Look at this! It's information about the Axis's military forces all across the Mediterranean!"

They studied the maps detailing the minefields under the surface of the sea, as well as the safe shipping lanes.

"What a great find, gentlemen! I'll wire it to Colonel Smith right away," Titolo announced.

Escape from Lampedusa

"Wake up, Enzo!" Marcello's loud voice roused me from my afternoon nap.

"What's wrong?" I sat up and listened hard, thinking I might have slept through a bomb attack.

"Your friend Klaus, who speaks a little Italian, just came from his shift at the telephone exchange. He looked very agitated, so I asked him what was wrong. Apparently, he and Werner listened in on an enemy radio message."

"An enemy radio message?" I rubbed my eyes.

"*Zitto!* It was top secret!" whispered Marcello conspiratorially.

"So, what did they find out?" I asked.

"The African campaign has failed! British and American units are now on African soil. Enzo, they're right round the corner, only a few miles away. Just think how quickly they could get here!"

Loud shouts and commands could be heard coming from Albero Sole.

Marcello ran to the barrack door. "I have to go, Enzo. Come on! I think it's the commander of the Felino Group."

The two of us hurried out of the barracks and arrived at the telephone exchange out of breath, where a number of soldiers were already in position. The commander of the Felino Group was in the process of explaining that he had received the order from high command for everyone to evacuate to the mainland.

Werner was sitting in front of the barracks, lost in thought. Klaus, silent and serious, was crouched down beside him. I had my suspicions as to what was bothering them. Quietly, I sat down with them and offered them cigarettes, and the three of us sat there for quite a while, smoking wordlessly. After a while, Werner interrupted the silence.

"Are you withdrawing with the others next week?"

I looked at him questioningly. "I haven't received any orders."

"Then you'll be staying here with us after all!" Klaus exclaimed sarcastically.

"What do you mean you have to stay here?" This was beyond belief. "I thought the whole company was leaving the island?"

"Unfortunately, we've been instructed to blow up the radar, then hide until the danger has passed."

I couldn't believe what I was hearing. A queasy feeling started to gnaw at my stomach. I felt scared and apprehensive. The war was becoming more and more of a reality. The island would be bombed. The rumours were true—the Allies would attack us and take us captive.

One thought was running through my head: *I've got to get out of here.*

The thought spurred me on. Time was running out. But how could I get off the island? I hadn't been allocated to the Italian unit nor to the Germans, I realised dejectedly. I was an exiled soldier who was supposed to be stationed in Rome. Shit! What was I going to do now? I had to get back to Rome. That's where I had originally been posted, and that's where I received my orders.

"How many days do you think it'll be until they get here?" I asked fearfully.

"No idea, but probably not long now," Klaus said. "It's just a pity things are getting serious now. I mean, we knew the day would come when we'd have to leave, but we had a lot of fun. We'll have to keep in touch, Enzo. When this damn war is over, we'll celebrate together!"

We exchanged addresses and concealed our fear of the unknown beneath visions of a future in which we were all together again, celebrating, drinking, eating, living good lives.

I was able to get hold of my superior in Rome via the German telephone line. He instructed me to leave the island too. So I waited for the marching orders, but they never arrived—neither by post nor by telegraph.

It was already mid-May. The entire German crew and most of the Italians from the Felino Group had already left. Fear crept through my body like a cancer.

"So you're staying here with me and Klaus after all, Enzo?"

"I don't know, Werner. Sorry. I'm still waiting for my marching orders," I explained.

"Then you'll probably be waiting till you're blue in the face, Enzo! The guys in Rome have completely forgotten about you. Listen, no one else is allowed to leave the island. Those orders came from the island commander himself."

"Werner, I have to talk to the island commander down at the harbour. Can you drive me down there?"

Werner fetched his motorbike, I jumped up onto the seat behind him, and before I knew it, we were hurtling down towards the port. Island Commander Bernini was standing in front of the navy command house conversing with two soldiers.

"Signore, I've been waiting for my marching orders for a fortnight now. My superior in Rome assured me that I'm also supposed to leave the island and report back to Rome. Can you please grant me permission to leave?" I gave him a beseeching look, struggling to catch my breath.

"Enzo," he said softly, "I'll gladly grant it to you. You really are cutting it fine by waiting till now to ask me. The last boat is leaving tonight. Hurry up and pack your things, quick as you can."

"I don't know how to thank you!" I exclaimed joyfully. My voice almost cracked as I told him.

He gave me a fatherly look, his eyes filled with tears. "You helped me telephone my family in Rome. This is my way of thanking you, but on one condition: I'm going to give you a letter to my wife. Please can you deliver it to her in Rome?"

What a weight off my mind. I thanked him profusely. We rushed up to the barracks to pack my things. Werner didn't mind driving me back down again.

"For you, my friend, I'd be happy to. Take care of yourself!"

"Keep your chin up, Werner, and don't let the Allies catch you!"

The last boat to Pantelleria and Sicily was transporting a few Italian soldiers who, like me, had been given special permission to leave. Most of the passengers were mainlanders who were being taken to Sicily first. I put the island commander's letter in the inside pocket of my jacket. I pushed my way through the crowd and spotted a space at the very front of the bow. My legs were still shaking long after the boat had set off. Fear lurked deep in my bones. Although we were in a flat-bottomed boat that should have been forearmed against mines, that was no guarantee. We were ordered to be quiet. Inch by inch, the boat glided through the gentle waves. The captain turned off the engine, and we drifted along in the silent darkness. He spoke quietly to his assistant, and we gradually floated on. Then he stopped the boat again. Everyone looked into the black water nervously.

"Can you hear it too?" whispered the young soldier next to me.

I listened intently, on high alert.

"We can't hear anything, Sergio. Those noises are just your imagination!" came someone's annoyed retort in the darkness.

"Zitto!" hissed a naval officer. "The sonar has detected something. It could be a submarine."

We all sat there on tenterhooks. The young soldier pressed up against me as if looking for support. I noticed his legs were shaking. I put my arm around his shoulders and held his trembling hand. "Calm yourself. They're only being cautious. We'll make it—everything will be fine," I whispered to him. I probably didn't sound all that convincing, as I was also stricken with fear. It felt as if we were walking on eggshells. The inky black night and the dark water all around settled over us like a heavy cloth, smothering us. After what felt like an eternity, the captain finally started the engine again, and we continued on our journey.

We travelled for several hours until the island of Pantelleria rose up before us. Everyone gazed, spellbound, at that shore we were all longing for. Suddenly, the dull roar of an engine swelled louder in my ears. *Are we going faster all of a sudden?* I wondered. The low rattling sound turned into a hum that grew louder and louder. Unable to locate the sound in the darkness, we all started to panic.

"It's the British bombers!" whispered one of the soldiers.

We all ducked down, as if that would protect us—but it was probably just an internal reflex. Some of the soldiers were quietly praying.

In the darkness, I could already make out the port of Pantelleria. But instead of heading into it, we steered towards a small bay on the other side of the island. We had only just entered it when we heard them again, the bombers, but this time the din was so loud that it pierced straight to the marrow. In no time at all, the sound grew nearer and nearer.

"Quick!" cried the captain.

We moored at the end of the bay and took shelter under a small rocky outcrop. No sooner had everyone left the boat than we heard the impact, as if it had struck right next to us. Over and over again, the bombs thundered down on the island, sending columns of smoke rising among the showers of sparks and flames. The deafening sound of boats and planes exploding in their hangar roared on and on. From our shelter in the bay, we could only guess at the scale of the bombing. We clung to each other, grateful to have moored our boat in the right place at the right time.

The hail of bombs lasted all through the night. We stayed in our hiding place all of the next day—only when night fell once more did we dare continue on our journey to Sicily.

When we reached harbour at Porto Empedocle, I called my aunt Maria immediately.

"Luca will pick you up in the car!" she said excitedly.

I breathed a sigh of relief.

"Hey, cugino. It's good to see you all in one piece! We just heard about the bomb attack on Pantelleria. That must have given you a fright! I'm glad you managed to get away in time." Luca gave me a warm hug.

"You said it, Luca. My heart is still in my mouth. Are you on leave?"

"Yes, for two more days. Then I have to go back to Rome."

"I have to go back to Rome too."

"Maybe I can arrange a flight for you. As a pilot, I've got connections—I can get you a permit to ride along with me. By the way, our cousins from America are here."

"Vince and Pete? How did they manage to travel to Sicily in wartime?" I couldn't make head nor tail of it.

"Between you and me, they were sent to Sicily on a secret mission. Pete told me he came to Sicily from Algiers. He was sent by the American secret services, and we've got to keep it top secret," Luca explained.

"Are they putting our family in danger by doing that?"

"They probably have connections with certain locals. It's definitely a dangerous business, but on the other hand, they can pretend to be Sicilians and are less conspicuous that way."

"And what do your parents and our grandparents think about all this?" I couldn't imagine Uncle Toni was too thrilled about it.

"Things are very tense between them. My grandfather is understandably sceptical of the two of them. Pete is sociable and friendly, but Vince is very reserved, although I think he's a bit of a hotshot. My father doesn't want them in the house under any circumstances. At the end of the day, Nonna is the kind soul who manages to find somewhere to put everyone up. She considers the pair of them part of the family, and I think the fact my father is remaining neutral makes the situation easier."

"What are they doing here exactly?"

"We've been wondering that too! Strictly between us, I don't think they're only working for the American secret services. You know we're not supposed to say the word 'mafia' out loud. They're probably making connections, and maybe they are for military purposes. They spend most of their time on the road. Nonna has invited them for dinner this evening."

"It definitely won't be long before the Allies invade. I realised that yesterday. On Lampedusa, we were always able to spot enemy planes over Malta, and sometimes we even shot some down. But the bombing raid on Pantelleria I experienced last night was a real eye-opener. When they come, that's it—everything will be reduced to rubble," I sighed.

The two of us were silent for a moment, lost in thought.

"I don't want to think about it. Pete and Vince are still our cousins, in spite of everything. I can't view them as the enemy, nor do I want to. But tell me, Luca, you're not being deployed for hand-to-hand combat, are you?" I asked, concerned.

"I hope it won't come to that. You know, flying is like an addiction for me. I just love the feeling of freedom when I'm in the air, like all of us—but nobody wants to fight. I get the wind up just thinking about it. With my youthful ambition, I never wanted to admit it. I had never considered the consequences of training as a pilot with the Regia Aeronautica; I was so cocky, I only thought about flying, about the super-fast Macchi jets. The reconnaissance flights were mostly harmless, and luckily I was never sent to Africa."

The road led along the rugged, rocky coast. The picture-perfect turquoise water stood out against the white sandy beaches in the bays. Colourful fishing boats rocked in the harbours of sleepy villages.

What I wouldn't give to make everything that's happened in the last few days turn out to be a dream, I thought.

We turned inland, away from the coast, and drove up into the hills. Vineyards rose either side of us as far as the eye could see.

"Our grandfather's Marsala!" Luca beamed with pride.

"I just remembered, I'm supposed to bring a bottle for my boss in Rome," I remarked, and at the same time, I felt a stab at my heart.

Nonna was sitting on the bench under the foliage, waving at us. With difficulty, she propped herself up on her cane and shuffled to the car. "Enzo, *amore mio*, I'm glad you made it! We just heard the news." She kissed me lovingly.

A slim young man stood in the doorway. I recognised him immediately; his features had hardly changed, his round glasses giving him a somewhat intellectual air.

"*Ciao, cugino!*" He gave me a friendly hug. "Tell us about your deployment on Lampedusa!"

Pete sat beside me at the table. Over a sumptuous meal, I relayed everything I had experienced. "It really was a stroke of luck I managed to catch the last boat. The problem was, I didn't belong to the Italian or German units. I was sent to the island as an individual, and the morons in Rome didn't give a damn about me."

"Do you want to report back to Rome, then?" Pete asked, uncomprehending.

"Do I want to? Not really, but it's an order. There's no getting around it."

Luca cut in. "Rome is safer than Sicily at the moment."

Vince stepped into the garden and came towards us. "Hello, Enzo!" He sat down opposite me. "Well, here we are, all of us together," he grinned. When I asked him what his and Pete's job was here in Sicily, he briefly explained that they were helping organise food shipments.

Somehow, we got to talking about my recruit training, and I told him that they had taken away my identity card.

"Listen, it's important that you have identification. You never know what might happen," Pete said, worried.

"I can help you," Vince replied curtly. "Let's go to Palermo tomorrow. I know someone at the town hall who can do it."

The next morning, we drove along rough country roads through the heart of the island, heading for Palermo. Wild fig trees and cacti grew on the barren hills. Between them were groves of fruit trees, alternating between olive, orange and lemon trees and small vineyards. Every now and then, we overtook farmers on their donkey carts. The villages appeared deserted, except for a few old women sitting on wooden benches in front of their dilapidated houses. The walls of the houses were daubed with slogans like *Noi sognamo l'Italia Romana* or *Credere, Obbedire, Combattere*.

"We'll have to make do with taking the scenic route on these dirt tracks, as there are more and more controls on the main roads. I don't want to take any risks," Vince explained. "I'm here on a secret mission, and I don't want to draw attention to myself. If we are stopped and questioned, worst-case scenario, we can defend ourselves with what's in the back seat."

He told me to lift up the cloth, and I glimpsed two large revolvers.

"I take it you learnt to shoot in your army training," he smirked.

I didn't find it funny at all. In fact, the longer I was in their presence, the more uncomfortable I felt. And Vince's secrecy unnerved me.

"I learnt to shoot in the Bronx," he told me, as if he were talking about the weather. I must have stared at him incredulously because he went on. "You can tell you're not Sicilian, kid! There are certain laws that apply here—maybe not elsewhere, but that's how it works here. When it comes to certain people, you have to make it very clear who's in charge. The acquaintance we're going to meet is influential, and people respect him because he protects and helps those who obey the laws. He'll help us get you an identity card."

I was a bundle of nerves. Of course, I understood what he was talking about, but it still scared me. In spite of this, I tried to see everything through the lens of the war. At that moment, it didn't matter to me in the slightest who exactly this acquaintance was. Here, the rule was: if you scratch my back, I'll scratch yours. I was just grateful to my American cousin for getting me my identity card. I tried not to think about how many people he might have killed in the past.

That same morning, Luca was summoned back to Rome at the last minute. I would have liked to spend more time with him, but we agreed to meet again once we were both there. After I had been issued with an identity card, Vince and I went our separate ways. I was glad to be in possession of this document, especially as it confirmed I was resident in Italy.

The last train from Palermo to Reggio di Calabria had already departed, and there wasn't another until the next day. I didn't want to wait that long, so I headed for the military airbase. Two German soldiers were standing in front of the airfield office, and they stared at me incredulously as I approached from a distance.

"Hey, you there! What's your business here?"

Only now did I realise that they were referring to my Italian uniform. I strode up to them and introduced myself.

"Heil Hitler! I'm a translator in the Luftwaffe, and I need to get back to Rome." I showed them my interpreter pass.

They examined the document and looked me up and down. Then they both laughed in unison. "You're the first Italian I've met who speaks perfect German! Amazing! Where are you from?"

I explained to them about Switzerland and my studies in Cottbus.

"The war threw a spanner in all our plans." They led me into the office and introduced me to a pilot called Georg. Georg would be taking a shipment to the mainland in two hours.

"Ever flown in a Ju 52 before?" he grinned.

I shook my head.

"The weather is good today. You can enjoy the view! We use the plane for transporting goods. For the past two weeks, I've done nothing but fly back and forth, from Reggio Calabria to Palermo and back."

"So I'm the only passenger?"

"It has space for 15 people, but you'll have today's flight all to yourself," he laughed. "I usually go alone. It'll be nice to have company today."

While I made myself comfortable in the seat, Georg checked the engines. After all the checks had been made, he sat down beside me in the cockpit. The propellers started to rotate, and we made our bumpy way towards the tarmac. Georg then pulled hard on the levers, the engines roared, and a moment later we were in the air. The Bay of Palermo now lay below us. The harbour was littered with warships. Colourful fishing boats bobbed further out to sea, and Monte Pellegrino was shrouded in a faint haze. The mountain loomed over the city like a colossal monument. The cathedral, framed by a leafy courtyard, stood out clearly amid the mishmash of pink roofs. Stately villas surrounded the squares and gardens, and countless church bell towers were strewn throughout the city. In the centre, I could clearly make out the Teatro Massimo Vittorio Emanuele.

"And? How do you like the view? The Teatro Massimo is the biggest opera house in Italy. Who would've thought?" he exclaimed.

"I didn't know that. It does look very impressive."

We approached the end of the Bay of Palermo. A long, sandy beach stretched out behind it.

"That's Cefalu up ahead," Georg explained. "Now we're going to head inland and set course for Taormina."

The flat coastal area soon transformed into a hilly landscape. Here, there were small lakes nestled in between wooded knolls.

"That's the Parco dei Nebrodi!"

"Unbelievable!" I cried, astonished. "The landscape in the southwest, where my grandparents live, is hilly too, but it's more barren, with fewer trees."

"I don't know the west coast at all," Georg informed me. "I've never gone further than Palermo. The area around Etna is mountainous and very green too, interestingly. Look, up there!"

In the distance, I could now make out the snow-capped peak of the mountain, enveloped in a hazy cloud of smoke.

"The volcano is still active. The last eruption was in 1928."

We were now heading for the Strait of Messina. Ferries were making their way through it, weaving between large cargo vessels and warships. Georg slowed down and steered the Junker over Reggio di Calabria, the southernmost coastal town on the mainland. The plane pitched as we approached the military airport. After a bumpy landing, Georg steered the plane towards the front of a large storage building.

"The next shipment is waiting for me already," he said. "Have a safe onward journey!"

I thanked Georg and assured him it had been a unique flying experience.

The Bombing of Rome, 1943

Va pensiero sull'ali dorate,
va ti posa sui clivi sui colli,
Ove olezzano tepide e molli,
l'aure dolci del suolo natal!

Fly, my thoughts, on wings of gold;
go settle upon the slopes and the hills,
where, soft and mild, the sweet airs
of my native land smell fragrant!
From Nabucco *by Giuseppe Verdi*

Nina drew the curtain aside an inch and peered worriedly out of the window of her *palazzo*. A car drove slowly by. Apart from that, all was still. She lingered behind the slightly open curtain until, at last, she spotted three shadows on the opposite side of the street. She waited. Nothing happened. The three figures were standing close together in the doorway of a house. Why were they just standing there? Something wasn't right. Nina was getting nervous, but she knew she had to remain calm at all costs. There—now she could hear a noise! The clicking came nearer, like the rhythmic beat from the heels of army shoes. They were two military men—clearly Germans. She could sense it, though she couldn't make out their uniforms. It was the way they marched over the cobblestones, keeping step— click, clack.

The footsteps fell silent. Then the doorbell rang. Nina felt her throat constrict. She gave herself a little shake and looked at her reflection in the mirror for a moment. Her black wavy hair fell softly over her shoulders, adorned by two gold hair clips on the sides. She was wearing a black wool dress, which accentuated her slender waist. She took a deep breath and left the room, head held high. As she opened the door, she heard voices from the entrance hall. She stopped behind the balustrade and listened to her maid's voice.

"Wait just a moment, please!" Flustered, the girl ran up the stairs, before spotting Nina behind the pillar. "Signora," she whispered hurriedly, "there are two German officers at the door! What can they want at this late hour?" Her voice quavered.

"Calm yourself, Angela. I'll deal with them. No need to worry—you can go to bed."

"But signora, the men aren't going to take you with them, are they?"

"No, Angela, certainly not. And you know what to do!" She briefly rested her hand on Angela's shoulder and looked at her gravely.

"Yes, say no more, signora. I know what to do."

Calmly, Nina descended the stairs and greeted the men.

"We need to ask you a few questions," said one of the soldiers in a brisk tone. He was rather stocky and had a round face, reminiscent of a piglet.

"Please come in," Nina responded cordially, eyeing the other man as she did so. He was a lieutenant and was tall and slim. He looked at her kindly with his deep blue eyes. "You are Princess Nina Pallavicini?"

"Yes, I am!"

He held out his hand to her and introduced himself with a slight bow of the head. "Karl Hissing, and this is Sergeant Weinstein." The latter just gave her a curt nod.

"You live here alone?" he asked directly.

"My husband served as a *capitano* in El-Alamein and was killed in an air battle there," Nina explained drily.

The piglet looked up the stairs, probably trying to work out how many rooms there were on the upper storey. His superior Hissing appraised the paintings and busts in the entrance hall with interest. Then his gaze wandered along the high walls lined with paintings by Velázquez, Rubens and van Dyck. He stood in front of a Botticelli and contemplated the scene in the painting.

Nina cleared her throat. "In the daytime, the palazzo is full of children. We've set up a school here." She opened the door to the dining room. In the middle of the large hall stood a long table laid with schoolbooks, slates and chalk. A blackboard hung above a desk, and there were piles of paints, brushes and paper in the corner. Pictures of children adorned the walls. The adjoining parlour was visible through the open double door, where they could make out an old piano on a raised platform. "That's the parlour, where we sing with the children and give them space to dance and play," she explained.

Sergeant Weinstein inspected the room and then went over to an old trunk, opening it without a qualm. To his displeasure, he saw it was filled with costumes and children's masks. "I'm going to investigate upstairs!" he called to his superior.

"Please take us there, signora," Karl Hissing requested, allowing her to take the lead.

The sergeant went from room to room while the lieutenant lingered in Nina's library. Nina stood off to the side, watching him. He stopped at the grand piano and leafed through the sheet music. He let his delicate hands glide dreamily over the keys. "*Aida!*" he exclaimed in delight. "Do you sing?"

"Not often."

He slowly walked along the shelves filled with books, drawing one out and leafing through it absentmindedly.

"I haven't found anything suspicious, lieutenant, but we should still inspect the cellar." The piglet was standing in the doorway.

"That's enough for today, Weinstein!" Hissing replaced the book on the shelf. Nina left the pair of them in the room and made her way downstairs.

"Why the rush, lieutenant? Now that we're here?" Weinstein whispered. "This palazzo has potential!"

Hissing waved him away. "We need to be diplomatic about this. Don't forget, Princess Pallavicini is a member of the aristocracy here in Rome. Write a short report stating the number of rooms and that it's being used as a school."

They departed from the library and took their leave.

No sooner had the door to the house snapped shut than Nina ran up the stairs. She peered through the library's small window, watching the men as they left. They were walking back in the direction they had come. Although it was very dark, Nina noticed the lieutenant looking up at her window. Had he seen her? She waited another moment until she was sure they were gone. Then she opened the curtain a crack and signalled to the three shadows that were still waiting in the doorway. They scurried swiftly across the street, then down the side staircase to the cellar entrance. Nina was already standing at the bottom, waiting for them.

"All clear?" asked Roberto.

"Yes," Nina breathed, "but we need to be careful. I'm certain the Germans will soon be back to search the cellar. Please show the men to the hidden summerhouse in the garden and explain our emergency plan to them."

Nina waited for Roberto in the dark sitting room. They proceeded cautiously to the window and checked the curtains were tightly closed. Then they lit a small oil lamp.

"Everything's fine, Nina. The men are in the loop." Roberto entered the room and slumped down into an armchair, exhausted.

She served him a cup of tea. "What's the situation, Roberto?" she asked quietly. "A friend of mine can take two refugees."

"Thank you, Nina. Every space counts. I have the support of an influential man, Sir D'Arcy Osborne; he's a British minister at the Papal See, one of the top representatives. He'll give us financial support. His butler, John May, is completely trustworthy too."

"His butler?" Nina looked perplexed and couldn't suppress a giggle.

Roberto laughed softly too. "He's still one of the old school! I'm sure you'll like him, Nina."

"Who? The butler or Sir D'Arcy Osborne?" She suddenly felt she was being swept up in a discussion that reminded her of her years at a girls' boarding school. And the fact that she was discussing men with a respected priest of the Vatican made her burst out laughing again.

Roberto chuckled, evidently amused. "I mean Osborne, naturally. I'll introduce you on our next visit to the Vatican."

"And what makes you think I'll like him?" Nina hadn't felt this cheerful and happy in a long time. Creating this underground organisation with Roberto had forged a deep trust between them, and that was especially evident to her in this moment.

"If something happens and you feel like you're in danger, come straight to the Collegio Teutonico. The Swiss guard knows everything. And if you come across anyone else who can provide somewhere for refugees to hide out, let me know right away. We urgently need more accommodation for our charges."

Nina nodded. "I'm sending Manolo to you with a shipment of cabbage. You know what I mean!"

Roberto smiled. "Your wealth of artistic ideas knows no bounds. That's what I call creative spirit!"

As they crept down the curved marble staircase, a satisfied smile flitted across Roberto's face. He remembered how the *principessa* had sent an errand boy with a handcart full of cabbages to the side entrance of the Vatican. In one of the cabbages, at the bottom of the pile, Nina had hidden a strip of paper. On it were the names and addresses of people that wanted to be involved in Roberto's secret mission. From then on, Roberto had christened his mission 'cabbage', and the codename for it was *crauti*.

Three days later, Karl Hissing was back. Alone. At that moment, Nina was in the parlour, lost in thought as she played the grand piano.

"Signora!" The housekeeper stood in the doorway, the German lieutenant beside her.

What does he want? Nina thought. How embarrassing that he had caught her playing the piano. She was annoyed that the housekeeper had just let him in. Was it possible he had caught her unawares and had already searched the cellar as she played music in blissful ignorance? Oh God, now she was trapped! Nina felt the hairs on the back of her neck stand on end, the fear of discovery paralysing her whole body.

"*Buongiorno, principessa!* Please keep playing—don't stop on my account! I have a few minutes to spare today and would love to spend them browsing your library. Will you grant me that privilege?" Karl Hissing strode confidently to the bookcase.

Nina was bewildered. Something about this man unsettled her.

"Are you alone? Did my housekeeper let you in?" she asked drily.

"I beg your pardon! Yes, I'm here alone; your housekeeper showed me upstairs. I was enchanted by your piano playing and simply had to follow the sound. Please continue. You play very well, principessa! I can call you that, can't I? In any case, I know that's what the locals call you."

"As you wish, lieutenant."

"Oh, call me Karl. Or, even better, Carlo!" he laughed.

Nina was still sitting stiffly on her piano stool. She couldn't make head nor tail of what was happening. Was he really here alone? Was he trying to distract her, or lure her into a trap? She scrutinised him out of the corner of her eye. He was tall and slim, and there was something cultured about him. His charming, easy manner didn't seem typically German. *Careful, he's your enemy!* she reminded herself.

"During my studies, I spent six months in Florence. My host family called me Carlo, and I liked it. I studied art history. When I was offered a place at a university in Florence, I didn't hesitate to enrol in an Italian course too. Since then, I've been reading books in Italian—I like the old poets best of all," he told her. His eyes roamed the bookshelves, fascinated. "Oh, I can't believe it! You have the collected works of Dante Alighieri!" Gingerly, he removed the book from the shelf, before taking a seat in the armchair by the window, lost in thought. Suddenly, he began to read aloud:

"Parev' me che nube ne coprisse
Lucida, spessa, solida e pulita,
Quasi adamante che lo sol ferisse.
Per entro sé l'eterna margarita
Ne ricevette, com'acqua recepe
Raggio di luce permanendo unita."

"Me seem'd as if a cloud had cover'd us,
Translucent, solid, firm, and polish'd bright,
Like adamant, which the sun's beam had smit
Within itself the ever-during pearl

Receiv'd us, as the wave a ray of light
Receives, and rests unbroken."

Nina stood rooted to the spot. His Italian, as she had remarked right from the off, was excellent. The devotion with which he spoke the words gave her a sense of his great passion for poetry. But what a strange situation she had found herself in! A German officer was reading Dante Alighieri in her parlour, while down in the cellar... My God, please let this not be a trap!

Nina moved cautiously to the door, opened it softly and stepped outside. "Angela! Please bring us a cup of coffee and some biscuits!" She stole a surreptitious glance down the sweeping marble staircase and strained her ears to try and figure out if anyone was in the house, but she couldn't hear anything.

"May I borrow this book?" Karl's voice roused her from her reverie.

"Keep it. Consider it a gift. I rarely read books these days," she said spontaneously.

"Oh, thank you very much! You have a beautiful library. Why don't you read anymore?"

Nina hesitated for a moment. "My husband collected books." No sooner had she said it than she immediately regretted it. She wondered why she had told this Carlo—this German lieutenant—about her husband. *Why aren't I more careful?* she thought, annoyed at her imprudence.

"Where is your husband?"

Nina realised bitterly that she would no longer be able to dodge his questions. "He's missing. He was a pilot in the Regia Aeronautica and hasn't been seen since 1 August 1940. His plane crashed and caught fire near Casablanca. They believe he perished in the flames."

"I'm so sorry, principessa." Karl cleared his throat and continued to peruse the bookshelves with his gaze. Nina sensed that the books were more interesting to him than her personal life.

"I'm so glad I found a library here at your home. It makes a nice change from my regular duties."

"Please don't hesitate to take as many books as you like."

Nina tried to sound friendly in the hope he would take plenty of books with him and then stay away from the house for a good long while. The thought that she would now be besieged by a German lieutenant and his soldiers was like a nightmare.

Coffee was served. Karl told her about his work as a curator at the Museum of Decorative Arts in Berlin. He was delighted to be stationed here in Rome because it meant he could spend his free time pursuing his interest in historical locations.

"Would you like to go to the opera with me? *La Traviata* is being performed next Thursday. I would love the company!"

Nina sipped her coffee and tried to compose herself. For three years now, she had kept herself away from Rome's social circles, and now she was suddenly expected to show her face in society by going to the opera with a German! What would they think of her? "That's very kind of you," she replied cautiously. "I'll think about it. I haven't been to the opera since the death of my husband."

"I understand, signora. I'll bring the books back at the end of the week, so you can give me an answer then."

A jeep was waiting in front of the Palazzo Pallavicini. The lieutenant took one last look up to the terrace where the library was, then climbed in.

Nina quickly changed her clothes, tied her hair up in a headscarf and made her way to the Vatican. St Peter's Square was practically empty. She only spotted two German soldiers under the right-hand colonnade, deep in conversation. She crept hurriedly along the left-hand colonnade. She had already reached the Swiss guardsmen when the soldiers spotted her.

"*Crauti*," she whispered. The guardsmen let her in. She hurried through the garden in front of the Collegio Teutonico. Roberto's study was in one of the adjacent buildings. Breathless, she slumped down into a leather armchair beside his desk.

"You look upset, Nina! What has happened?"

She described the incident with Lieutenant Karl Hissing. "He wants to take me to the opera! What should I do?"

Roberto hesitated a moment. "What do you think of him, Nina? I mean, what does your gut tell you? Did he question you? Did he want information?"

"No, he didn't say a word about any impending house search, or anything like that. In fact, he only seemed interested in my library. Strange, isn't it? He studied art history in Florence and seems to be taken with our culture. I just can't put my finger on it—I can't tell if we're walking into a trap here."

"Did he mention the name Kappler?"

"No, the name didn't come up. He didn't mention anything to do with the military."

"I think you should go with him to the opera. *Fai una bella figura!* We might be able to find some way to use this. Keep your ears open! Herbert Kappler will certainly be there too."

A shiver ran down Nina's spine. She would be meeting Kappler, the German chief of police and the local SS commander of Rome's Gestapo. The Vatican's greatest enemy. The worst rumours were circulating about him. His close collaboration with the OVRA, the *Organisazione per la Vigilanza e la Repressione dell'Antifascismo*, only increased his influence. People lived in fear of his raids, and he was quick to quash his opponents, arranging for suspicious persons to disappear at lightning speed.

There was a knock at the door, and Sir D'Arcy Osborne entered. "*Signora, buongiorno. Monsignore,* may I speak with you a moment? There are three British soldiers here, and they have some interesting information for you," he asked politely.

The British representative to the Holy See cut an impressive figure. He was immaculately dressed, and Nina could immediately tell that his leather shoes were of the highest quality.

"Of course, but wait a minute! I've just had an idea, sir! Do you like the opera? I was thinking that we could send you to the opera to shadow our principessa, so to speak. What do you think? Signora Pallavicini has been invited to accompany Lieutenant Karl Hissing to the opera. Because she hasn't moved in social circles for a long time, she is feeling rather uneasy, especially as she'll be in the company of a German, if you catch my drift. And it occurs to me that you, sir, could be there in an official capacity. Keep an eye and an ear open for our principessa, and always stay within reach so she can feel safe." Roberto was quite taken with his plan and gave Sir Osborne a friendly pat on the shoulder.

"It would be my pleasure, signora! No need to be intimidated by the German authorities." Sir D'Arcy Osborne gave a slight bow and, placing his left hand behind his back, he took her right hand and kissed it. "It would be a great honour, Principessa Pallavicini." Nina couldn't help smelling the subtle scent of his cologne.

The door opened, and a white terrier bounded into the room, jumping up at the English diplomat, until he gave the young dog a gruff command. "Sit!"

"He escaped from me again, sir. I'm sorry!" The butler went to pick up the dog with his white-gloved hands.

"Leave it, John. The little chap needs to learn better manners."

"Can I get you anything, sir, madam?"

Nina declined. She was still feeling a little dizzy.

"You'll be in the best hands, Nina, believe me. Nothing can possibly happen to you. Just remember to put your feelers out, trust your intuition and keep track of where the dangers lie. You have a knack for recognising and sizing up people and their intentions. You'll be able to get some important information for us. And when the lights go down and the curtain rises, just enjoy the music and the singers, the beautiful set, the costumes," Roberto reassured her.

Nina smiled tensely. "Yes, Roberto. I will. I'll think of the beautiful music and that will keep me calm. But I'll be on the lookout and make a mental note of anything that catches my attention."

"*Brava!* I'm proud of you!"

"Thank you for accompanying me, Sir Osborne. I must be going now."

The butler led the terrier out of the room. Sir D'Arcy Osborne stood at the door and held it open for Nina.

"Goodbye, Roberto. Manolo will bring you another delivery of cabbage at the weekend." She couldn't say any more than that, because they had to be careful, even in the Vatican. "There are spies everywhere," Roberto had once told her. "Even in the Holy See!"

"See you on the night of the opera, signora. I'm pleased to be able to go with you, even at a distance. I will talk to you at some point, discreetly of course. No need to worry. I'm sure you'll turn some heads among the audience." He gave her a reverent look.

"Thank you very much, Sir Osborne!"

A guardsman led Nina through the building and down some stairs to the garden. In the cool shadow of the great, ancient pines, they made their way along the narrow paths that wound their way up the hill, along flowerbeds and bushes laden with blossom. The imposing form of St Peter's Basilica now lay below them.

"I have been instructed to take you to the outbuilding, where there is an inconspicuous exit leading into a small alley. It will be safer for you. St Peter's Square is too dangerous in the evening. They're watching our every move—we have to be careful," the guardsman explained.

They descended a steep flight of stairs to the cathedral. Another guardsman was keeping watch at the rear entrance gate. They hastened past the chancel. They mounted a wooden staircase that led to a narrow balcony, before making their way along the elongated chancel arch, high above the nave of the church. From up there, they had a breathtaking view of the painted ceiling and the dome. The monotonous chanting during vespers lent the massive building an aura of peace and calm. Nina wanted to stop and listen, but the guardsman urged her to keep moving.

"It will soon be dark. You must hurry!" he whispered.

"Oh, yes," said Nina. The guardsmen were very responsible—she knew she could rely on them.

After taking a detour along passages and staircases, they reached the exit. The alleyway was deserted. Nina covered her face with a veil. In the twilight, she crept past the rows of houses as she made her way home. Just as she was about to round the corner by the palazzo, she grew alert and froze in the doorway of a house by the square. From her vantage point, she was able to examine her house without being disturbed. Something was wrong. Why were there so many soldiers in the street all of a sudden? And why were there two soldiers standing guard outside the palazzo? She removed her veil and hurried to the entrance of her property.

"Halt!" someone shouted. "Who goes there?" The soldier stood in a wide-legged stance, blocking her path. Another appeared and prodded him in the ribs, snapping at him.

"Hey, let the signora through. She's the lady of the house! The principessa!"

"Oh, excuse me, my dear princess! Please enter your palace!" cried the other mockingly, bowing with a grin.

Head held high, Nina entered the house. Angela, the housekeeper, ran up to her and explained that a lieutenant and three soldiers had ordered a search of the house.

At the top of the stairs stood a stocky man, eyeing Nina sternly. Almost at once, the front door flew open, and Karl Hissing marched angrily up the stairs at a brisk pace. He nodded at Nina and said briefly, "Excuse me, signora, I will settle this in a moment. Allow me!"

"Thank you," Nina whispered fearfully.

"What's going on here, Lieutenant Kessler?" Hissing snapped at him sternly.

"I ordered the search, Lieutenant Hissing! The house is on the investigation list."

"Listen, Kessler, this house, as you call it, is under my jurisdiction! We just searched it ten days ago."

"Oh, you don't say! That's not what I was told. I heard you were here, but you did not search all the rooms and certainly not the cellar. Instead, you ordered the officer present to leave the house. And no report was made," Kessler replied dismissively.

"I had planned to carry out a search the day after tomorrow and was also planning to investigate whether this residence could be used as accommodation. During the day, it is used as a school for children. I'm accusing you of interfering in my affairs, Lieutenant Kessler, do you understand? Stick to worrying about the tasks that are assigned to you. Now get out of here!" Hissing's voice cracked. Outraged, he chivvied the lieutenant down the stairs.

"Terminate the search! Get those two out of the cellar and give me a detailed report!" Kessler ordered his soldiers.

Hissing stood on the landing, his voice ringing down the stairs. "Don't let me catch you here again, Kessler!"

Kessler and the soldiers left the palace as fast as they could. Then, suddenly, all was quiet. Hissing was still standing at the top of the stairs, looking at Nina with concern.

Slowly, he descended the stairs step by step. When he was standing before her, he took her shaking hand. "I'm awfully sorry. You've been given a fright, and those scoundrels have absolutely no respect for a person like you. May I ask you to sit with me in your library for a moment?"

Nina swallowed and could only nod. Still holding her hand, he led her gently up the stairs.

Angela came running. "Signora, what can I get for you?"

"Wine, Angela. Bring a bottle of red wine. And some bread and prosciutto to go with it. I need to recover from the shock."

"Right away, ma'am!" Angela hurried into the kitchen.

They sat down in the parlour, facing one another. Karl Hissing was smoking a cigarette, looking at Nina intently.

"It was a misunderstanding. Kessler has no reason to search here. Those weren't my instructions. As I already told you, I did want to come by with my people at the end of this week." He stood up and went over to the bookcase.

Nina couldn't make head nor tail of what had just happened. Why was he apologising? He was being very courteous and treating her respectfully—*unlike the other Germans*, she thought.

Angela brought the wine and food. Gradually, Nina started to relax. The wine did her good, but she was still battling with her thoughts. How was she supposed to sit there in her armchair and drink wine while there was a German standing next to her, browsing her bookshelves?

Hissing took an illustrated volume entitled *Michelangelo and His Works* from the shelf, sat back down and began to leaf through it. Nina offered him the dish with the bread, olives and Parma ham.

"Will you accompany me to the opera?" he asked casually.

Nina looked him in the eye. "Yes, I'll join you."

A satisfied smile flitted over his lips. "I'm glad. I'll pick you up at 7 p.m. May I borrow this book?"

"You don't need to ask. You may take as many books as you like."

After he had left, Angela hurried up the stairs, flustered. "Signora, the German soldiers forced their way into the cellar. That Kessler is an arrogant, pushy man. He practically beat down the front door. It was all so unexpected. I couldn't keep them out!" She was still very upset.

"Calm yourself, Angela. Everything is all right. Karl Hissing just informed me that he'll be back at the end of the week to search the house more thoroughly. Of course, I find it all very unpleasant, but there's nothing we can do about it. We are at his mercy. We just need to keep a cool head."

"Our men have done good work. They haven't left any traces. They are still in the summerhouse for the time being. Should we keep them there?"

Nina nodded. "Yes, definitely. The best thing is for them to set up a place to stay in the connecting walkway. Who knows? Maybe our garden will soon be searched as well!"

The next few days passed without any visitors. Nina expected Karl to turn up to fetch more books any day now. Sometimes, she found that she was almost waiting to see him. Her thoughts drifted back and forth between feelings and reality. He was, in fact, very kind to her, courteous, respectful, and his passion for the Italian language and art fascinated her. But then the fear would resurface again. What was she getting herself dragged into? How could this possibly end? She pushed down any feelings for this man that she felt arising in her, yet she realised she was secretly looking forward to going to the opera. But she also felt an unexpected nervousness that was almost like stage fright. The idea that she would be facing all the senior Nazi military officers and probably SS men, accompanied by a lieutenant, made her feel almost faint. What should she ask? What would she observe?

Then she gave herself a shake. *Stop this! Who am I? I, a respected Roman noblewoman, will not allow myself to be intimidated by a few Nazi officers and silly SS losers! My pride will set me head and shoulders above them. And—wait a moment—my educated, aristocratic conversation will put them all to shame. That's how this visit to the opera is going to go!*

Nina sat in front of the mirror and considered her simple black evening dress and her hair piled high on her head, emphasising her fine, noble features. "Chin up!" she whispered to her reflection. Then she strode to the door, where Karl Hissing was already waiting for her, holding his car door open in anticipation.

The building of the Teatro Reale dell'Opera was brightly lit. A great crowd had gathered before the entrance, forming a collage of grey-green uniforms and black or subtly colourful evening dresses. A clamour of boisterous chatter and laughter rang out. The car weaved through the crowd and drew up directly in front of the stairs. Karl climbed out and opened the door for Nina. She had to pause for a moment to take a deep breath. Gallantly, he held out a hand to help her out.

"You look charming, principessa!" he whispered.

Her black evening dress had a short train that swept along behind her. Nina climbed the stairs slowly, the lieutenant's hand offering gentle support. She could feel all eyes on her.

Champagne was being served in the large saloon bar; Karl snapped up two glasses. "To the Italian opera! I hope you enjoy it."

Nina sipped the cool, sparkling drink.

"Principessa!"

She recognised the high, clear voice instantly.

"What an honour to run into you at the opera!"

"Oh, Isabella, lovely to see you!"

Isabella Colonna embraced her warmly. "I can hardly wait to hear Paolo Silveri. How about you?"

Isabella's husband approached the two women. "Principessa!" He kissed Nina's hand. "I heard about your husband's tragic accident. We're all so sorry about it." His right hand was resting on the knob of a walking stick.

"Antonio has been back at home for three months now. He was shot in the leg, but it's starting to heal, and of course I'm delighted to be able to nurse him back to health," Isabella gushed. "I miss the big parties. Don't you?"

"Well, I withdrew from social circles after Marcello's death," Nina replied simply.

"I can well understand that. What brings you to the opera tonight? You're in the company of a German officer?"

Karl Hissing was standing a little apart from them, engaged in conversation with two men in uniform. Isabella eyed him surreptitiously.

"That's Karl Hissing. He has visited me a few times and has borrowed some books from my library."

Isabella raised her eyebrows quizzically.

"He studied art history in Florence and enjoys reading Italian literature."

Isabella was still looking at her in disbelief.

"Of course, the palazzo has been searched—they're trying to decide whether some of the rooms could be used as offices. But I think all the available rooms should be left for the children to use."

"It's very generous of you to have taken in the schoolchildren. It's a disgrace that two of our schools are now in ruins."

"Yes, I quite agree. But the lessons with the children make a nice change for me. I sing with them, we put on plays, and I've engaged three teachers to try and follow a curriculum as best they can. How are things with you?"

"Our top floor is occupied by sick and wounded patients. It's a bit of a burden, if I'm honest. Nurses are hard to come by, but we've temporarily employed two young women from Sicily who are very attentive and are doing what they can. They come two days a week. Luckily, this means Antonio can be cared for directly. That's the one positive to come out of all this," said Isabella soberly.

"Why did the two nurses from Sicily come here? I'm astonished."

"Carina and Francesca are the daughters of Roberto's family friends. He brought them here because he believes they will be safer in Rome." Nina nodded silently. Both women understood what she was talking about. "They go back and forth between the hospital, Ciampino Airport and our palazzo," explained Isabella.

"Principessa, would you like some more champagne?" Karl approached the two women.

"Allow me to introduce Isabella Colonna!" Nina gestured to her friend.

"Delighted, signora. Would you like some more champagne?" He waved to a waiter, who came to fill up their glasses. "To the opera!" He toasted the two women happily.

Then Nina spotted Sir D'Arcy Osborne. He was standing beneath a palm, and he winked at her discreetly as he conversed with Vito Borghese.

A man in German uniform came over to them. "I was sure I would run into you here, Karl!" he exclaimed, while at the same time eyeing Nina and Isabella with interest.

"Yes, we love the opera, don't we?" Karl replied. "May I introduce the ladies? Principessa Nina Pallavicini, Signora Isabella Colonna."

The newcomer surveyed the two women. "Herbert Kappler! It's an honour to meet you, signora, principessa! Yes, we love the Italian opera! Isn't it fascinating how Verdi is performed more than Wagner?" He laughed. "It was always understood that Wagner was the Führer's favourite, but now it seems he has found a rival. I quite agree with him. *La Traviata* in particular is very diverting, isn't that right, Hissing?"

His appearance, the blond hair plastered firmly to his brow with pomade, the cold, pale blue eyes, coupled with his hard military tone sent a shiver down Nina's spine. She froze and gave a tense, mask-like smile.

"Where did you study, Hissing? I heard you're an Italian history buff," he asked, interested, while not letting the women out of his line of sight.

"I studied art history in Florence, and Italian language and literature alongside," Karl explained.

"When was that?" Kappler probed.

"That was in 1932," Hissing replied.

Kappler turned and greeted a young Italian. "There you are, Giorgio! Wonderful! And armed with your camera too! Just the way I like it. Giorgio is my new cameraman. I've commissioned him to work on a photography exhibition about the Colosseum. Photography is my passion, and sadly I have far too little time to dedicate to it, but naturally I will accompany Giorgio in his work from time to time. We need inspiration, don't we, Hissing?"

Karl nodded approvingly. "The Colosseum truly is a breathtaking piece of architecture," he remarked.

"Oh, the architecture is part of it. But what I really want to do with the exhibition is show our Italian soldiers what the fighters in Rome did back then, the honour with which they fought. I want it to symbolise our fighting spirit! We don't need any more inspiration, do we, Hissing? Our soldiers have fighting spirit, but the Italians? They desperately need to be reminded of what their ancestors achieved!" cried Kappler enthusiastically.

"*Veni, vidi, vici!*" shouted an SS officer.

"Bravo, bravo!" Kappler laughed derisively.

A gong sounded. Nina breathed again. It was time to take their seats. Kappler gave her a piercing look.

"Enjoy the opera, ladies. Hissing, we'll see each other later."

Karl saluted.

"I'm sure we'll see each other again in the intervals, Nina," murmured Isabella.

Antonio took her arm and, turning to Nina, said, "Enjoy the show, principessa!"

Karl led Nina to the box. "I last saw *La Traviata* five years ago at the Deutsche Oper in Berlin. But seeing the opera here in Rome is a very special experience for me."

Nina was suddenly caught up in Karl's infectious enthusiasm. She peered over the railing of the box at the orchestra pit and the rows of spectators below. The stalls were dominated by grey uniforms. Directly opposite, in one of the boxes on the other side, she caught sight of Sir D'Arcy Osborne. He was sitting bolt upright, looking directly at her. He held up his hand slightly in slow motion. Nina did likewise, and she felt as if an invisible bond were being forged between the two boxes. She couldn't help smiling.

Then the lights gradually dimmed, and the violins rang out, playing the Prelude in a minor key. The melody of the higher violin parts exuded the profound sadness of the tragic tale about to be told; but then, as the lower parts joined in, the music took on a certain lightness that foreshadowed the joyous celebration of the first act.

The curtain opened. Violetta greeted her guests, and Gastone introduced her to Alfredo. The exuberant mood in Alfredo and Violetta's duet *Libiamo ne lieti calici* made Nina completely forget where she was. The audience clapped enthusiastically to the rhythm, and Karl Hissing joined in too, singing along softly while giving her an impish look.

"Beautiful!" he exclaimed, delighted.

The story took its course; Violetta's singing touched Nina in every way, and the addition of Alfredo with his dark, beautifully rich tenor filled her with a deep longing.

"I take it you're enjoying the opera as much as I am?" Karl asked during the interval.

"Yes, very much," Nina replied.

In the saloon bar, she was offered more champagne, but she only sipped a little from her glass. It was as if she had been jolted back to harsh reality, and the presence of the German military caused the music, which was still ringing in her ears, to die away. Fortunately, she was able to find Isabella and Antonio

Colonna again, and they were joined by the Orsini family.

"The cast is fabulous!" exclaimed Antonio.

"I couldn't imagine a better tenor than Beniamino Gigli for the role of Alfredo," Isabella gushed.

"Yes, I agree," said Nina. "And then there's Paolo Silveri as Giorgio Germont—he was simply jaw-dropping."

They were all in agreement that the performance, both the acting and the singing, was sensational.

Karl Hissing politely excused himself from the Roman opera guests, and Nina felt much more relaxed.

"Good evening, *signore e signori*. Isn't it a wonderful production?" Nina heard a familiar voice behind her.

"Ah, Sir Osborne, what an honour to see you here," Vito Orsini declared. "Laura, this is Sir D'Arcy Osborne, British attaché to the Papal See."

"Delighted, signora!" Osborne replied.

"I didn't know you were an opera fan, Sir Osborne?" Vito Orsini seemed to know Osborne personally.

"Yes, I am. I'm particularly fond of Verdi, but who isn't? Back in London, I used to go to Verdi operas at Covent Garden as often as I could. Of course, the atmosphere here in Rome makes for a particularly unique experience." He nodded at the ladies and withdrew back into the crowd.

Nina couldn't help smiling inwardly at his correct, respectful attitude towards her. She hadn't known what to expect from his 'shadowing' her, but his approach was as professional as could be. From behind a flower arrangement, he indicated to her that Kappler was behind the pillar and was able to draw her attention in the direction of the senior Gestapo officers just by walking past them.

"I'm just going to the loo before it starts again." Nina excused herself from her friends, meaning she could escape the gazes of Kappler and his officers.

Back in the box, Karl passed her a programme. "A little souvenir for you."

"Oh, thank you, Carlo. I look forward to looking back fondly on this wonderful evening."

Then the orchestra started up again.

Oh, thought Nina, *I'm acting rather giddy*, and she chided herself for it. It was probably the champagne. When was the last time she'd had a glass? It seemed to her as if the orchestra were breathing with the singers, and she grew more and more entranced by the tragic love story, Violetta's despair and Giorgio's bitterness. *I know the libretto inside out*, she said to herself, *but it's touching me so close to my heart, cutting so deep, that it's almost painful. The music is tearing me apart inside, quite literally.* Then she suddenly noticed the connection between the tragedy in *La Traviata* and that of the war. How unbelievable that they mirrored each other so exactly! Violetta, the woman hounded to death, excluded, despised by society and forced to renounce love. But, at the same moment, Nina was struck by the fact that the brutal emotional blackmailer, portrayed by Giorgio, was ultimately being driven by external forces himself, the victim of the mendacious social morality he created. Nina was overcome by a deep sadness and, without realising it, a tear ran down her cheek.

Karl lay a hand softly over hers. "Music touches our souls. And every time I hear *La Traviata*, I end up just like you—all that remains is sadness."

Roberto slumped down into his chair, his breath still coming in gasps. "I need a glass of water, please, Nina! You know how running strains my lungs." He was wearing a suit and tie today. With a grin, he explained to Nina that he needed to vary his disguise wardrobe a little. "Now, tell me, Nina, how was the opera?"

"Oh, Roberto, it was wonderful. I had completely forgotten how much I love the music and the arias. I also felt I was in good hands with Sir D'Arcy Osborne shadowing me. He's a true professional." Then she explained about the meeting with Herbert Kappler.

Roberto listened attentively. "Herbert Kappler, my nemesis. Yes, he's rather fond of culture. But it worries me that you came so close to him."

"I'm telling you, Roberto, I can still feel the fear in my bones! His eyes were so cold and brutal, and he had that dreadful scar on his face. I excused myself to use the loo. I sat in the cubicle trying to stop my whole body from shaking."

"How did Hissing act with Kappler around?"

"He was tense, I could tell. But they didn't say much. Tell me more about Kappler, Roberto!" she said.

Roberto settled back in his armchair. "Kappler. He is a solitary person, has few friends, was in an unhappy marriage, kept getting caught up in affairs, opposes the church. When he came to Rome, he started out as the German embassy's police attaché, then he turned to the Fascist police. Skilled and ambitious as he is, he made it to the head of the Gestapo in Rome. And now he hunts down whoever he can, especially the Jews. We're complicit, so we're particularly vulnerable. And I'm probably at the top of his list. Tell me about Hissing, Nina! What do you think of him?"

Nina sighed. "I don't know, Roberto. I have the feeling that he's trying to woo me, and that it's not just my library he's after," she chuckled, then grew serious again. "The more he shows up, the more dangerous things will get for me, Roberto. Of course, I was delighted to go to the opera, but I can feel that we're growing closer, and it frightens me. Even if he's only doing his duty, he is a Nazi—our enemy. I sometimes wonder if he suspects I'm hiding people, and he wants to protect me by coming to the library often so he can tell his bosses that everything is fine with me."

"Either way, Nina, listen to your instincts. If you smell danger, come to the Vatican immediately. We can put you up in the Monastero Benedettine Santa Cecilia."

After Roberto had left, Nina sat at her desk, lost in thought. She wondered if she had shared too much. Was Karl Hissing really a threat? Her gut told her that he was a courteous, respectful and warm person. His interest in Italian culture was sincere; it fitted his profession, after all. And she had to admit, she always looked forward to his visits. After their evening at the opera, he had driven her to her front door and kissed first her hand, then her cheek, drawing her near to him. And as she played that moment again before her eyes, she felt a great, profound affection. She went into the library, sitting at the grand piano and starting to play, to give her feelings free rein.

It was Monday morning, and Nina was getting ready for the schoolchildren to arrive. She wanted to sing with them today. Since her visit to the opera, she felt more drawn to music again.

"Come and stand round the piano! Who knows who wrote this song?" Some of the children raised their hands.

"Giuseppe Verdi!" cried a little boy proudly.

"Correct. Your parents and grandparents all know this song. It's beautiful—let's sing it together." She struck the first note, played the introduction, then began to sing, together with the schoolchildren.

"*Va pensiero, sull'ali dorate,*
va, ti posa sui clivi, sui colli,
ove olezzano tepide e molli,
l'aure dolci del suolo natal!
Del Giordano le rive saluta, die Sionne le torri
  atterrate.
Oh, mia patria sì bella e perduta!
Oh, membranza sì cara e fatal!"

"Fly, my thoughts, on wings of gold;
go settle upon the slopes and the hills,
where, soft and mild, the sweet airs
of my native land smell fragrant!
Greet the banks of the Jordan
and Zion's toppled towers.
Oh, my homeland, so lovely and so lost!
Oh memory, so dear and so dead!"

The young singers were interrupted by an impatient knocking. In the doorway stood Karl Hissing. Nina asked Anna to watch the children. His countenance was fraught with anxiety.

"I need to speak to you urgently, Nina," he said shortly. He seemed very upset. As soon as they were in the library, he took her hand and looked at her beseechingly. "Nina, everything I'm about to tell you must remain between us. Please trust me. Your house will soon be used as quarters. I heard that today. Things will soon become too dangerous for you here, Nina. I want to help you. I have a plan. I can arrange a ticket and papers for you to take a train to Turin. My friend, who is a curator in Geneva, can pick you up and take you to Geneva. You'll be safe there." He spoke very quickly and seemed to be in a great hurry.

Nina just looked at him in shock. "I can't just leave here and run away!"

"Nina, please understand, things are getting too dangerous for you here. You'll be safe in Geneva until the end of the war. I'll arrange everything; my friend and his wife will take care of you. Believe me, time is running out!"

Nina looked at him, distraught. He put his arms around her and whispered in her ear. "Nina, when the war is over, I'll come to you. Let's build a life together. I love you, Nina, and I want you to be safe." He looked deep into her eyes, then kissed her tenderly. "I wish I could stay with you, but I have to go." He stroked her hair gently. "I'll be back tomorrow night, with more information. I have to go. Take care of yourself." He kissed her, then hurried to the door. Just as he was about to open it, he turned back, pulled an envelope from his trouser pocket and placed it on the piano. A mischievous smile played on his lips. "I almost forgot the most important thing!"

Nina felt utterly dazed. Carlo. How he cared for her. Did he have any idea the kind of people she was hiding under her roof? No, she couldn't accept his offer. It was too risky. She snatched up the envelope, threw a scarf over her head and crept quietly down the stairs. She could still hear the children's singing. "Fly, my thoughts, on wings of gold..." The melody drifted along behind her as she silently opened the front door and hurried through the twilight towards the Vatican.

She entered Roberto's study in a state of agitation, her face streaked with tears. He gave her a friendly hug.

"I can't leave, Roberto! But it's getting too dangerous for me here!"

"I have somewhere you can hide, Nina. You'll be safe in the monastery up in the mountains. I'll send Manolo to the house right away and have the refugees you're hiding housed elsewhere. Time is of the essence."

Nina was led to a chamber where she would be able to spend the night. Her head was still spinning from the day's events. In bed, when she was finally able to rest, she remembered the envelope. 'My dear Nina' was written neatly on it. Her heart grew warm as she carefully opened it.

My beloved Nina, I am not good at writing and certainly not at writing poetry, but I hope this poem by Goethe will convey how much I love you.

Your Karl.

Nina paused for a moment. Her thoughts drifted back to her house. Should she have stayed put and followed his instructions? How she wished at that moment that there was no war. She knew her heart wasn't filled with fear, but with trust in him. He was not her enemy. She knew, in that moment, that he meant it sincerely—but the circumstances meant she had to act against her instincts. Travelling to Geneva would have been far too risky. She would be safe at the monastery. With a heavy heart, she read the poem.

Ich denke dein, wenn mir der Sonne Schimmer vom Meer erstrahlt.
Ich denke dein, wenn sich des Mondes Flimmer in Quellen malt.
Ich sehe dich, wenn auf dem fernen Wege der Staub sich hebt.
In tiefer Nacht, wenn auf dem schmalen Stege der Wanderer bebt.
Ich höre dich, wenn dort mit dumpfem Rauschen die Welle steigt.
Im stillen Haine geh ich oft, zu lauschen, wenn alles schweigt.
Ich bin bei dir, du seist auch noch so ferne, du bist mir nah!
Du bist mir nah! Die Sonne sinkt, bald leuchten mir die Sterne,
Oh, wärst du da!

I think of thee, when golden sunbeams shimmer across the sea;
And when the waves reflect the moon's pale glimmer, I think of thee.
I see thy form, when down the distant highway the dust-clouds rise;
In deepest night, above the mountain by-way, I see thine eyes.
I hear thee when the ocean-tides returning loudly rejoice;

*And on the lonely moor, in stillness yearning, I hear
   thy voice.
I dwell with thee: though thou art far removed, yet
   art thou near!
The sun goes down, the stars shine out, beloved,
Ah, wert thou here!*

There came a muffled whirring sound. Nina paused. It grew louder, morphing into a hum that swelled to a roar. Nina listened, got up and went to the window. The muffled sound became deafening, the windowpanes shook, and the floorboards vibrated under her feet.

"My God!"

The sky was strewn with aeroplanes and, below them, swarms of flying objects floated towards the city.

"They're bombing our Eternal City!"

"Quick, Enzo, we need to get out of here!" Maurizio dragged me onto his motorbike.

"What are you going to do? Isn't it too dangerous?" I shouted frantically.

"We'll be quicker on the bike!" he called back. "I'll take you with me to my parents. Hopefully the hotel will remain unscathed."

We had just been sitting in the office at Ciampino Airport, checking the inventory of a food delivery, when we heard the muffled sound of an engine and knew immediately what it was. We pelted down the stairs to the forecourt where Maurizio had parked his motorbike. Maurizio's parents ran a hotel in town—that's where we were going. Cold sweat ran down my back.

"But that's crazy! We should look for a better place to shelter!" I yelled.

Maurizio didn't listen. He raced as fast as he could along side streets and down alleyways. A house exploded right behind us. The vibration caused the motorbike to skid dangerously over a curb. I just managed to hold on. Maurizio drove like mad in a slalom to avoid the hail of bombs. The closer we got to the city, the further we seemed to get from the explosions. I didn't dare look back; the noise was bloodcurdling. People were running into churches in their panic, hoping to find shelter in the crypts.

At long last, Maurizio slowed down. He drove into a narrow lane and stopped the motorbike. "Come on!" He shunted me through a heavy oak door.

"Maurizio! There you are! Quick!" His mother hugged him, then hustled us down the stairs into the cellar.

After hours of waiting, the noise of the explosions finally died away, and we crept out of the cellar. The fiery smell of burning hung in the air.

"You can stay here for the time being, Enzo," said Maurizio's mother kindly.

"Thank you, signora. I'll gladly stay for two nights, then I need to go to Southern Italy, where I'm being redeployed. Those are my marching orders."

We went out into the street. Here in the centre, there was only minor damage. I wanted to head straight to the Vatican to see Roberto and find out more.

Accompanied by two gendarmes, Roberto and Pope Pius XII drove to the San Lorenzo quarter of the city. Both had looked on in horror from the Vatican as the bombs dropped and had seen the columns of smoke rising over the east of the city. In the forecourt of the Basilica di San Lorenzo, the head of the Catholic Church met with the shocked victims. Amidst the rubble, he knelt down and prayed the *De profundis* lament. People touched him, kissed his ring—children clung to his cassock, which was smeared with blood.

"We want peace!" the crowds wailed.

The pope spoke to the wounded and comforted the survivors. He was in a state of shock himself. He raised his outstretched arms to heaven, with a plea and a warning.

On the way back, Pope Pius XII declared indignantly, "I will telegraph President Franklin Roosevelt directly! The capital of Holy Christendom must be respected and spared any further attacks. I will order the military to evacuate the high command from the city. Rome is to be declared an 'open city'!"

"Quick, out of the way!" cried Dr Bernardo. Assisted by his two helpers, he hoisted the blood-soaked body onto a hospital bed. "We need to operate immediately!" It only took a moment for the doctor to realise the injured man's legs, which had been torn to shreds by bombs, would have to be amputated. On the next stretcher lay a patient with severe head injuries.

"Give him a dose of morphine!" he ordered.

A continuous stream of bomb victims arrived at the hospital, overwhelming the operating theatres.

"This man here must be operated on immediately or he won't survive." Francesca looked at Dr Bernardo questioningly.

"All the doctors have their hands full right now. Do what you can, Francesca!" He looked worn out. There were cavernous dark circles around his watery eyes. He had been on his feet for twenty-four hours, operating on the victims of the bomb attack.

Francesca spoke softly to the soldier. His intestines were hanging out of his stomach; he was screaming so loudly that it pierced her right to the marrow. As she was giving him an injection of morphine, she caught sight of Carina tending to a patient with a severe wound in his arm. When Carina looked up and saw the next wounded man being brought in, she doubled over under the nausea that overcame her. The stench of burnt flesh and blood was overwhelming. Francesca quickly rushed to her and embraced her.

"Come here, Carina!" She led Carina into a room where patients from the operating theatre were brought for observation and nursing. Francesca explained to the head nurse that Carina wouldn't be able to work with the emergency admissions.

"I understand," the head nurse replied.

The room was full to bursting. The nurses could only just squeeze in between the rows of beds. Carina felt better here. The injured patients wore bandages, so she could only guess what had happened to them. Someone was crying quietly, many lay motionless, some stared at the ceiling. The horror of the previous night was engraved on every face.

"Is there room for one more person here?" A voice snapped her out of her reverie. The doctor was looking at her questioningly.

"I'll wheel him into the back corner over there, but after that, this room is full." Carina pushed the sickbed down the narrow aisle. Then she leaned over the patient. "Luca, my God, Luca! Is that you? Yes, it's you! What happened, Luca? Help! Help! It's my husband!" she cried out. "Fetch Francesca, quickly!" she shouted to the nurse. "Luca, my darling! No, no! What have they done to you? Luca, can you hear me? Oh Luca, my love, I'm here. It's me, Carina. I'll nurse you back to health. My Luca! Everything will be okay." She looked at Luca's closed eyelids, tears streaming down her face. She kissed him, held his hand—but he remained motionless.

I waited impatiently in Roberto's study. Clerks, clergymen and guardsmen buzzed up and down the corridors like swarms of bees. I was told that Roberto had gone with the pope to the ruins of the Basilica di San Lorenzo to pray with the victims. But I still wanted to wait for him to return so I could ask him exactly what had happened.

The door flew open, and Roberto hurried into the study. "Enzo! I'm glad you survived the attack in one piece!"

Never had I seen him so agitated. He usually faced any troubles with a calm and prudent demeanour, but today he was falling apart.

"It's terrible, Enzo, what happened last night! The San Lorenzo neighbourhood is in ruins," he explained. "Now the pope will finally make sure the city of Rome is spared any future attacks."

The telephone rang. "Oh, hello, Francesca!" said Roberto, surprised. "Oh no, my God! Enzo and I will be there right away!" He hung up. The shocking sights he had seen in San Lorenzo were still etched over his face, but now he looked up at me with tears in his eyes. He howled in despair. "It's Luca. Let's go to the hospital immediately!"

The Funeral in Sicily

The long funeral procession made its way silently up the hill. The path leading through a wrought iron gate into the cemetery was lined with cypress trees.

At the heart of the graveyard was a mighty statue of an angel sitting on a throne. Behind the marble tombstones stood large family crypts, with elaborately carved stone figures in between. The marble slabs of the worn and weather-beaten sliding graves bore inscriptions in gold, with photographs of the deceased inlaid in the centre of the stone. The graves were adorned with brightly coloured flowers—some were entwined with hibiscus bushes, others with round shrubs. At the end of the path, fresh graves had just been dug on either side. The many small crosses told of just how many soldiers had fallen in recent months.

I still couldn't believe Luca had been killed in the bombing. When we got to the hospital, they told us he was already dead when he was brought in. Carina was beside herself, wracked with sobs that shook her whole body. Roberto took her back to the Vatican with him, where two nuns would look after her.

When I saw Luca lying so rigid and pale on the hospital bed, I felt an indescribable sadness rise up inside me. I felt numb, and I embraced him and cried for a long time. He had been like a brother to me. We had often met in Rome and had conversations that stretched into the small hours. I admired him more than anything; his cheerful, open manner, his friendly way with people, his passion for flying, and his fondness for Italian poetry, something that had surprised me about him. The first time he had recited a poem had been at his wedding, and it touched me a great deal. Later he told me that he sometimes wrote poems in his barracks in the evening. It helped him relax and drive the war from his mind.

"You know, as much as I love flying, it has also brought home the fact that we're at war, and the longer it goes on, the more it bothers me. If there were no war, Carina and I could live in a nice place in the city. She could start studying history, and we could have a nice life, going out, meeting up with friends. Sometimes I get so angry that I feel like packing it all in. I've been wondering if I would soon become depressed because of being billeted at the airfield. Carina has had to give up her studies, and now she works endless shifts at the hospital. We rent a hotel room whenever we want some time to ourselves, but we rarely get the chance. Writing calms me down; it helps me drift away into another world. Dreaming does me good."

I was completely blindsided. It surprised me to hear him confess that he was in a bad way, because he always seemed to be in such a good mood. And the anger he described, I felt it too. I was angry that Luise had to die and that I had to break off my studies. And having to obey my superiors in the military just went completely against the grain for me.

"I know exactly how you feel, Luca. We've had to give up so many things—the best years of our lives have been spoiled," I said sympathetically. "I think it's amazing that your writing helps you find peace. In Lampedusa, in my spare time, I sometimes just sat on a rock and looked out into the open sea to forget everything."

I remembered him taking me on a sightseeing trip in his plane. It wasn't allowed, of course, but Luca urged me to come along. The idea made me uncomfortable, but he managed to convince me with all his talk of flying being the best feeling in the world. He just wanted to take a quick flight over the city and the Apennines. Thinking about it now almost made me feel dizzy. Of course, Luca was best friends with everyone, including the air traffic controllers. He had them all wound round his little finger. He was simply a darling of fortune, having always succeeded in everything he turned his hand to. He had his dream job, his dream woman, and the respect of everyone wherever he went. Happiness seemed to fall right into his lap. Even that short sightseeing flight over the city could have got him in serious trouble, but he was always so confident, so satisfied with himself and the world, that he never shied away from anything. Oh, how I missed him!

I felt a hand on my arm. Francesca was looking at me with great compassion. She linked her arm through mine. I felt good when I was around her, as if she could rescue me from my darkest thoughts.

"Just think, Enzo, Luca's spirit lives on in us."

"It's tearing me apart just thinking about him, Francesca. For a moment, I was remembering all the good times we had together in Rome. We were so close."

Deep in thought, we walked along behind the other mourners.

"How is Carina?"

"The nuns at the Vatican have been taking care of her. She was in shock for a few days, but she's started to calm down now," Francesca told me as we approached the burial plot. Then she whispered softly in my ear. "She's expecting Luca's baby!"

I stopped abruptly. "Really?"

Francesca laughed quietly. "Yes, really, my dear Enzo. The doctor confirmed it!"

"Sorry for the stupid question, Francesca. I'm just so surprised." The news filled me with both joy and sadness. "How cruel that Luca won't be here to see it." My eyes filled with tears. Francesca hugged me sympathetically.

People gathered around the grave, which was decorated with sumptuous wreaths of flowers. My grandparents were sitting on folding chairs, and next to them were Carina, her mother and Aunt Maria with Uncle Toni. Vince and Pete were in the background, where a whole crowd of Regia Aeronautica pilots were standing in a row. Francesca stood beside Carina. Roberto devoutly opened his prayer book and made the sign of the cross.

Thinking about the child filled me with indescribable joy, and at that moment, I stood at the graveside and swore to Luca I would do everything in my power to make sure no harm came to Carina or the baby. I understood what Francesca meant when she said that Luca's spirit would live on in us.

I looked up. My eyes met Francesca's. For a moment, our gazes were locked together, and I felt as if she could read my thoughts.

The Walk Along the Apulian Aqueduct

Acqua di monte, aqua di fonte,
aqua que squilli, acqua que brilli,
acqua che canti e piangi, aqua che ridi
e muggi, tu sei la vita, e
sempre, sempre fuggi.

Water of the mountain, water of the spring,
water, you ring, water, you shine, water
you sing and cry, water, you laugh and low,
you are life, and on and on you flow.
Gabriele d'Annunzio

The Luftwaffe operations centre in Rome ordered me to return to Southern Italy, to the Italian fighter airbase in Matera. They were just trying to get rid of me, that much was clear. There was no place for me in Rome, I was told. It annoyed me that I'd come all the way up to Rome and was now being sent back. I felt like a marionette that had been left in a corner, still dangling from its strings but abandoned to gather dust. My one comfort was that I would be near my relatives again.

When I reported to the command office at Matera airfield, my superior seemed to be very busy. "What do you want?" he asked gruffly.

"The Ministry of Aviation in Rome has transferred me to your unit," I explained.

He looked up briefly, eyed me, then continued to rummage through his papers. After a while he asked, "Do you speak English?"

I told him I didn't.

"Then there's nothing for you to do here. We're all just hanging around waiting for the Brits. Those idiots in Rome have no idea what's going on down here in the South. Yesterday, the armistice was declared, and the Allies landed in Salerno and Taranto. Take my advice: go back home!"

I saluted and departed from my irritable superior. I was thoroughly fed up too. Time to go home, back to Switzerland! Outside, I went and got changed in the toilets—luckily, I had civilian clothes with me. I stowed the uniform in my suitcase and hurried out of the airport building.

I could go to Bari and take the train north from there, I thought. I weighed up the options, and this seemed like the best solution.

A short while later, I found myself in the centre of Matera. The last rays of the setting sun fell across the countless cave dwellings carved into the rock. There were no more trains at this time of day, so I inquired about the bus station and tried my luck there. It really felt as though fortune were smiling on me that day, because a long-distance bus to Bari was just about to depart. I managed to find a free spot, and I sat down with relief next to a young woman holding a toddler in her arms. A few youths got on and took seats behind us.

"Guys, it's going to be a blast! I'm going to a baseball game at the Bambino Stadium!"

"Do you even know the rules of baseball, Gino?"

"Nope, not a clue, Nino. We'll find out. It'll be a surprise!"

Their enthusiasm was contagious and quickly spread to the other passengers on the bus. The news about the Italian armistice and the Allied invasion had spread like wildfire.

"If those boys only knew why Mussolini had the biggest football stadium in Italy built in Bari," my neighbour giggled. I must have looked confused, so she explained further. "Statistically, the women of Bari have given birth to more boys than any other Italian city. Mussolini had the stadium built in honour of that. Ha, if it weren't for us women!" She chucked her little boy under the chin.

Then the girls piped up. "We're going to Porto-Vecchio!"

"You lot are probably planning on making friends with some GIs, eh?" one of the boys teased.

"Maybe, why not? But first we're going to see a film," they retorted cockily.

The woman next to me swivelled round. "A film?"

"Yes! *Sergeant York* is being shown in the piazza. It's got Gary Cooper in it!" The girls squealed with excitement.

The woman turned to me. "I don't speak English, but I'm going to go and see the film anyway. There are going to be some great festivities in Bari!"

I wasn't the slightest bit interested in their conversation. But I gathered that the Allies had advanced as far as the city of Bari, and the Italians were celebrating being liberated. Fortunately, the woman next to me was busy with her toddler, and it didn't occur to her to ask questions.

The bus crawled at a snail's pace through the crowds of people that had gathered on the streets of Bari to celebrate the Allies' arrival. People were handing out flowers to the GIs, speeches rang out through megaphones, and I could hear music blaring. Women crowded into shops selling silk stockings and Palmolive soap, old women dressed in black laid out fresh pasta on tables, officers sat on benches sipping their gin while an Italian singer warbled arias in the background. I pushed my way through the throng at the harbourside. The boisterous atmosphere felt good, and the light breeze refreshed me. It was already dark when I approached the harbour pier. The dazzling floodlights swept over the harbour and circled in wide arcs over the bay in the dark evening sky. An impressive number of ships lay at anchor; I had never seen an armada on this scale before. Further away in the distance, I could just make out an aircraft carrier. I picked up snatches of conversation from the crowd.

"The Eighth Army's main line of supply is going to run via our port. Apparently, the Allied air forces are planning to build four dozen landing fields for the fighter bombers in Foggia."

"Ah, so that's what all that steel is for. Look at that— they're loading up tonnes and tonnes of steel plates!"

I strolled back to the main street, where I stopped at a stall and bought a bread roll filled with grilled sardines. It tasted delicious! Relishing in my little luxury, I continued to make my way through the euphoric crowd. All around me people were laughing, drinking and celebrating, and distant shouts and hoots could be heard coming from Bambino Stadium. The baseball game seemed to be in full swing. But I didn't want to linger here long—I was keen to catch the next train north as quickly as I could.

At the main station, they informed me that trains were only running from Macchie station at the moment. That station was outside the city, so I started to head there on foot.

Crowds of people were still strolling about the streets. All of a sudden, I heard a woman cry out. She was standing on the roof terrace of her house. "Help! They're coming!" She pointed at the sky and hustled her children inside. The muffled thrumming I could hear was all too familiar. An American peered up through his binoculars. "Move it, folks! Hurry! They're German Ju 88 bombers!" The news tore through the crowd, and people started running as fast as they could to their homes and shelters. The aircraft flew briefly over the city, then disappeared again.

"Mummy, look! It's snowing!" I heard a child say through a window. It was pointing in the direction of the harbour. Thousands of tiny foil strips flashed in the spotlights. We all watched the harbour, spellbound, the children shrieking ecstatically. And then, out of the blue, the roar of the bombers sounded again, but much louder this time. Barely fifty metres above our heads, around twenty planes were flying towards the harbour. I hid in a doorway. A second later, the ground shook from the first detonation, then another and another. I peered round the corner of the house. The harbour was burning—ships' hulls were torn open, and sailors were leaping overboard amid the flames that licked above the water. A bomber started to approach the aircraft carrier. I felt my throat constrict. Fire swept across the deck, dragging everything in its wake as planes exploded, and burning steel plates were thrown into the air, only to crash into the ships docked nearby, which flared up in seconds as more flames engulfed them. Screams and cries for help mingled with more explosions. A wave of fire tore along the harbour quay at lightning speed.

"That's probably a crude oil pipe," I heard someone shout in horror. I ran behind the house. An old man was hitching a donkey to his cart.

"Where are you headed?" I asked on a whim.

"Back to my farm. Away from this chaos! This morning I was selling my vegetables at the market. Who would have thought those damned Germans would be back!" He swung himself up onto his perch.

"Please can you take me as far as the railway station?"

"Have a seat!" He urged the donkey onwards, and I was glad to be making my way out of the city. Down by the harbour, pillars of smoke the size of skyscrapers billowed up as sirens wailed incessantly amid the blasts from more explosions.

"The station will have been shut down by now, lad. Where are you going?" The old man seemed friendly, so I told him that I wanted to get as far north as possible.

"Does your family live there?"

"Yes, I want to get to Como. I have relatives there, an aunt and cousins."

He tutted. "*Dio mio!*" he exclaimed. "That's going to be quite a feat, my dear. There won't be any more trains, believe you me. At least not from here. Maybe they're still running further up."

After an hour, we reached a small farm. It was already late in the evening, so he invited me to stay the night. His kind wife served up a simple meal of beans and potatoes, then they showed me to the barn where I could spend the night. The next morning, we discussed how I would be able to get to the North.

"You'll be lost without a map or compass. But I've got an idea, lad. Once you get further up, you'll find the Acquedotto Pugliese. It's a Roman water conduit that supplies drinking water to a lot of Apulia and smaller areas of Campania. It leads into Abruzzo and ends in Molise near Campobasso."

He drove me there in his cart. I was so grateful for his hospitality and his help with my onward journey—his natural inclination to help a stranger was very moving.

The aqueduct was an impressive structure. I imagined the Romans of the past dragging vast quantities of stone into this impassable area, then building the structure piece by piece. Lucky I would have it there to guide me, I thought.

The curved arches of the wall were surrounded by tall grass. To the sides, casting shady patches beneath them, stood an array of wild fruit trees. I trudged through the bushes. As long as I stayed out of sight of the road, there was little chance of me meeting anyone. Even so, I soon started searching for a well-hidden place to sleep, as I deemed it too risky to walk during the day. I decided I would move on once it got dark, then I crawled through the dense undergrowth under one of the arches and leant against the cool wall. The sun was already high above the horizon. *It's lunchtime*, I thought, and soon dozed off.

The monotonous humming of mosquitos roused me from my slumber, and I shooed them away from my face. Dusk was closing in. I stretched my limbs and listened intently. I couldn't hear a sound, so I set off again. A while later, I stopped for a break and ate a piece of bread and cheese that the farmer's wife had packed for me. I wanted to walk as far as possible, because I would need to stop at a farmhouse at some point to replenish my provisions. I avoided exposed tracks and instead followed the path of the aqueduct closely. The evening sky was clear, and the bright moonlight made it easy to see where I was going.

I spent two more days sleeping in the shelter of the walls, and when darkness fell, I would walk until dawn, always remaining close to the water conduit. I was exhausted, as I had managed to make the portion of bread and cheese last for three days. Luckily, there was enough water in the wells that tapped directly into the water supply. The landscape had started to open up, and the path led over a field that was cleaved in half by a dried-out riverbed. On the other side of the furrow, I spotted a cluster of tents. I crouched behind a bush to try and figure out who was staying there. All was dark and still. There was no movement from the tents.

Strange, I thought. Suddenly, I heard footsteps. A farmer was trotting across the field on his donkey. He was shouting in Italian to drive the lazy animal onwards. I plucked up my courage, left my hiding place and went out into the field.

"*Porca miseria!*" the man started in dismay. "You gave me a fright! What do you want?"

"Sorry. I just wanted to ask who is staying in those tents on the other side of the river."

The man laughed. "I've just come from there. The Germans all left yesterday before nightfall, as if they'd been stung by bees. No idea why. Word travelled fast in the village. I managed to get hold of some of the things they left behind in their haste. I'd get a move on if I were you, if you want to find anything useful." He stomped past me, dragging the frail donkey along behind him by the halter. I crept quietly along the riverbed, constantly ducking down behind the boulders that lay scattered among the gravel. I wondered why the villagers hadn't taken down the tents yet. Maybe the locals were more interested in food and clothes. Many of the tents hadn't been completely emptied yet. I spotted boxes, blankets and cooking utensils beside paraffin lamps, aluminium plates and empty cans. I quickly searched through them in the darkness. When I stepped into the third tent, I discovered an open box of woollen blankets and tarpaulins in one corner. *Maybe I'll find a map or a compass—those would help me the most*, I thought. I rummaged in the box and lifted out the woollen blankets. Just then something hard fell into my hand. Oh! A hunting rifle—not bad! I found some ammunition rolled up in a woollen blanket, which I immediately stowed in my pocket. There were no maps to be found, but the rifle was a stroke of luck. Then I slipped away as quickly as I had come.

In an olive grove, I caught sight of a small tumbledown stone house. Hens were pecking between the wheels of a ramshackle cart, and a cock crowed hoarsely from a shed nearby. The first rays of sunlight were streaming down into the valley. I knocked at the door.

"*Signori*, I'm an Italian soldier on the run. Could I trouble you for something to eat?"

They were probably starving themselves. The wooden gate in front of the shed groaned softly in the wind. No answer. I knocked again and was about to repeat my little speech when the door opened a tiny crack. An old man peered back at me with wide, fearful eyes. I repeated my question. A calloused hand opened the door a little further to reveal a face marked by toil.

"*Vieni!*" he said softly with his toothless mouth. The interior of the stone house was a sorry sight. Two broken chairs stood around a crooked wooden table. In the corner, a small flame blazed in the open cooker. It smelled of rancid oil and stale air.

"My wife is ill in bed." He pointed towards the adjoining room, where I could just make out a head poking out from a mound of blankets on a cot.

"What's wrong with her?" I asked.

"Fever." He offered me a seat, then fetched a small pan from the fire. "Bean soup—that's all I've got. I can boil you a couple of eggs for the road," he offered kindly.

"That would be wonderful. Thank you!" I replied.

The cot in the next room gave a squeak, and I heard a low cough. I could just make out the old woman's red, wrinkled face. Her eyes were closed, and her gnarled hands clung to the blankets.

The bean soup tasted better than I'd expected.

"I have some tablets I can give your wife. They might help. They're for malaria, but in the army we used them for all sorts of things." I took the small box out of my pack and laid it on the table.

The old man looked at me gratefully. Then he stood up laboriously and fetched two wine glasses with a grin. "My own wine, from the vineyards up on the hill."

The wine had a sour taste, but I enjoyed the warm feeling that spread through my body, nonetheless. After dinner, the old man boiled the eggs and wrapped them up in an old newspaper, along with a piece of bread, two tomatoes and a handful of grapes. I asked him how far it was to Rimini. He looked at me in disbelief and said it would take at least seven or eight days to walk there.

"Here," I said, and handed him the hunting rifle I had found in the abandoned German tents. "Take this as a thank you."

His watery eyes lit up as he laughed with joy. "It's like Christmas, lad! And you're sure you won't be needing the rifle yourself? Your journey might be dangerous—there's all sorts of riffraff roaming about the country right now, and if you get caught by a German, you could end up in prison." He shook his head, worried.

"Don't worry. I have my revolver with me."

"*Bravo, ragazzo. Buona fortuna!*" He embraced me warmly, hobbled out with me to the front of the hut and waved me on my way. "And thank you for the medicine, too!"

As I reached the Abruzzo hills the following night, I considered how I would continue my journey once I reached the end of the aqueduct. Walking at night was exhausting. I set off after sunset and walked until dawn. The path led me into the Apennine mountains, and the aqueduct ended near Molise. As I walked along a dusty country road, I came across several Italian soldiers. They were on their way to Calabria, Puglia and Sicily. They told me that the train connections to the South had been stopped, but that they were still running northbound from Rimini. After about an hour, I saw a small delivery truck turning into the road from a side path. I flagged it down. The driver opened the window.

"Where do you want to go?"

"To Rimini, to the station!"

As luck would have it, he was also driving in the direction of Rimini. On the way, he told me about the many people from Southern Italy that had been stationed up north and were now fleeing south to make their way home.

"The armistice has caused mass migration—it's total chaos. I don't trust all this euphoria. Everyone's talking about the Germans surrendering. But I'd advise you to be careful," he warned.

"I completely agree. They bombed the harbour in Bari. Luckily, I was on the outskirts of the city. It was awful!"

We arrived in Rimini that evening. I managed to catch the last train to Como. I was sitting in a compartment with an elderly couple, their grandson and a businessman. I flopped down into the seat and immediately fell asleep. As we were approaching Milan, the compartment door was flung open with a jerk. A German security official filled the doorframe. "Tickets and ID cards!" He took the businessman to task first and examined his luggage, which consisted of a box and a briefcase.

"What's in the box?" he asked sharply.

"Cigars. I'm delivering them to a business in Milan."

"Oh, cigars!" The official smiled, suddenly relaxed. A cold shiver ran down my spine. I secretly prayed that my suitcase wouldn't be searched. I held out my ticket and identity card, which had been issued in Palermo. He pored over the identity card for what seemed like an eternity. He only gave my suitcase a cursory glance, then turned to the couple. Before he left, he asked the businessman, "I'm sure you can spare a couple of cigars. My colleagues would be delighted." The man opened the box and handed him a carton. *What an arsehole*, I thought angrily. The poor man would probably have to pay for the cigars himself.

I couldn't sleep for the rest of the journey. I pretended to so I wouldn't have to talk to my fellow passengers, but I was listening on tenterhooks the entire time. I felt a gnawing fear deep in my bones, but luckily the officials didn't return.

I had to change in Milan. At the station exit, I found a phone box. I squeezed into the booth and dialled the number of my aunt Chiara, whom I hardly knew. Nonna had scribbled her address on a piece of paper for me at the last minute before I returned to Rome.

"Unfortunately, Nonno never forgave his daughter for having a child out of wedlock. That was probably the reason she ran away. But I always stayed in contact with her via letters. I have photographs of her children Bianca and Alfredo that I kept in secret. Here, take this photograph! She sent it to me just recently. Who knows, maybe it'll be useful to know what they look like and where they live." Then she gave me an envelope and whispered, "I'm sure you could do with some money too. Keep it safe. There are thieves lurking round every corner! Oh yes, I almost forgot. Watch out for Alfredo. He's only eighteen, but he's already involved in politics."

I took a closer look at the photograph. My aunt had delicate features, and she was the spitting image of my nonna. She had little dimples either side of her mouth. In the picture, she was hugging her two adolescent children. Alfredo wore a moustache, like me. His hair, which grew in short, unruly waves, was combed back severely with pomade. His narrow eyes and angular features gave him a stern impression, despite his youthful age. His sister wore a dark skirt and a checked blouse, her long curls tied back in a ponytail. Alfredo had a very suspicious look about him, and if anyone discovered the photo, I would certainly have been considered suspicious too. I remembered that my mother used to talk to Aunt Chiara on the phone at Christmas. We visited her once in Como when I was very little. That had been my first time riding a train.

"*Pronto!*" I heard a woman's voice say through the receiver.

"*Ciao, zia!*" I said excitedly. "Is that you, Chiara?"

There was a moment's silence. Had we been cut off?

"Who is this?" asked the voice.

"It's Enzo Dorigo," I replied quietly, almost whispering. I suddenly wondered if it had been a mistake to call her. Someone might be listening in. My hand holding the receiver was drenched in sweat.

"You have our address, Enzo?" asked the woman's voice.

"Yes. I'm in Milan, and it'll take me an hour to get to Como by train."

"There's a road map on the wall in the waiting room at Como station. I'll wait for you at home."

The line crackled. She had hung up. Deep in thought, I stowed the photograph with the address in my jacket pocket. I bought myself a copy of *Corriere della Sera* at the newsstand and sat down on a bench. On the front page, there was a picture of the burning harbour in Bari, and below were the words:

Last Friday, there was a bomb attack at the port of Bari. Seventeen ships were sunk, and eight more ships were severely damaged. The oil pipeline along the harbourside exploded, meaning the fire spread quickly along the quay. About a thousand soldiers and as many civilians were killed. They were not just victims of the fire. Many civilians developed huge, pus-filled blisters all over their bodies fifteen hours after the attack took place. It was not possible to treat them, and the doctors could not make any clear diagnosis.

I stared at the newspaper. The man next to me pointed to the article. "It's obvious that the press is keeping something from us. I'm sure there was gas involved," he insisted. I looked at him in surprise. It only just hit me what a narrow escape I'd had. The thought of it made my blood run cold. Thousands of people had been killed and, as luck would have it, I was far enough away from the site of the attack not to be injured or killed as well. Word had spread among the soldiers that Hitler had threatened to use gas, but where had the gas come from? The bombs they dropped didn't look like gas bombs. In my mind's eye, I pictured the happy young people enjoying themselves and celebrating their liberation, full of hope for a new life. And these were the people who had suffered an agonising death.

"All aboard, the train to Como leaves in two minutes! All aboard!"

The announcement startled me. Hurriedly, I snatched up my suitcase and jumped into the carriage.

Partisans

The repetitive motion of the train's wheels felt like the ticking of a time bomb. Every turn of the wheels brought me a little closer to the border, yet time seemed to be moving unbearably slowly, as if I would never reach my destination. I had already come so far; I was so close. Why did it feel so impossibly far away? Impatience gnawed away at me. My nerves were frayed to breaking point. I felt as if I were trapped in a bad dream.

The sight of the autumn landscape surprised me. Had it really been that long since I'd left on the last boat out of Lampedusa? It must have been—it was now autumn. In the warm sunlight, the leaves of the chestnut trees glowed in a palette of golden yellow hues. They reminded me of the earthy scent of roasted chestnuts as my aunt prepared them over the fire. Small fields were laid out in a step formation on the barren hills, with a few vineyards in between like splashes of colour.

The train drew slowly into Como station. "Last stop, Como. All change!" shouted the ticket inspector. With a jolt, the train came to a complete stop.

The station was situated slightly above the town. A quick glance at the map in the waiting room was enough for me to figure out how to get to my aunt's house. I strolled along the street that led down to the town centre. The cool air did me good and invigorated my senses. In the distance, I could see rugged mountain peaks dusted with snow.

I needed to get hold of a map so I could find my way around. Perhaps my aunt or my cousin would be able to help me. The thought shot through me like a lightning bolt. Tension gripped me again and wouldn't let go, digging its claws into my body. I sat down on the edge of a well to regain my composure. Then I washed my face and let the ice-cold water flow over my neck. I had a long drink, then felt revived enough to walk the rest of the way.

A German jeep with two armed soldiers was parked in the corner of the piazza. I immediately turned into a side street, then down an alleyway. I felt safer there, as the alley was too narrow for a car to drive down. At the other end, I came to another busy street, which I had to cross before turning into Via di Foscolo. As soon as I was in front of my aunt's house, I suddenly recognised the front door and the palm trees in the front garden. They had probably seemed very impressive to me as a young boy. It had been so many years since I'd last visited. This brief moment of recollection filled me with a sense of happiness and home—I would have a safe place to spend the night and plan my onward journey. I knocked at the door in joyful anticipation. Nothing stirred. I glanced around me. The residential street seemed to be taking a siesta. Just as I was about to knock again, the door opened a crack.

Recognising me, my aunt Chiara hastily exclaimed, "Come in quickly, Enzo!" I squeezed through the small gap into the entrance hall. Only once the door had been closed and locked again did the expression on her face relax. She hugged me warmly, kissed me and whispered, "Enzo, I'm so glad you're here! Be careful, you're taking a bit of a risk by staying with us. I'll explain everything, but first I'll run you a warm bath and show you where you'll sleep. I'll give your clothes a thorough wash right away. You can wear something of Alfredo's in the meantime." She led me upstairs to the bathroom.

It was only as I took off my filthy clothes that I realised I had been wearing them day and night for weeks on end. What a luxury it was to sink into a warm bath! The thought of a clean shirt, a fresh shave and a soft feather bed filled me with delight, and I relished in the indescribable feeling of immersing myself in the warm water.

Afterwards, I felt like a new man. In the kitchen, I sat down by the blazing hearth. My aunt was busying herself with kitchen utensils, and the smell of polenta spread through the cosy living room.

"Take a piece of cheese, Enzo!" she passed me a plate with a thick chunk of Taleggio. "You must be hungry after your long journey," she said thoughtfully.

"It wasn't so bad. I met so many friendly people who welcomed me, mostly poor farmers who were hungry themselves, but they shared what little food they had with me, gave me places to sleep, and were often kind enough to spare a little something for the road."

My aunt looked at me in wonder.

"I'm so proud of you, Enzo, and so happy that you made it here in one piece. You're not out of the woods yet. Here in the North, we have enough to eat, but the political situation is growing increasingly tense. More and more Germans are streaming over the Brenner Pass and heading south. The borders are being strictly guarded. You can stay here for the time being, but I'll take you to my sister-in-law the day after tomorrow. It's too dangerous here."

"Has Alfredo been drafted too?"

She gave a deep sigh. "No, fortunately. Our family doctor classed him as unfit because of his lung disease. But he had to work at the steel mill in Dongo where he had an accident two months ago, and now he's on sick leave. He's still limping, and we don't know if his leg will ever fully recover. Your uncle Mauro was a staunch anti-Fascist and was politically active in the *resistenza*." Her sad eyes filled with tears.

"He was the leader of a brigade of the Republic of Ossola. They were mainly doing reconnaissance work. He was being investigated, and one night, when he was on his way into the hills, he was ambushed by a troop of German border guards who took him prisoner. They wanted him to give names of partisans and tell them where the weapons were hidden. But Mauro refused. I was so worried about him. It was awful. Three weeks later, we received the news that he had died in prison."

She bowed her head.

"Oh my God, Chiara! What did he die of?"

"They didn't say. Alfredo was beside himself, and his anger spurred him on to follow in his father's footsteps. He believes his father was hanged. Mauro's body was wrapped in a shroud, and when we opened it, we could see what they had done to him. I can still picture it now. His face was completely disfigured, and his body covered with bruises and festering wounds." She paused. "There's more reason to fear even now, Enzo. Alfredo and Bianca have become active partisans too. They're playing with fire and fighting for freedom. Be careful nothing happens to you, Enzo."

She lowered her voice to a whisper. "Al has come up with a plan for you. He knows some people who can take you across the lake and then over the unfenced section of the border."

She kissed me on the forehead and then started ladling polenta onto a large plate.

The noise sounded familiar. Where had I heard it before? I listened. Gradually, it grew louder, as if there were balls rolling through the sky. I looked up. The skies were strewn with bombers, swarming through the air like birds in the autumn breeze. They crisscrossed over each other, emitting a great buzzing sound. I tried to follow one of the planes with my eyes, but it twisted and turned at breakneck speed in all directions, so fast that I couldn't keep up. I felt dizzy. I closed my eyes. Everything was spinning around me, faster and faster, like a merry-go-round.

Where was I? When I opened my eyes again, I noticed tiny dots slowly floating down from the planes. The aircraft were still veering this way and that, up and down in a wild rollercoaster ride—but now they were heading my way. I could make out the dots more clearly now.

"Oh no!" I held my breath and took off at a run. A second later, I heard the impact, then another in quick succession—one after another, the bombs crashed into the asphalt, tearing apart roads and blocks of houses, like deadly blades. I could feel the heat. The fire from the explosions spread at lightning speed. On and on I ran. Suddenly, I felt a cold hand on my shoulder. It pulled me backwards with a jerk.

"Stop! You can't go any further!" The soldier's distorted face screamed in pain, and he lunged towards me and pulled me down with him. The echoes of rifle shots rang in my ears, over and over, until it became so loud that I was deafened. Had I lost my hearing? The sounds were muffled and distant. Suddenly, there was water all around me. Oh, so that's why everything sounded so muffled. I flailed my arms around me wildly. There! I saw rays of sunlight dancing on the surface of the water to the rhythm of the waves. That's where I needed to go! I swam towards the light with all the strength I had left. I came so close to the surface that I instinctively knew that one more stroke would do it. But no, I was still too far away. As if from nowhere, something silver sped past me. And again. More and more of them—they were getting bigger and bigger. Tuna. They were swimming in circles around me.

Slowly, they drew nearer. A huge fish swam straight towards me. At the last moment, it veered away. I felt as though some of its fighting spirit swept over me. It swam in a wide arc, then turned back, zooming towards me even faster. I tried to dodge, but it slammed into my side. I looked on in horror as blood slowly leaked into the water. Loud shouts rang out as the tuna raced wildly around me in panic. I felt another slam into me, this time into my back. I could hear the shouts clearly now. I could make out dark, rectangular shadows on the surface above me. More and more blood was pouring into the water.

"My God, I'm bleeding to death!" Only then did I notice the gaffs hacking through the bloody water, fish carcasses writhing beneath their blows as they rammed into the flesh of the tuna in rhythm with the shouts. I froze in shock as a gaff fell on my head like a guillotine.

"Enzo! Enzo!" a voice called out.

I looked up. Luca was looking at me with an expression distorted by pain. His face was streaked with wounds that had been torn open.

"Oh my God, Luca!" I screamed, hysterical.

I fell into his arms, wracked with sobs. Then darkness closed in around me.

My eyes were blinded by a pale beam of light. I slowly opened them. I shivered, even though I was bundled up in two thick woollen blankets. "Where am I?" My damp head ached. I felt so weak that I couldn't sit up. Then the door opened, and I caught sight of Susanna, my aunt's sister-in-law.

"Enzo, *amore*! You're sweating again. Come on, I'll help you out of bed. After you've had a wash, I'll change the bedclothes. *Dio mio!* That fever's got you bad!"

When I reached the bathroom, the first thing I did was throw up.

Since the fever still hadn't improved after two days, Aunt Chiara called a doctor. He diagnosed a stomach flu and prescribed bed rest and a light diet.

I was so glad the fever didn't take me while I was still on my journey. Here, I would be able to lie in a comfortable bed while I recovered, with Aunt Susanna bringing me food and Alfredo and Bianca visiting me every day. They told me about their work in the partisan movement. During the daytime, Alfredo worked on forged documents and propaganda materials down in the cellar.

"That's why my mother didn't want you to stay with us. She's afraid our house will be searched and that something could happen to you."

"What we're doing is dangerous," Bianca said, "but our fighting spirit is so strong we carry on regardless. We're fighting for freedom, for justice." She explained how she and other women sewed clothes for deserters and refugees. "The soldiers from Southern Italy can't go home now. They would be taken prisoner immediately. The Germans send them to the labour camps in Germany. Every Italian soldier we save counts. We give them weapons and provide them with hiding places and shelters. Many of them join the *resistenza*."

"Your bravery is amazing! And I can sense the strength and resilience inside you both," I assured them.

"I'm so proud of you, *cugino*, that you walked all the way up here from Southern Italy," Alfredo gushed.

"And you escaped so many bomb attacks unscathed!" Bianca agreed with him. "We're lucky too that we're not in Milan," she went on. "The city has been bombed several times. The Allies targeted the Savoia-Marchetti factories, but often they just ended up hitting regular civilians."

Alfredo had come up with an escape plan for me.

"I have connections with various people who'll be able to help us. Even up in the mountains, the border is heavily guarded. But our groups know every path, and they've set up bunkers in the mountains. You can take a passenger ship to Dervio, where my uncle Giulio will be waiting for you."

"I see what you're planning, Al!" cried Bianca, delighted. "You want Enzo to take a fishing boat over to Dongo?" she grinned.

"Exactly, dear sister, you've rumbled me! As Bianca just said, you'll cross from Dervio to Dongo with Giulio in a fishing boat. My uncle Giulio runs a motorcycle shop, and he also trades in smuggled goods on the side. One of his smugglers will take you to Switzerland via the San Jorio Pass."

"How long will it take to walk?" Just the thought of dragging myself up a mountain made me feel numb. I was still so weak. My limbs ached, and I could hardly sit up in bed. I was afraid of being caught off guard by another bout of fever. Bianca seemed to read my thoughts and turned to Alfredo.

"Enzo needs to get completely back on his feet first. What did the doctor say?" she asked.

"He thinks the fever will break within the next couple of days. He says it's probably stomach flu, which might last up to 48 hours."

Bianca lay a wet cloth on my brow.

"I've just thought of something, Enzo. Your fever might be malaria," said Alfredo.

"Malaria?" I asked in disbelief. "One of my German comrades gave me a bottle of Atabrine tablets as a preventive measure, but I gave them to a poor farmer. His wife also had a fever, and I explained to him that the tablets might not be of any use because they were for prophylaxis."

"We'll nurse you back to health, Enzo, don't worry," Bianca assured me. Turning to Alfredo, she remarked, "They'll have to stop along the way. What do you think, Al, maybe in our bunker up by the forest? The hike up to Roveredo in Switzerland takes seven hours."

Alfredo weighed up Bianca's suggestion. "The bunker isn't really suitable. I think it would be better for them to have their rest in the alpine hut at the top of the pass."

After two days, I did start to feel much better. Aunt Chiara had looked after me very lovingly. Although food was being rationed here in the North too, there seemed to be no shortage of meat, eggs, butter, sugar or flour in the house. She even served me real coffee for breakfast. "We have our connections, you know, Enzo," she said, laughing.

"Uncle Giulio?" I inquired with interest.

"He's one of them. He recently got me some nylon stockings. What a luxury!" She showed me her legs proudly. Like all widows, she was dressed in black.

"Black stockings are particularly hard to find. I'll give the others to the girls."

"What does he exchange them for?"

"Anything and everything—mainly luxury items, but also weapons. Money is practically worthless now, so his wages are partially paid in food. The weapons are the only things that make me suspicious—or, shall we say, uncomfortable. Alfredo is mixed up in it too. The partisans up in the mountains have whole stores of weapons in their bunkers. They recently found a parachute up on a hill."

"A parachute?" No sooner had I asked the question than I had an inkling of the answer. "Of course, the British!"

"You said it! The British are supporting the partisans by providing weapons," Chiara explained. "Only, they will soon be in an even more vulnerable position, as more and more Germans will be coming across the border. They're heading south, so you can imagine what that means for our resistance fighters." She sighed. "Let's hope it ends soon." She stood up and ladled a second helping of risotto onto my plate. "Eat up! It'll give you the strength to face the final hurdle!"

Lake Como

It was six o'clock in the morning. Although I had recovered by now, I still felt exhausted. The past two weeks had been a dreadful ordeal for me. I told myself again and again to just relax, that everything would be okay. But lying in bed wasn't relaxing for me at all. The fever was nothing compared to the constant swirling thoughts that consumed my mind. I couldn't switch them off. They just spun faster and faster, and I fell more and more under their spell with each passing day. It was as if the memories of the last few months were rising up within me, hammering holes into my skull, which spread like a cancer through my body. The nights were the worst. I tossed and turned in my sodden sheets for hours on end, images flashing before my eyes and paralysing me with fear. I thrashed my aching limbs until the early hours of the morning, when I finally fell asleep. I sat on the bed, lost in thought.

I pulled myself together and set about packing my suitcase. Aunt Chiara had stuffed coffee, rice and polenta between my clothes. I opened a small box. Underneath my certificate of citizenship was a 20-franc note. Oh yeah, I'd almost forgotten about that! Mother had given it to me in case of emergency. It felt good to hold the note in my hands. A piece of home, of

Switzerland! It was so close I could almost touch it. I rejoiced that I would be able to put the money to good use and buy a train ticket with it.

There were envelopes under the note, and I pulled one of them out. Gently, I ran my fingers over the curved writing. Luise. I was overcome by sadness and anger at her death. My thoughts moved on to Wolfgang and his family. How everything had changed. Where were they now? How were they doing? I resolved to contact Wolfgang as soon as I got home.

I was roused from my thoughts by a knock at the door.

"Are you ready, Enzo?"

Alfredo was standing expectantly at the door.

He strapped my suitcase onto the back of the motorbike.

"*Vai!*" he called out to me. We drove across Piazza Vittoria, past the monument to Giuseppe Garibaldi and into the centre of Como. Various army vehicles sped by. I felt comfortable and safe wearing my new trousers, a clean shirt and Alfredo's jacket. A weekly market was set up in the Piazza del Duomo. Farmers from nearby farms were hawking their wares, and the smell of roasting chestnuts filled the air. Long queues of people lined the colourful stalls. The deep chimes of the cathedral rang out—seven o'clock. I glanced at the impressive façade.

"God protect me!" I whispered. "Hopefully, in two days' time, I'll be safe on the other side of the mountains." I took a deep breath. "And I'll probably make it too."

We were now driving along the promenade by the lake. He parked the motorbike behind a bar.

"Come on! Let's go in."

"Hey, Alfredo!" the waiter called out, coming over to us. "Masetto is already waiting for you." He pointed towards the back.

In the semi-darkness sat a young man at a small table. He stood up, clapped Alfredo on the back and held out his hand to me. "Ciao!"

"*Mio cugino Enzo!*" Alfredo introduced me.

Masetto gave me a friendly look.

The waiter brought us some lemonade. "The coffee ran out yesterday. Hopefully we'll get another delivery soon."

"How long does it take to get to Dervio?" I asked.

"Almost two hours. You can sit with me in the captain's cabin—it's warm and has the best view," he said enthusiastically. Then he lowered his voice to a whisper. "And no one will ask awkward questions. You can count on me. Alfredo and I have discussed everything in great detail."

Alfredo had told me about Masetto the night before. He was probably a member of the partisan group too.

As a captain, he had the opportunity to smuggle goods across the lake. It seemed to me that they were all involved in the resistenza in some way.

"My uncle Giulio will be waiting for you on the jetty in Dervio. He knows the lake like the back of his hand, so you can rely on him. Masetto will show you where he's waiting," Alfredo said quietly. Then he pushed a banknote across the table, which Masetto immediately put into his pocket.

"Thanks, Al," I whispered.

"Of course, *cugino*! Come and see us again soon!"

We hugged.

"I'll be in touch," I said.

My heart was pounding. We were off!

The waiter gave me a bag. "Bread and cheese for the journey."

I thanked him. Masetto picked up my suitcase.

"Ciao, and take care of yourself, and of Bianca!" I called to Alfredo.

I followed Masetto to where the boat was moored. We were greeted by his two assistant captains. No one seemed to notice that he was walking boldly up the stairs to the captain's cabin with a suitcase in his hand and me in tow.

"Make yourself comfortable in the seat by the window!"

Masetto slid the suitcase under the wooden bench and placed a blanket over it. Then he started the engine and checked the dials. He pointed up at the blue sky.

"Perfect weather," he winked at me.

The boat filled up with passengers. I had a great vantage point from my spot in the window and could see everything without anyone being able to identify me. The crew hauled up the ropes and Masetto manoeuvred the boat out of the harbour. My gaze fell on a large paddle steamer anchored at the far end of the docks. It was obviously a luxury ship.

"That paddle steamer there wasn't designed for foot soldiers!" Masetto laughed. "She's a great ship, isn't she? I love her—her name's the *Plinio*! She's been in service for almost twenty years and is the fastest ship on the Lario. In May 1927, she even carried King Vittorio Emanuele along with the 28 Ottobre militia division. I was still a small child back then, but I remember very well how my whole family stood on the quay watching and waving to the fleet. I had a little flag," he reminisced. "The king was going for a cruise on the *Savoia*. It was quite a sensation!"

"Have you ever had the honour of setting foot on the luxury liner?"

"No, sadly not. But a friend of mine works as a waiter on board. They have a top-notch restaurant, and there's even a ballroom."

I looked back at the city. The magnificent façade of the Palazzo Lago di Como was eye-catching, and the curved, pointed windows were reminiscent of Venetian stately homes. Next to it, the cathedral rose up proudly, its pastel green dome enthroned above it like a great jewel. In the bright sunlight, the silhouette of the promenade was reflected in the surface of the water. It was a lovely sight.

"Get under the bench while we're in the port!"

I started out of my reverie. I was so busy marvelling at the lake's beautiful landscape that I'd completely forgotten I was on a mission. Quick as a flash, I crawled into the narrow opening, pushed the suitcase up above my head and covered myself with the blanket.

Masetto steered towards the port of Cernobbio. I heard shouts from the deck, then there was a sudden jolt, and I heard the rattle of the passenger bridge being lowered.

"Masetto, ciao! *Come va?*"

I listened tensely.

"*Ben, ben!*" said Masetto.

Soon after, I heard the sound of the bridge being drawn up again. I waited until Masetto assured me the coast was clear.

"Good job you were hidden."

I didn't want to ask who had called out to him. I was just glad that I could travel all the way to Dervio without being spotted.

The tiny village of Cernobbio was dwarfed by a magnificent villa standing on its shores. "The Villa d'Este," explained Masetto, following my gaze. "A luxury hotel! The aristocrats of Europe stayed here, before the war."

Masetto was now zigzagging across the lake, heading for the towns on the eastern shore. I lay down under the bench, covered myself with the blanket and dozed off. Eventually, the hard wooden floor grew uncomfortable, and my back hurt from lying hunched up on my side.

"Can I stand up or are we about to enter another port?" I asked.

"Have a seat. Our next stop isn't for a while."

Various opulent villas kept cropping up among the tranquil medieval villages. I saw old churches atop steep flights of stairs, the clanging of their monotonous bells ringing out across the lake. Individual houses clung to the slopes, with grassy areas stretching between them to the edge of the forest. I spotted an olive grove between the terraced vineyards that led up the hill.

"Are there really olive trees here, or am I imagining things?"

"That really is a little olive grove, *Zoca d'Oli*, on the hill above the bay of Ossuccio." Masetto pointed to a small island. "That's Isola Comacino!"

I could hardly make out the island at this distance. It was covered with a dense thatch of trees, which blended with the vegetation on the shore. The island seemed to be uninhabited. A modest church peeped out from behind the dense conifers.

"And you must take a look at Villa Carlotta from further up!" he exclaimed. "We're lucky that prominent members of the upper classes took care of the villa. It used to be owned by the German nobility, after all. Imagine if that were still the case. Hitler might have settled here. The villa is full of valuable works of art!"

Masetto seemed to be a mine of information.

"And who runs it now?"

"It was confiscated by the state after the First World War. It was supposed to be sold at auction in 1922, but enthusiasts such as Giuseppe Bianchini were dead set against it. He teamed up with Milanese industrialist Giovanni Silvestri, engineer Luigi Negretti, and textile entrepreneurs Guido Ravasi and Enrico Stucchi, and together they founded the Ente Autonomo Villa Carlotta, a charity that preserves the villa's cultural heritage and allows it to be opened to the public."

The villa resembled the kind of palazzo I had only seen in Rome. Behind the elaborate wrought iron gate was a sweeping flight of stairs, framed by a balustrade, that wound up to the entrance. The fountain at the centre was hemmed with carefully trimmed hedges. The dash of colour from the blossoming azaleas, camellias and rhododendrons stood out like a painting against the otherwise neutral colours of the villa.

The lake opened out as we reached the point where it forked.

"Behind us on the left is Lago di Como, and on the right, Lago di Lecco. The upper section of the lake is known as Lario," Masetto remarked.

My eyes wandered over to the right-hand shore of the lake. On a small outcrop at the foot of a cliff, rows of pastel-coloured houses formed a colourful mosaic, with an ancient castle towering above them. The tranquil spot looked like something out of a dream—it almost made me forget about the war. The whole scene captivated me, and I couldn't take my eyes off it.

"What's the village over there called?" I asked absentmindedly.

"That's Varenna."

After the war, when all this is over, I'll come and visit Varenna, I thought dreamily. *I'll bring Alfredo and Bianca gifts to say thank you, then I'll travel on to Varenna.*

I couldn't help smiling at my musings. They gave me a glimmer of hope. And as I sat there with the sun on my cheeks, lost in thought, I suddenly saw a joyful face before my eyes. It smiled at me and blew me a kiss. I laughed out loud.

"What is it, Enzo?" Masetto turned to face me.

"Oh, nothing, Masetto," I replied. "I just remembered a funny thing that happened!"

I couldn't get the friendly face out of my mind. It warmed my heart. Francesca. The rambunctious celebration after Luca and Carina's wedding, the loving embrace at the grave, and the joy that she was soon to become an aunt brought the memories flooding back. My guilty conscience nagged at me—I could have got in touch with her. I hadn't even asked her if she had to go back to Rome. She was probably in Sicily with Carina, helping her sister with the baby. I felt such a strong connection to the two sisters, and it was as if Luca were sitting next to me, his strong arm wrapped around my shoulders.

I felt him saying to me, "You can do this."

Half an hour later, we arrived in Dervio. Masetto advised me to wrap my suitcase up in the woollen blanket and carry it on my shoulders like a package. No one seemed bothered by it, as most of the passengers had baskets or crates with them.

Giulio had moored his small boat at the far end of the pier. In the bow of the boat was a tottering pile of nets, and he stowed my suitcase under it. I sat down on a box in the stern while he untied the rope. Then he took a seat in the middle of the boat.

"*Pronto?*" He smiled at me, then started rowing.

The dark lake stretched out before us, a light breeze rippling the surface, and we glided softly over the water in the rhythm of the oar strokes. I found the cool air from the lake both refreshing and calming. Giulio rowed in silence. I was glad he wasn't asking me any questions. Apart from the passenger ships, our only companions on the water were fishing boats.

"Where do you cast the nets?" I inquired.

Giulio glanced back at me. "Further down, where the lake forks. That's where most of the fish are—redfish, whitefish and tench."

"Would you like a piece of bread with some cheese?" I opened the bag containing my provisions.

Giulio lifted the oars. "Please. I could do with a break. There's a bottle of wine in the box." He pulled out a canvas bag from under the pile of nets, which contained two aluminium cups and a knife. We cut slices of bread and cheese and toasted each other with the red wine.

"We'll arrive in Dongo in an hour. Then I'll put out the nets on the way back." The waves lapped softly against the hull of the boat. "If we're stopped and questioned, we'll just say we're going fishing," he said casually. "But it's not usually a problem during the day. See that little black boat across the lake? It's a police boat. The Carabinieri patrol the lake, but even they take breaks." He gave a low chuckle. "I know those fellows, and they know me, so they'll leave us alone. I've given them plenty of fish already," he grinned.

I was so grateful to Alfredo. Without his contacts, there was no way I would have found safe passage across the lake and into the massif. And yet, I could feel a restlessness slowly building within me, despite the calming sound of lapping water all around me. I closed my eyes and concentrated on the gentle rocking of the fishing boat.

Giulio took up the oars again.

We approached the bank, where a rickety jetty led up to a curved gravel path. The village was out of sight.

"Are you going to moor here?" I asked, roused from my thoughts.

"The port of Dongo is a little further on, but Alfredo asked me to set you down here."

I must have looked frightened.

"Don't worry, I'll wait with you until Mario gets here."

It didn't take long, and soon we heard the rattle of an Apetta. The three-wheeled vehicle pulled up behind a plane tree.

The cargo area was filled with potatoes. Giulio took my suitcase out from under the nets and carefully stepped out of the swaying fishing boat.

"Ciao! That went like clockwork!"

Mario greeted me. In his left hand he held a potato sack. "Some supplies for you, Giulio!"

The pair looked at each other conspiratorially.

I wondered what else was in the bag. But I didn't really care—I just wanted to leave this place. I sat down in the Apetta. The two of them chatted for a while as my impatience grew. They probably noticed I was fidgeting in anticipation on the passenger seat. Mario took the suitcase from my lap and stowed it under the potatoes. He waved to Giulio one last time, then turned to me. "We're going to my house first. Cleglia will prepare a hearty meal for you. Then Nevio will pick you up after dark."

The stone house stood at a crossroads above Dongo. Mario parked the Apetta behind the chicken coop to keep it out of sight of the road. His wife greeted me coolly and barely said a word to me all afternoon. Only once, when Mario had gone to the chicken coop, did she remark sharply, "I wish this war would be over soon! I'm fed up with this constant game of hide and seek. How many more will we have to feed and take in? I see things quite differently to my husband, you know. I think we should stay out of all this. It'll only cause trouble. Mario is trying to curry favour with everyone so that we can keep our heads above water. It's miserable! And what are we going to do when the Germans come? Then we'll all be shot because we belong to the traitors!" Her distorted face was hard and bitter.

"I'm sorry," I mumbled. "When it gets dark, I'll be out of your hair." I sat in the corner by the stove. A minestrone soup was bubbling in the pot. Mario trudged into the kitchen with a basket of eggs and sat down at the table. He, too, was at a loss for words. He fetched two glasses and a bottle of wine. He put a piece of bread and cheese on a plate and handed them to me. "*Saluti!*" he whispered.

I felt like a cat on a hot tin roof as I waited for nightfall. It was moments like these that I really missed my watch. What time was it? The loud bleating of the goats began to get on my nerves.

"Cleglia, get the pannier out of the shed! We need it," Mario called to his wife. "Come on, Enzo, let's put your suitcase in it!"

He stuffed my suitcase into the basket with such force that I cried out in fright, "Watch out! I want the suitcase to get home in one piece!"

"*Zitto!* Not so loud, lad! We still need room for blankets on top of it. You don't want to stroll up the mountain carrying a suitcase bold as brass, do you?" he snapped back.

I gave up. He furtively took some small packages from a shelf and shoved them into the gaps. I couldn't see what they were, but I didn't need to—I could smell them. Coffee beans. Then he filled some canvas bags with rice and stowed them in the box as well. Last but not least, he pulled out an object wrapped in newspaper from a drawer. He sat down gravely at the table and unfolded the packages. Two brand new revolvers. I gave him a questioning look. "I'll put one in the basket; the other is yours. Alfredo told me to give it to you."

He placed the weapon into my hand. "Careful, it's loaded!"

I wondered how much Alfredo had paid him for it. Did I really need it? I already owed Alfredo so much. How much had he had to pay for the pistol?

"Don't be stupid. You need a gun." He laughed scornfully. "I thought you were in the army and knew how to use one. You can stow it in your belt."

I didn't feel like replying. I didn't want to explain to him that I had never had to use a gun except in military training school, and I was even more reluctant to tell him that I already had a revolver in my suitcase. For some reason, Mario made me feel uneasy. I only hoped that the smuggler would be trustworthy—I didn't care about anything else now. One day I would show my gratitude to Alfredo, that was for sure. Francesca's face appeared before me again. I suddenly felt strong and invincible.

Thank you, Francesca, I thought silently.

Finally, the sun was hovering just above the horizon. I was sitting on a bench behind the house as wisps of cloud scudded across the sky. It was still warm for the time of year. What luck! That meant I wouldn't have to trek across the mountains through mud and rain. For the first time, it struck me just how important the weather would be for my mountain crossing. There could be some quite frightening thunderstorms, especially here in the southern part of the Alps, but they normally only happened in summer. *I'm here at the perfect time*, I mused thoughtfully. I said a prayer of thanks and felt a fortifying strength flare up inside me. It was hard to believe that just a week ago I'd been lying in bed, half dead from fever.

The glowing yellow orb above the horizon bathed the water in golden light. On the other side of the lake, windows flashed in the glow from the last rays of the sun. There, further down, was Varenna, the enchanting place I planned to visit with Francesca. I couldn't help smiling at the longing that suddenly welled up in me. My mind wandered down the boot of Italy, all the way to Sicily.

"*Buona fortuna, mia cara!*" I whispered to her. I felt on top of the world.

Half an hour later, the smuggler arrived.

Across the Mountain Border

The smuggler came into the house without saying a word. He spoke with Mario quietly in dialect. I could only make out scraps of the conversation. After a while, Mario waved me over to the table.

"Listen, Enzo! Nevio won't be talking to you directly. He says you have to maintain absolute silence as you walk. You can use hand signals to communicate, if necessary."

I nodded.

"Time to go!" He hefted the pannier onto Nevio's back.

Nothing more was said. I thanked him, but Mario dismissed me with a wave.

Nevio strode briskly ahead. In the evening light, we crossed a field behind the house and then entered the forest. The path led us through the undergrowth, veering away from the usual route. The tangy scent of resin filled the air. When we reached a low hill, Nevio pointed to the mountain massif that now loomed up sharply and towered above us. The trees thinned as we neared the forest line, with only individual pines left. Craggy rocks rose up as far as the eye could see. We walked along the steep path without saying a word. I concentrated hard on every step. I felt as if I were being forced to pass an exam under time pressure. I gulped great lungfuls of the fresh mountain air to calm myself. *In peacetime, this would certainly be a very picturesque hike*, I thought.

We stepped out of the undergrowth into an alpine pasture. The mountain slopes were covered with lush green grass. I looked at the lake, nestled peacefully in between the mountains. A passenger ship was approaching a mooring, probably the last one of the night. A motorboat glided along the right-hand shore of the lake, leaving a white trail. I turned my gaze back to the mountain massif in front of us. The path was lined with rows of bushes that stretched up to the cliffs. The forest line was now behind us. We zigzagged through the bushes until we came to a scree slope. Nevio pointed to a rock. I took that to mean he wanted to take a break. He set the pannier down, then pulled a small canteen out of his jacket pocket and held it out to me. I took a sip. The grappa burned in my throat but gave me a pleasant, warm feeling in my stomach. We leaned against the stone boulder and looked up at the evening sky in silence. Nevio took one last sip, then hoisted the pannier back onto his back. He listened attentively and looked around him before giving me the signal to walk on. To our right, the crest of the mountain loomed up dimly in the twilight. The lake was far below us now, and we could only make out a smattering of lights. I took one last look at the black water, then turned and followed Nevio. The path took us steeply uphill. I silently thanked Alfredo for his mountain boots. He really had thought of everything. My army boots were worn through from my long march along the aqueduct, and besides, they would have made me stand out like a sore thumb.

"You can't possibly hike up the mountain with your shoes falling to bits!" he had exclaimed. "I'll get a pair of real hiking boots for you."

I counted myself lucky—the hiking boots gave me support as I walked on the slippery scree and climbed over the rocks. Suddenly, Nevio stopped and signalled to lie down. I looked up questioningly, but he remained as silent as the grave. He just held up his index finger in front of his mouth. The pannier was now hanging crookedly on his back. I put my left arm over it and tried to keep it from tipping over. No matter how intently I pricked up my ears, I couldn't hear anything suspicious. I hid my head behind the pannier. After a while, just as I was about to raise myself up a little, Nevio tutted softly and jerked his head in the direction of the mountain range. I could clearly make out two figures at the top. Were they coming towards us or heading the other way? They moved slowly along the ridge, then stopped and looked around. We ducked down and remained in our position. After what felt like an eternity, Nevio dared take another look. He tilted his head back and forth again, then clucked his tongue softly, indicating to me that we could sit up. I heaved myself up and settled down beside him, relieved. My limbs ached. We waited a little while longer until the two silhouettes had completely disappeared from view. Then Nevio signalled that the coast was clear. He swung the pannier back onto his back, and I stretched my limbs and followed him. The scree grew denser and denser, and soon we could barely make out the path, but Nevio kept walking purposefully towards the pass. I started to feel really exhausted from clambering over the boulders. I whistled softly to let him know I wanted to stop for a moment. I pulled my water bottle out of my jacket pocket and drank some water. That felt good! Then Nevio gave the signal to go on. I paid close attention to every step I took. A cool breeze blew over the ridge. The last stretch curved around a rocky outcrop, then Nevio stopped and pointed ahead.

"The San Jorio Pass!"

I stopped and looked around me. The clouds that had so far been covering the full moon drew aside to reveal a white orb. My gaze roamed over the mountain massif that stretched to the horizon, radiating an indescribable beauty in the pale moonlight. The sky was scattered with hundreds of stars, more than I had ever seen. The view left me spellbound. I reminisced about my experiences in Italy, this incomparable, enchanting country, and about the warm-hearted people I had met. At the same time, I was overcome with pain and sadness for all those who could not escape to safety and freedom like I could.

Behind the knoll was a narrow path that veered off and led to an alpine hut. There was a crooked bench in front of the entrance. Nevio bent down and pulled a key out from under it. Inside the hut, he lit a candle and pointed to the wooden cot in the corner. "We'll set off again at four in the morning. Get some rest!" he said curtly.

Exhausted, I lay down on the creaky bed and fell asleep in an instant.

It was still dark when Nevio woke me. The descent led over a long, rocky desert. There was no path, so we were forced to slither across the scree. It was getting lighter, and dawn was tingeing the clouds on the horizon a soft pink. Nevio walked quickly and was already further down. I had to tie my shoelace and bent down. As I rose again, I caught sight of two children walking towards Nevio. Nevio whistled impatiently. He put down his pannier and rummaged in it.

"Do you have anything to trade?" asked the girl. "We have nylon stockings."

Nevio took out two bags of rice and cigarettes and handed them to the children. Then he stuffed the bag with the stockings into the pannier. He heaved my suitcase out and said, "I'm handing you over to the children, Enzo. They'll take you to the next alpine hut and past customs to Roveredo."

I was gobsmacked. "What? You were supposed to take me to Roveredo!" I shouted in dismay.

"Not so loud!" he hissed. "Listen, Enzo! Never mind what I was supposed to do—I'm not going any further.

Every other week, the customs officials take one of us prisoner and lock us up for a couple of days. I don't want to risk it!" He grabbed the pannier and turned away.

I seized his sleeve. "You rotten bastard! You take my cousin's money then make off like a coward!"

He looked at me angrily and shoved me roughly aside.

"Count yourself lucky you got this far in one piece!" Then he ran up the slope.

There I was, stranded on the mountainside, forced to entrust myself to two shepherd children.

The boy led the way. He couldn't have been older than twelve. Nimbly, he found us a path through the scree. He carried a small basket on his back. The girl was younger. Every now and then, she would turn to look at me. "Before we reach the border, we'll stop at an alpine hut. We can eat something there," she explained kindly. She, too, had a basket with her.

We crisscrossed the rocky desert, weaving this way and that. I carried the suitcase on my shoulders. As we approached the foot of the mountain, the gravel started to thin, and soon we were walking on grassy hillsides. The further down the slope we walked, the more tense I became. We would soon be at the border, and it was highly likely we would encounter someone here. It wasn't just the border guards who would be a danger to us; we were also at risk of attack from partisans or smugglers, especially since I was visibly carrying a suitcase.

I scrutinised my surroundings carefully, feeling like a wild animal on the prowl. We soon came upon a forest that stretched out before us. The children led me through the undergrowth to a clearing. We reached the alpine hut, which was more comfortable than the hut I had stayed in on the pass. The boy brought wood from the shed and lit the fire, while the girl hung a pot of water over it. I sat down at the table and watched the pair of them. They were siblings—that much was obvious. The girl took a loaf of bread and cheese from a cupboard. She sliced the bread neatly and brought it to the table on a plate.

"Help yourself! Here's some cheese to go with it." She poured some coffee and milk into a cup and sat down opposite me at the table. "It's only two hours to the customs house from here. We'll hide in a nearby forest and wait. When the customs officials go into the house to take a break, we can sneak past the border post," she explained.

I put my trust wholeheartedly in the two children; they really seemed to know their stuff. They didn't talk much, but they did explain that they lived in Roveredo. Their uncle was a railway guard and could arrange a ticket for me.

It was time to set off. The path led us downhill over alpine pastures and through forests. After two hours, the children stopped.

"You need to wait up there, behind that dense thicket," the boy said. "My sister and I will hide there, behind the fir trees, and watch the customs house. When the coast is clear, we'll come back and get you."

They crept to the fir trees on tiptoe, while I froze, rooted to the spot, behind my bush. The hazel's leaves moved gently in the wind. My gaze was fixed on the children, who were now crouched on the roots of a fir tree. I could make out the customs house in the distance, two officials standing in front of it. Freedom was so close I could almost taste it. This was the final hurdle. I could only hope the children chose the right moment.

I stared, transfixed, at the customs officers, vigilantly watching their every move. Then what we had waited so long for finally happened. They retreated into the house. The children turned and signalled to me to go. Quiet as mice, we stalked between the fir trees to the meadow. We ran over the hill, hunched over, before creeping along the edge of the forest behind the customs house. I didn't look round, keeping my gaze fixed instead on the children's heels in front of me. My fate was in their hands. Hunched over, they made their nimble way along the edge of the forest until we were far enough away from the customs house. At the end of the forest, we stepped out into the open meadow again. We swiftly followed the path that led down into the valley. I didn't dare look back; I only wanted to look ahead now. At the bottom of the valley was a railway line, running in parallel to a raging mountain river. Our path wound this way and that, down into the depths of the valley. I drew water from a spring and washed my face.

We reached Roveredo as evening was drawing in. The children brought me to their uncle's house. He looked me up and down.

"The last train has already left, but you can stay with us tonight. I'll take the suitcase to the station and stow it there. You'll be too conspicuous walking through the village with it. I'll take you to the first train tomorrow morning."

I was so grateful to the children. I would have loved to give them a gift to say thank you. But I didn't have enough money on me. I needed the 20-franc note for my train ticket.

"Do you have a gun for us?" the boy asked me directly. I was flabbergasted. I couldn't get my head around his asking for a weapon. He couldn't have been more than eleven or twelve years old!

I looked at him regretfully. "I'd like to give you money, kid, but sadly I don't have any. When the war is over, I'll come by and bring you money and presents," I promised.

Their uncle told me more about the customs officials and the business of smuggling. "They know very well that there are smugglers going back and forth every day. They put one of them behind bars every now and then to keep the authorities happy."

"How long do they spend in jail?"

"Normally only one or two days, but that's far too long for most smugglers. They need the money."

As I lay in bed that night, snippets of my escape over the mountain pass flashed before my eyes like a film. I could hardly believe I was now on Swiss soil and would be taking the train home tomorrow.

The train journey took me via Bellinzona. When I was waiting for my connecting train, I went to a barbershop to get a shave, as I wanted to look halfway decent when I saw my mother again. I had just enough money to buy a train ticket to Lucerne. I needed to call my mother, so I made my way to a telephone booth, tossed what little change I had left into the slot and dialled the number. We didn't have a telephone in our flat, but we could use the one in the restaurant on the ground floor of our building. The waitress answered and told me my mother was out shopping.

"Please tell her to meet me at the station in Lucerne. I need money for the train ticket home!" I shouted into the phone. The employee assured me she would tell my mother as soon as she returned home.

No sooner had the train pulled out of the station in Bellinzona than the doors to my compartment were opened by two armed police.

"Passport control! Please present your identity documents!"

Luckily, I had my certificate of citizenship with me all these months, which confirmed my right to reside in Switzerland.

"My passport expired. I need to renew it," I lied, "but I have my certificate of citizenship with me. Here!"

I had deliberately altered the certificate's expiry date so that it was still valid. The armed police didn't seem to notice. They handed back the document and closed the door.

I breathed a sigh of relief. Everything seemed to be going according to plan.

The train was approaching the Gotthard and was now winding its way through the loop tunnels. As we crossed the bridges, I looked down at Wassen Church. Seeing it every time from different perspectives was quite an experience, because the train climbed 200 metres in elevation in a short space of time here. The church sat enthroned upon a small rocky outcrop and was the main landmark of the train journey through the Gotthard tunnel. Thoughts of the war whirled through my mind. Here in the Alps, there were secret military defences—known as the National Redoubt— because the Gotthard massif was one of the most important connections between the North and the South. I remembered when several divisions had been mobilised and moved to various military defence facilities in the Alps. We could only guess what those facilities looked like.

It felt odd to now be in a country that rose above the chaos of warfare like an island sanctuary. People went about their work and planted crops in every green piece of land in order to survive. I couldn't help thinking of my German and Italian friends in Italy. Where were they now? Had Klaus and Werner managed to escape the attacks? What was the situation in Rome? At that moment, I hoped against hope that this miserable war would soon be at an end.

The train was now travelling through the Swiss Plateau. The familiar landscape made me feel at home. "I'll be there soon!"

My mother was standing on the platform, suitcase in hand.

"Mum! Ciao!"

Tears of joy ran down her face. She pulled me close, hugged me and kissed me. "Enzo, I'm so happy to see you safe and sound! Where are they sending you now?"

"What? Oh, Mum! I'm back, I'm home—I'm not going anywhere!"

My mother looked at me in astonishment. "I thought you needed clothes, food and money because you were on your way to another deployment," she said, astounded.

"I'm not going back to war, Mum. All I need is the money for a train ticket home."

"You're really coming home?" my mother still couldn't believe it.

"Yes, Mum!"

At home, Rinaldo, my little brother, greeted me with utmost delight. "You'll have to tell us everything, Enzo! I'm so proud of you! You're a hero!" He hugged me enthusiastically. Rinaldo wanted to know every detail, and I was recounting my tale until late in the evening. He listened intently to my descriptions, completely beside himself with amazement.

"Enzo needs to relax, Rinaldo. He can tell you more tomorrow," my mother warned him.

It was only when I lay down in bed that I realised just how exhausted I was. All I wanted to do was sleep.

The next day I had to report to the immigration authorities. The official was the father of one of my school friends. I greeted him warmly and asked how his son was doing. He didn't answer and instead looked at me coldly. "You fled to Switzerland as a deserter! How were you able to just run away from the army like that?" He gave a short laugh and went on condescendingly. "And then you think you can get off scot-free and return to safe, peaceful Switzerland, just like that? That's not the way us Swiss see it. You're still a foreigner after all!"

I couldn't believe it. This man, who knew me and my family, whose son had been my school friend, was treating me like a piece of dirt on his shoe.

"Switzerland is my home. I grew up here!"

"Report for agricultural service immediately so you can do something useful for our country! Goodbye!" he scolded.

I felt wretched. My mother and brother tried to comfort me, but the discrimination I had faced in my own country was deeply humiliating.

Two days later, a major of the general staff contacted us at home. He greeted me courteously and asked politely if I could give him some information. He was particularly interested in my deployment in Lampedusa.

"Could you do me a sketch of the radar unit?"

I tried my best. As I drew, I explained to him how the equipment worked. "We used the radar unit to monitor enemy aircraft. We had to watch all movements in the airspace. British bombers would fly towards Italy three or four times a week. Our observations had to be reported immediately to the telephone exchange, which then alerted all the Italian airfields. Some fighter bombers flew in from Malta, others from Africa. I had to translate the announcements into Italian, and the messages were then forwarded on to Rome and Munich via Taormina. The Allies must have known about the installation, which meant we weren't able to detect all the attacks. They would fly low, around 50 or 60 metres over the sea, allowing them to pass unnoticed under the radar and head for the mainland."

"During your stay on Lampedusa, were there any bomb attacks on the island?" he asked, interested.

"Yes. We were attacked three times. I remember quite clearly. One bomb fell into the sea 50 metres away from the port. A German transport ship and an Italian passenger ship were sunk during the other attacks."

"We're aware of some of the German military's radar installations, but this Freya device seems to be a more recent development. What you've told me is very interesting. We at the general staff will file your sketch in our records and archive it accordingly. Don't worry, it will be sent via secure channels to a secret military address. You're a good draughtsman by the way," he said appreciatively.

"I studied at the textile training college in Cottbus before I received my marching orders. I particularly liked the design department there. Developing ideas and making patterns allows you to play with shapes and colours," I said enthusiastically.

The major inquired about the rest of my army service in Italy. I told him how I had escaped the Allied attack and fled along the Apulian Aqueduct.

"You've really had a terrible time of it! I hope things are going better for you back in Switzerland."

I told him about the insults and harassment I had suffered at the hands of the immigration official.

"That officer was wrong to do that. It isn't his place to judge your desertion in Italy. I'll take care of it."

When I had to report to the office again a few days later, I was received in an extremely friendly manner. The official's behaviour was the polar opposite to what it had been. He even told me about his son, who sent his regards.

The major had probably had a thing or two to say to that philistine.

The next night, I woke up drenched in sweat. Was I trapped in a nightmare? My head was on fire, and my body was wracked with shivers. My mother made me cold compresses. The fever lasted for two days. I lay limply between the sheets, sweat pouring out of my body almost without reprieve. My mother called a doctor who had me admitted to hospital, where they examined me but found nothing. I was discharged after three days.

When the fever returned a month later, it was clear to me that I had malaria. I contacted a specialist in Zurich, who confirmed the diagnosis and gave me medication that finally cured my fever.

Epilogue

Sicily, 1947

"*Padrino, padrino!*" Little Luca leapt into my arms, overjoyed. He looked at me mischievously with his dark, round eyes. "Come and play with me!" He dragged me by the hand out into the garden, where he showed me his ball, beaming with pride, and rolled it in front of him, trying to kick it with his foot. He scampered after it tirelessly, kicking it again. He would fall down every once in a while, but he kept getting right back up. I watched the little tyke absentmindedly. We spent every minute together, in the garden, on the beach, with the chickens. Riding in the car was his absolute favourite. There was a small tin aeroplane on the bookcase in his room.

"*Di nonno!*" he explained.

Carina stood in the doorway as I looked at a book with little Luca. "Yes, Luca, that's right! Nonno gave it to you for your birthday. Your dad flew planes." She looked up momentarily, and our eyes met.

After little Luca was in bed, we went out onto the veranda.

"Little Luca has really taken a shine to you. He loves you more than anything!" Carina smiled at me contentedly. "He's very sweet, and I enjoy spending time with him. Although he reminds me so much of Luca, playing with him helps me forget what I've lost."

I paused for a moment, trying to find the right words. "How are you, Carina?" I asked quietly.

"I miss him every day."

I knew exactly how she felt. The house, the surroundings, the beach—wherever I went, I could feel the emptiness inside. Something was missing. Even now, especially now, having dinner with my grandparents, aunts, uncles and cousins, his absence was particularly noticeable.

"I'm so happy you could come and spend a few days with us. Francesca is especially happy," Carina said, grinning.

It was already evening when I made my way through the village towards the cemetery. The piazza was bustling with activity, and people were chatting, laughing and drinking in front of the Bar di Domenico. Old people were sitting on benches in the cool shade of the tall palm trees. Music was playing from an open window. As I walked across the cobblestones, lost in thought, I recognised the melancholy voice of Sergio Endrigo.

"Non so perché sta sera penso a te,
strada fiorita della gioventù…"

"I don't know why I'm thinking of you tonight,
flowery road of youth…"

The words moved me, and the melody put me in a pensive mood. He was singing about the flowery road of youth.

Our youth. It was stolen from us.

All that remained was a generation's deep longing for its happy years, a generation that had been robbed of its vitality, whose desires were left unfulfilled. They were flowers that never bloomed. They faded, withered and died beneath the mourning cloak of war.

On the long train journey to Sicily, I saw places that were still in ruins. Impassable bridges, stations that were destroyed, unable to be used, villages and sections of towns that had fallen victim to the bomb attacks—a bleak sight. The residents had been forced to flee and leave their homes behind. All that remained were gutted houses lined up like skeletons beside the rubble. The reconstruction work would take years.

Fortunately, the centre of Rome and the Vatican had been spared. Alighting from the train in Rome felt like a miracle. I had planned my trip so that I could attend the canonisation of Brother Klaus in St Peter's Basilica. Brother Klaus, the fifteenth-century hermit and mystic, was considered the patron saint of Switzerland. My local church back home was even named after him. Several of my Swiss friends and acquaintances wanted to attend this unique event—the thought of it made me smile. It was practically impossible to get a ticket, as half of Switzerland seemed to be making the pilgrimage to Rome to attend the canonisation. What's more, only a few trains were running there, and all the tickets from Switzerland to Rome were sold out.

I telegrammed the stationmaster in Milan asking if he could issue me a train ticket from Milan to Rome, specifying the exact arrival and departure times. I went to Milan on the off chance and reported to the stationmaster's office. I brought cigarettes and chocolate with me in my luggage.

"We have prepared a train ticket for you. We thought it would be best if you took the express train," he said.

"There's an express train running to Rome?" I asked in disbelief.

The man laughed. "The newest, fastest train, the *Frecciarossa*! You'll be in Rome in eight hours."

"That's unbelievable!" I cried excitedly.

"The normal trains take up to eleven hours. Lots of the bridges that were destroyed in the war are still impassable, and we can only use one side of the tracks because the lines haven't been repaired yet either. The *Frecciarossa* has right of way," he explained.

I took the cigarettes and chocolate out of my luggage and handed them to the men in the office. "Thank you very much! You've done me a huge favour!"

When I arrived in Rome, I immediately made my way to the Vatican.

"You think I'd leave my Swiss cousin without a ticket?" Roberto grinned at me, delighted. "By the way, Enzo, the tickets are numbered. Your seat is in the front row!"

"My Swiss friends will be amazed. They only just managed to get tickets right at the back. I'm lucky to have a *cugino* in the Vatican. By the way, I'm meeting Marcello tonight at the Trattoria del Orso. Why don't you come too?" I asked him.

"Sure. For you, cugino, I will. You know, I haven't been there since the bombings. Over the last few years, I've avoided a lot of places that remind me of Luca."

I looked at him sympathetically.

Life in Rome was the same as it had always been. It felt as if I'd only just left. And I could sense a palpable spirit of optimism, a *joie de vivre* that was starting to blossom again.

Before I set off on my onward journey to Sicily, I wanted to visit Island Commander Bernini. I had brought some chocolate for him too. His stately home was in a fashionable district of Rome, near Villa Borghese park.

A maid opened the door for me and led me into the large living room, where she introduced me to Bernini's wife, Violetta.

"Oh, what a lovely surprise, getting to meet you like this! I'm so sorry, but my husband is in a meeting at the ministry. What a shame!"

I told her that I had come for the canonisation of Brother Klaus and was on my way to Sicily. "Your husband helped me get on the last boat off Lampedusa before the Allies landed."

"And you managed to get home in one piece?" she said, amazed.

"Yes. It was a long journey. What happened to your husband after the Allied invasion?" I asked.

"He was captured like all the others. He was lucky. Who would have thought then that the war would last another two years? He was safe in prison. He went on and on about how well he was treated."

"I managed to find out what happened to my two German comrades from the radar unit. They had to stay on the island with orders to blow up the radar station. Unfortunately, they both died in the bomb attacks."

"The war took so many young lives. That must have been awful for you to learn of your friends' deaths," she said sadly.

We chatted for a while about Lampedusa and my relatives in Sicily. Then I gave her the chocolate and bid her farewell.

The entrance to the graveyard was open. A light breeze ruffled my hair. I remembered the statue clearly, the narrow path leading up to the hill, and the scent of the flowering jasmine. Four years had passed and yet it seemed like only yesterday we were standing here in mourning.

Behind the family crypts, between old myrtle trees, were rows upon rows of little crosses, all lined up like a sea of white stars.

"My God," I gasped. At Luca's funeral there had been just two rows of crosses here, now there were so many it was impossible to count them. I stopped at the top of the hill. As I tried to work out where Luca's grave was, my gaze wandered to the horizon. Far in the distance, I could see the deep blue of the sea. The sun hung like a fiery red orb above the horizon, the warm evening light exuding a profound sense of calm.

I made my way through the long rows of graves. There was a sense of purity about the white of the crosses, as if the fallen soldiers had been freed from the dirt and blood of war, lain to rest here in innocence and humility. The crosses radiated an infinite peace. And as I walked slowly along, my mind calm and absorbed in this aura, the names blurred before my eyes, dissolving, leaving only the silence that enveloped the place. Finding Luca's cross no longer mattered to me. I felt his presence so clearly anyway, and the power of that moment made me feel as if I were united not only with him, but with all the young fallen men of our generation. I thought of Klaus and Werner, my German comrades in the radar unit, who were given no chance of escape and were then killed by bombs. We were all part of a sacred friendship, which everybody was a part of, no matter what side they were on. We were brothers of our youth, divided between war and home. Our homeland had betrayed us and had been ripped away from us. Our childhood memories were all that reminded us how happy and loving it had been, before the machinery of war had slowly eroded it away. The feeling of familiarity, security and home was transformed into defencelessness and the fear of death. And we fought and succumbed to madness in the hope of finding our way back.

I wished I could tell my friends who had been laid to rest here that justice had prevailed, that life was blossoming again, and that we were reclaiming our old, familiar home.

It was almost dark when a shadow approached the hill. The slender silhouette moved, light-footed, towards me. Her long curls danced in the wind. Francesca.

I stood up and slowly made my way towards her. We embraced.

"You found Luca's grave," she whispered.

I knelt down and read the inscription on the cross before us. I looked at her in surprise. "I didn't even notice." I took hold of her hand, and we remained standing there for a while, in front of the cross.

"Come on, I'll show you my father's grave," she said, breaking the silence. She led me towards the family plots. "Our hearts are finally at peace. After all these years, his killer has now been identified—it was a member of the Gambino family."

We left the graveyard and walked along the coastal path.

"I'm really glad you're coming to Switzerland with me. When we get to Lake Como, I'll show you a place that's particularly beautiful. It's a small, picturesque village called Varenna," I told her. "From there, you can see the San Jorio Pass, where I crossed the border."

"I want to hear all about your escape, Enzo," she said, excited.

I led her through an olive grove to an old, dilapidated farmhouse. "Look! I have a little surprise for you, Francesca!"

"A farm?" she said, laughing.

"Something like that! This is where our holiday villa will be—here, where this house is now." I strode across the field behind it. "This is where the pool will be, and we can put a garden back here. Come on!"

I led her down to the end of the plot. Beneath an orange tree drenched in blossom stood an old wooden bench. We sat down and gazed out to sea, oblivious to anything else. I put my arm around her.

"And? What do you think of my plan?" I whispered.

"It's wonderful, Enzo!"

Surrounded by the scent of orange blossom, we dreamed of our future together.

Annex

Explanations and Facts

Mattanza: The mattanza was the traditional tuna fishing ritual off the west coast of Sicily, between Trapani and the island of Favignana. The people of the island relied on a good catch to survive. The process of canning tuna with olive oil was invented in the *Tonnara Florio* tuna factory. The last mattanza took place in 2007. The *Ex Stabilmento Florio delle Tonnare di Favignana e Formica* tuna factory is now a museum.

Rome/The Vatican, 1943: The Irish priest Monsignor Hugh O'Flaherty saved more than six thousand people from arrest, torture and death in German-occupied Rome in 1943–44. He hid prisoners of war who had escaped, those who were persecuted, and Jews in the Vatican as well as private houses and villas belonging to Roman aristocrats, who provided financial support to his underground organisation. Hugh O'Flaherty was supported in his rescue operation by British envoy Sir D'Arcy Osborne and his butler John May. British officer Sam Derry also joined the organisation. O'Flaherty engaged in a murderous showdown with his adversary Herbert Kappler, the head of the Gestapo in Rome.

ISABELLA PALLAVICINI

Operation 'Husky', the Allied landing in Sicily in 1943:
At the conference in Casablanca in January 1943,
British Prime Minister Winston Churchill and American
President Franklin D. Roosevelt agreed to open a second
front in Europe. They decided to land in Southern Italy,
using the code word 'Operation Husky'. It was agreed
that the Normandy landings would take place fifty
weeks after the invasion of Sicily. The planning stages of
'Operation Husky' began at the end of January 1943 in
Algiers. The Allied victory over German and Italian
troops in the African Campaign and their almost total
control of the Mediterranean created the optimum
conditions for the British and Americans to carry out
their landing operation. The intention was that Italy,
demoralised by its defeat in North Africa, would be
overcome and the powerful German Wehrmacht taken
down before the Allied invasion of France that was
scheduled for the spring of 1944.

Lampedusa was bombed on 6 and 7 June 1943.
Before the attack on Sicily, the Allies occupied the
islands of Pantelleria, Lampedusa, Lampione and
Linosa from 2 to 14 June 1943. The British Eighth
Army and American Seventh Army, which had set off
from North Africa, landed in Sicily on 10 July 1943.
The attack took the Axis powers by surprise. Thanks to
false information that had been spread ('Operation
Mincemeat'), they had assumed the landing would take
place in Sardinia. After the armistice between Italy and
the Allies was announced on 8 September 1943, the
Germans resorted to countermeasures. They disarmed
and imprisoned Italian soldiers, and Rome was occupied
by German troops.

The Bombing of Rome on 19 July 1943: A few days after the Allied landing in Sicily, Rome was attacked by American long-range bombers. Whole swathes of the city were razed to the ground, including the San Lorenzo neighbourhood and the Basilica of St Lawrence. Littorio and Ciampino airfields were also bombed at the same time. It was the heaviest air raid on Rome that took place during the Second World War. Pope Pius XII comforted the wounded while praying to heaven with outstretched arms. The gesture is one of the most expressive images of his pontificate. A life-sized bronze statue in this stance can be found near the entrance to Verano cemetery.

Pope Pius XII called upon President Franklin D. Roosevelt to respect Catholic Christendom and protect the city from further bomb attacks. He demanded that the city's military commandos be evacuated to eliminate any cause for attack. Rome was declared an 'open city'.

German air raid on Bari, 1943: After the Allied occupation, the port of Bari was used for ammunition and transport ships to enable supplies to be delivered to the troops. The American army ship SS *John Harvey* was carrying a dangerous cargo, 540 tonnes of mustard gas, but neither the captain nor the crew knew anything about it. The ship was anchored in the port of Bari when German Ju 88 bombers launched a surprise attack on the port on 2 December 1943. Seventeen naval vessels were sunk and another eight set on fire. The SS *John Harvey* also caught fire and exploded. Thousands of soldiers and civilians perished in the swathes of the highly toxic agent, while hundreds of wounded patients were admitted to hospitals with unexplained symptoms. They had skin rashes with pus-filled blisters, high fevers and breathing difficulties that caused death by asphyxiation.

The Allied forces feared a gas attack by the Axis powers. American chemical factories had been instructed to produce enough warfare agent as a precautionary measure, in case the German Wehrmacht initiated chemical attacks. Hitler's intelligence services knew about this, and they also learned that warfare agents were continuously being shipped to North Africa.

The Allies hushed up the mass deaths, and the Bari disaster remained a well-kept secret for decades after the war ended.

Partisans—a historical overview: Fascist Italy under Benito Mussolini entered the Second World War on 10 July 1940 as an ally of Nazi Germany. Many Italians did not understand the point of the war. By early March 1943, it seemed as though Italy had already lost the war. The first strikes were organised at factories in Northern Italy. The Allies met little resistance in their invasion of Sicily, and Mussolini's power waned. On 25 July 1943, Mussolini was ousted by his colleagues in the Fascist government and imprisoned. Chief of General Staff Pietro Badoglio took over control of the military government and negotiated an armistice with the Allies. At the same time, he reiterated to Germany that Italy would continue fighting the war as its ally. Then—under protest from the Italian government—Germany moved more troops across the Brenner Pass. The 'Rome-Berlin axis', Mussolini's term for the close ties between the two countries, was broken. On 3 September 1943, Italy reached an armistice with the Allies, which plunged Italian forces into chaos when it was announced. In the absence of any military orders, many soldiers decided to return home. Within a few days, Nazi Germany had occupied Italy right down into the South, with many Italian troops being disarmed and deported to Germany. A total of 730,000 Italian soldiers were deported, 16,000 of whom died in German camps.

Civilians started helping soldiers disguise themselves, with women playing a key role in procuring civilian clothing for the troops, organising shelters, and helping them escape and get home. Many men retreated into the mountains to avoid deportation, forming the first partisan groups. From their high-altitude hiding places, they kept tabs on the German troops' movements and relied on surprise attacks. Deserters and escaped British and American prisoners of war joined the partisans. As the Allies continued to advance in Italy, partisan groups joined them and were used in their units mostly for reconnaissance purposes. Mussolini, his companion and some others were captured and shot by partisans at Lake Como on 28 April 1945. The bodies were publicly hanged in Milan.

The role of the mafia: Since 1924, Mussolini had been employing every means at his disposal to tackle organised crime. Several mafiosi were put behind bars, while others moved to the USA. Many Sicilians felt drawn to the Americans because of their family ties there. By 1943, two million Sicilians were living prosperously in America. They sent money back to support their relatives in Sicily and were highly esteemed among the population as a result.

After the USA joined the war in 1941, the American government came to an agreement with the mafia. The Allies used the mafia's connections in Sicily to their advantage, and the US Secret Service collaborated with mafia bosses in secret. The American intelligence services ensured that fifteen percent of invading soldiers were of Sicilian heritage, because the *Cosa Nostra* were sworn enemies of the Mussolini regime, so they had good reason to cooperate with the Americans. US troops, with the help of the mafia, paved the way for the invasion of Sicily. The mafia also helped the American army with the administration of the conquered territories. Because, until then, the mayors of many Sicilian towns had been representatives of the Fascist party, the US military authorities needed the support of the administration. This meant that mafiosi were promoted to public office. The mafia boss Don 'Calò' Vizzini submitted a list of names of anti-Fascists eligible for office after the Sicilian landings. Many of these men were in prison at the time. His services earnt him the title of honorary colonel in the US army, awarded to him by the Allies.

Author's Note

My father's real-life experiences of the war inspired me to write this novel. His actual encounters have been incorporated into the story. However, places and names have been changed and family members are mainly fictional; plot points, historical events and well-known figures have been freely embellished.

In 2001, I took a trip to Lampedusa with my father. It was his first time visiting the island in 58 years. We stayed at the Hotel Martello, visited the Albero Sole and chatted to the locals.

While researching the book, I stumbled across the website *Die Funkstunde*, where I found a picture of the radar from 1943. My father contacted the person running the website, and they engaged in an animated email exchange. Because the website owner often went on holiday to Lampedusa and considered the island his second home, he asked my father for photographs and an account of his experiences on Lampedusa during the Second World War. The photographs and my father's article can be found in the *Museo Archivo Storico di Lampedusa*.

My father celebrated his 100th birthday in March 2021.

About the Author

I sabella Pallavicini grew up in Switzerland.

After working as a primary school teacher for many years, she retrained as a drama educator and storyteller.

Since then, she has been writing and directing plays, as well as running workshops for schoolchildren on storytelling and creative writing.

She lives with her family in London.

Please visit the website for more information about the book and the historical events!

www.isabella-pallavicini.com

About the Translator

Rachel Farmer is a translator and conference interpreter working from French and German into English.

Her translations have been published by *No Man's Land*, *SAND* and Two Lines Press, among others. She also reviews books for online publications and works as chief executive assistant for *Asymptote* literary journal.

She currently lives with her partner in Bristol.

www.rachelfarmertranslation.com

Lightning Source UK Ltd.
Milton Keynes UK
UKHW041603190122
397396UK00002B/136